BLOODY FOREIGNERS

T0149030

BLOODY FOREIGNERS

An Inspector Low novel

Neil Humphreys

MUSWELL
PRESS

First published by Muswell Press in 2021
This edition published 2022
Copyright © Neil Humphreys 2021

Neil Humphreys has asserted his right to be identified as
the author of this work in accordance with under the Copyright,
Designs and Patents Act, 1988

A CIP catalogue record for this book is available from the British Library

ISBN: 9781838340131
eISBN: 9781916207745

Typeset by M Rules
Printed and bound by CPI Group (UK) Ltd, Croydon CR0 4YY

Muswell Press
London N6 5HQ
www.muswell-press.co.uk

PROLOGUE

Mohamed Kamal knew he was dying. The puddle told him. He was sitting in his own blood. He tried to move, but the pain stopped him. His body was shutting down.

The other voice was no longer shouting. It was quivering. Kamal's stabbing was deliberate, but his death would be an accident.

The voice turned away from him and faced the ugly black bricks. The wall was built in a different century, a different time, a different London.

Kamal watched his killer take the bloody knife and scrawl four capital letters into the Victorian brickwork.

MEGA.

Kamal knew what the acronym meant.

Make England Great Again.

Written in his blood.

Make England Great Again.

Kamal almost smiled at the irony, but the blood swirled around the back of his mouth and choked him. He was going to be another racist statistic, another opportunity for thoughts and prayers. He'd be a Facebook page, a candle in the park, a poster boy for the oppressed and a puerile chant outside every student union. He didn't want any of these things.

He just wanted to live.

He wanted to see her. One more time. Once would be enough. He knew exactly what he'd say, too.

Thanks and sorry.

That's it.

Thanks and sorry.

He looked up at the Chinese lanterns. They swayed peacefully in the chilly air. *Bloody Chinese lanterns.*

Even in death, in London, the Chinese surrounded him. That was too much.

He was not going to die in Chinatown. He was born an Indian man in Singapore. He had lived most of his Singaporean life on Chinese terms. But he was going to die an Indian man, on his terms.

He allowed the blood to dribble down his chin, clearing his throat, giving him a chance to breathe, a chance to drag his broken body through the puddle.

His puddle. *His* blood.

He didn't know where he was going, but he wasn't dying in an alleyway with those words on the wall.

Make England Great Again.

Fuck you.

I'll write my own obituary.

But his crawling was slow and loud and cumbersome. He pressed his hand against the black dustbin, catching the smell of yesterday's leftovers, disturbing the rats. He heard scraping footsteps along the narrow path.

'No, no, no, not out there,' a voice said.

Kamal felt his hair being pulled back. She had always liked his long hair. In Singapore, he was a rebel with long hair. He tried to think of her, stroking his hair, fooling around, but he couldn't see anything now.

The pain closed his eyes. He was slipping away, desperate for sleep, waiting for peace.

And then he saw the graffiti again.

The anger revived him. Suddenly, his eyes were open. He allowed himself to be dragged deeper into the alleyway's darkness. He found the energy to turn his head, spitting the blood from his mouth, readying himself for a final act of futile defiance.

His teeth tore into a leg. He bit through the jeans, ignoring the wild, unfocused blows raining down on his head. He reached the flesh and clamped down hard, a rabid dog with lockjaw, no longer in control, no longer caring, oblivious to the punches and the sudden screaming. Blood filled his mouth, but it wasn't his. He was fighting back, overcome with euphoria. He chewed through hair and skin and tendons, shaking his head to spread the pain, wounding his enemy and cutting him down, following internal orders to take back his dignity. Kamal saw his younger self in the Singaporean jungle, the green-faced national serviceman playing at soldiery. He thought the phoney exercises were pointless then, but the training was sustaining him now, fooling him into thinking that this was a fight he could win.

He suddenly saw himself in uniform, his boots and buttons polished, raising the flag, singing the same, uplifting song of hope.

'Majulah Singapura'. 'Onward Singapore'.

He was not going to die at the hands of a racist lunatic in a London alleyway.

'Majulah Singapura'. 'Onward Singapore'.

But he didn't see the knife coming for him a second time.

He just felt it, somewhere in his back, twisting, cracking a rib. Stopping him. Defeating him. Kamal spat out the foreign blood and slumped backwards, lying on his back, staring up at the brick archway. His fight was gone.

But he still had a choice. He could control his death, even in another country, even in Chinatown, beneath those bloody Chinese lanterns.

He could close his eyes and see his father at their *roti prata* stall, tossing the dough in the air, showing off for Arab Street tourists, working sixteen hours a day for his beloved son.

And he could see her beautiful, tender face. One more time.

His last moments belonged to her, the woman he was going to marry, the woman who was going to have their children, the woman who had taken his heart.

And as Mohamed Kamal slipped away from this life, he barely felt the knife being wrenched from his back.

But he heard the words.

'Fucking foreigners,' the voice said.

CHAPTER 1

Stanley Low stared at the carpet. An airport's carpet defined its country. Fourteen hours earlier, he'd left Changi Airport's carpet. It was new, vibrant, clean and sanitised. The carpet was the work of Asian hands, designed in an Asian country and maintained by migrant labour.

That was Singapore.

The carpet at Heathrow Airport was faded and frayed; once bright and confident, it was now coming away at the edges. Attempts had obviously been made to cover the corners and hide the decay.

This was England.

Huge, garish banners greeted new arrivals. The words of an enthusiastic PR executive were slapped optimistically across Union Jacks.

Britain is Great.

Low considered his own slogan to pass the time.

Britain is History.

His history.

An hour had passed, but the arrivals queue for non-citizens had barely moved. Low watched the Brits swagger through their queue, basking in their inherent superiority, oblivious to the foreigners around them.

'Stay in line, please; have your passports ready.'

The voice was husky and lyrical and belonged in the Jamaican sunshine. The voice was far too cheery and welcoming for 6 a.m. arrivals at a gloomy airport.

He was round-faced and smiley, a foreigner-turned-British citizen who would always be grateful for a steady job and free healthcare. He had a past. So he had perspective.

'How much longer? Low asked.

'It will take as long as it takes,' the plump immigration officer replied.

'What does that mean?'

'Excuse me, sir?'

'It will take as long as it takes. Does that mean an hour, a day, a week? Should I make plans for Christmas?'

The officer stopped. 'Are you British, sir?'

'No. Do I look British?'

'Well, your accent is . . .'

'Educated?'

'No, I just think your English is really good.'

'Thank you. So is yours.'

The immigration officer paused, as if searching for an explanation for the scruffy, well-spoken Chinese gentleman. Low's English really was impeccable when it needed to be. But he was tattooed and sweaty. The sight and sound didn't match.

He was carrying nothing but a passport.

The immigration officer replayed the same thought.

He's carrying nothing but a passport.

'Where have you just travelled from, sir?' the officer asked finally.

'The toilet. Which was cleaner than this carpet. Maybe you should just let people piss on the carpet and cut the middle man out.'

Chinese faces in the queue turned to face their belligerent countryman.

Low saw the minor explosions in his head, the dizzying, wearying fireworks and took a deep breath, waiting for them to fizzle out.

He heard the words of Dr Tracy Lai.

Count to ten and start again.

He watched the immigration officer nod to a colleague, calling for backup.

'Look, I didn't mean to be sarcastic, OK? It's just that we're all tired, this queue isn't moving and I need to get to an event in central London.'

Low couldn't miss the officer heading towards him, a member of the Aviation Policing Command with the semiautomatic across his vest, the Glock 17 hugging his hipbone and the sculpted biceps peeking through the uniform. Low knew the type. Some wanted to serve the community. Some wanted to serve the American movie forever playing in their heads.

'Is there a problem here, sir?' The Bulging Bicep enquired.

Low rolled his eyes. The crop-headed clown borrowed his lines from shit movies. The soothing words of Dr Tracy Lai faded. The fireworks sparkled and danced. Low was bored and angry. The Bulging Bicep offered a target, a chance to vent.

'No, but I have a question. How do you get muscles like that? Do police stations here have gyms?'

The officer tapped his finger against the side of the trigger of his semiautomatic. He couldn't make sense of the Chinese runt's aggression. The new arrival was engaging in an argument he obviously couldn't win. The officer settled on a routine line of questioning.

'Where are you from, sir?'

'You know where I'm from. I'm standing with three hundred other people who just arrived on the same plane. From Singapore. You've already seen it on my passport. Singapore. And I've got a Chinese face. So, let's consider the facts, shall we? A Chinese guy with a Singaporean passport has just landed on a Singapore Airlines flight from Singapore. Clearly, I'm from Zimbabwe.'

The officer considered his options. There were eyes everywhere. Foreign passengers. Returning citizens. Fellow officers. Airport staff. Liberal snowflakes. Everyone had an agenda. Everyone had a camera phone. He was white. The twat was Chinese. He had no choice. Stick to the routine line of questioning. Play the robot.

'There's no need for the sarcasm, sir. Where are you staying in the UK?'

'At the London School of Economics, *sir.*'

'You're a university lecturer,' the immigration officer exclaimed.

'Nope.'

'Then what are you?' The police officer spat the words at Low, emphasising his indifference to academia.

'Well, PC Bicep, I am, hold on a second,' he said, fumbling around in his wallet before producing an identity card, 'ah, there we are. I am Detective Inspector Stanley Low from the Singapore Police Force. My wonderful government has sent me here to give some really boring lectures on criminology at the London School of Economics.'

The police officer moved his semiautomatic to one side and examined the card. Even his well-drilled line of questioning had deserted him.

'I didn't expect that,' he mumbled, returning the card. 'You don't look like . . .

'A detective inspector?' Low interrupted. 'No, I look like what I am. An arsehole. That's why I'm here.'

CHAPTER 2

Through the pre-dawn fog, Detective Inspector Mistry noticed the two uniforms giggling. Two white men protecting an Asian corpse in Chinatown in front of all those phones. They were stupid, but not malicious. They were scared. Their bullshit made up for a lack of bravado. That's why she was in plain clothes and they were in uniform, standing in the drizzle. Besides, she recognised them from the station. They were almost half her age.

'PC Cook, PC Bishop,' she said, ducking beneath the police cordon.

'Yes, Sergeant,' said Cook, clearing his throat.

'What's so funny, lads?'

'Nothing, Sergeant, just passing the time.'

Cook was the talkative constable, the thicker one. So she glared at the smarter Bishop.

'No, you're making jokes to take your mind off the dead bloke behind you. Look where we are. Fruit and veg deliveries are on their way, wholesalers, then office workers and early-morning tourists. Do you wanna go viral?'

'No, Sergeant,' Cook replied.

Mistry ignored him, still staring at Bishop, still waiting.

'No, Sergeant,' he said finally.

'Good. No one comes in without clearing it with me first, OK? No one.'

Dansey Place was an alleyway like any other in central London, except it was particularly long, running like a discreet artery through Chinatown, feeding the restaurants on either side. The city's wealthiest had surrounded the narrow walkway years ago, with the theatres of Shaftesbury Avenue and Leicester Square's red-carpet premieres a reminder of a world away from fried noodles and chopped garlic.

But Dansey Place's high brick walls blocked out both the sun and the globalised metropolis. Victorian London still reigned here and some things never changed. Strangers were still being stabbed.

Mistry loved London just before dawn. The night owls had dragged their hangovers back to the suburbs. The office minions had yet to arrive. In the in-between hours, London offered the illusion of peace, the promise of something better.

And then, through the fog, it spat out another victim.

Mistry pulled her latex gloves tighter and smiled at a tall, slim man in a dark suit crouching over the body.

'So?'

Detective Constable Tom Devonshire didn't look up. 'Two stab wounds, both in the back, quite close to each other. The surgeon is on his way. Some grit and shit on his hands, blood along the floor, on his face. He put up a fight and tried to escape, poor bastard.'

Mistry crouched beside the dead man. 'Grit and shit?'

Devonshire sighed. 'Yeah, all right. It's five-thirty in the morning, had to sort Ben out and I haven't had any coffee yet.'

'Is he all right?'

'Yeah, he's fine. Hasn't got much choice, has he?'

Mistry moved past the question and focused on the body for the first time. The dead man was young, olive-skinned and remarkably handsome.

Those eyes.

She had seen those eyes too many times before. They always

captured the moment of revelation, a terrifying acceptance that death was on its way. Those eyes had followed her from one murder scene to another. From a rookie homicide detective in Dagenham to running her own murder investigation team at Charing Cross, the eyes always had it.

They saw the end.

But his brown eyes belonged on a puppy dog, not a corpse. They were beautiful. He was a beautiful boy.

'Such a waste,' she murmured.

'Yeah, good-looking bugger,' Devonshire agreed. 'With a face like that, he should've been on the stage over the road, not in a gang.'

'You think he was in gang?'

'He's a stabbed teenager with a brown face.'

'I've got a brown face.'

Devonshire didn't take the bait. 'You know what I mean.'

Mistry flicked her ponytail away from her shoulder and reached for her torch. 'Nah, I'm not having it.'

'Look, don't get all PC about it. They're happening every day. We had one yesterday, in your bloody neighbourhood.'

'That was outside the train station. Revenge attack. This is theatreland. Who killed him? A pensioner pissed off she didn't meet Benedict Cumberbatch at the stage door?'

Devonshire looked over at his boss. 'Benedict Cumberbatch is playing in the West End?'

'Shut up. Teenagers don't kill each other in the theatre district.'

'This isn't really the theatre distrct, is it? It's Chinatown. And he's a dead Asian.'

'He's Indian. Had an identity card in his wallet.'

'Meaning he's Indian?

'He's Singaporean.'

'What the hell's a Singaporean Indian? And how would you know?'

Mistry stood up. 'How do you think?'

Devonshire sighed. 'Ah yeah, of course. *Him.*'

Mistry ignored the sarcasm and followed the torchlight along the chipped brickwork. 'He wasn't stabbed against the wall,' she said. 'There's no blood on the walls.'

'Of course not. Rival gang members follow him in to the alley, stab, stab and he's gone.'

The torch stopped moving. The carved letters glowed in the spotlight. Faint blood streaks trailed each letter.

'Oh shit,' Mistry muttered. 'Look at this.'

Devonshire turned and faced the bloodied letters on the wall behind him.

MEGA.

'Yeah, I know,' he said. 'Thought I'd save that for you. Bet you wish it was a gang killing now.'

CHAPTER 3

Charing Cross Police Station didn't look like one from the outside. The façade fitted its environment rather than the profession. The imposing colonnade was more in keeping with the Roman Empire than coppers on the cobbles. The Agar Street building had once housed a Victorian hospital, a noble attempt to heal the sick in the surrounding slums.

Now the place aimed to provide peace for the dead.

Detective Chief Inspector Charlie Wickes enjoyed working at Charing Cross. He was a middle-aged man of simple pleasures, edging towards a well-deserved pension. He'd worked his way through the ranks at Tottenham, Tower Hamlets and Newham. Different gangs. Different races. Same endgame.

But he came through the other end with a few promotions, a detached house in Chigwell and two teenagers in a private school. He was a proud comprehensive-school kid, but the job had changed his education philosophy.

Stabbing victims didn't go to private school.

Stabbing victims always looked like Mohamed Kamal.

DCI Wickes sipped his tea and focused on the blown-up images of Kamal's body on the whiteboard. The dead kid promised to be a real pain in Wickes's pension. Central London didn't have the teenage knife-crime stats of north and east London, but central London did have the omnipresent threat of terrorism. Radicalised nutcases preferred to kill innocent people around tourist attractions. The footage played better on social media.

Wickes heard their shuffling footsteps. He downed his tea. He was never going to make tee-off time at Hainault now.

'Morning, everyone. Take a seat,' Wickes said, as DC Devonshire followed DI Mistry into the office. PC Cook and PC Bishop soon followed. The room filled quickly. Dead bodies didn't really count, but he was given plenty of resources for one word on a wall.

'OK, let's start. Yes, you've already noticed that there are a lot of you and I'd like to say it's because of that poor sod there,' Wickes said, pointing to Kamal's broken body on the whiteboard. 'But we all know it isn't. It's because of this bloody thing here.'

Wickes nodded towards a photo of the graffiti found in the alleyway.

'Make England Great Again. Counterterrorism are jittery about this, obviously. This kid was killed on our patch, so it's our homicide. But it's already been made very clear to me that we're on the clock. No delays. No press leaks and no discussing the bloody graffiti. Ramila?'

Mistry cleared her throat. 'Well, sir, he had his ID in his pocket, as you know. Luckily for us, Singaporeans carry identity cards with them.'

'Should have them here,' a voice in the group muttered.

'Yes, all right,' Wickes said. 'Carry on.'

'Yes, sir. His name was Mohamed Kamal. He was twenty-two years old, a Singaporean Indian. And he was a Muslim.'

Mistry heard the murmurings.

'Yes, he was a Muslim. Doesn't mean he should be dead. He'd completed his national service in Singapore and was a first-year student at King's College, studying engineering. We're working with the Singaporean authorities to get in touch with next of kin.'

'Was he rich? Poor?'

'Don't know yet, sir.'

'Well, someone was paying for him to study here. Find out who and why.'

'We all know why,' another voice muttered. Others nodded in agreement.

'No, we don't know why,' Mistry snapped. 'He was just a student, a kid, and now he's dead. And I'm not sure what his financial status has to do with him being stabbed twice in the back.'

'Ramila, come on,' Devonshire said. 'It's a reasonable line of inquiry.'

'It's DI Mistry and I really don't think a kid from squeaky-clean Singapore is going to be funded by the fragments of ISIS. And besides, terrorists kill strangers. Strangers don't kill terrorists.'

Wickes raised his hands. 'All right, enough. We all know he's likely to have some sort of income, either here or coming in from Singapore. Find out and speak to them. Now, what about the graffiti? What do we know, Tom?'

Devonshire shrugged. 'Only the obvious stuff so far: Make England Great Again, a far-right group run by Billy Evans, a nightclub promoter turned Oswald Mosley, supported by mostly white blokes who beat up brown people at weekends. Evans is on a tour of the Midlands at the moment, doing grooming gangs. Again.'

'What? Pet-grooming gangs?'

Wickes didn't mind Cook's puerile joke. Cheeky constables were usually good for paperwork and bad punchlines on murder investigations. Wickes figured he'd need both with the Kamal killing.

'Look, jokes aside, leave your politics at home. I'm not

15

interested. In this room, as far I'm concerned, this is a hate crime and I want this boy's killer found, all right? Who's looking at the CCTV?'

'I am, sir,' said Bishop, 'with a fine toothcomb.'

'Yeah, all right, it's a dull job. Just get it done with less sarcasm. Rule nothing out at this stage: strangers, residents and— DI Mistry . . . am I boring you?'

Mistry raised her phone. 'No, sir. It's on the radio. They already know.'

Margaret Jones savoured the silence. Just for a moment. Anything more than five seconds and the light flashed on her panel and the producer started banging on the glass partition. Silence was the death of a radio presenter's career. London Call-In was a talkback radio station. She knew the in-house mantra.

Don't talk. Don't come back.

Three seconds was enough. It was time. Time to kill off the snowflake.

'Well, if you won't answer the question, Mark, then I will,' she said, peering up at her co-presenter. 'But I can't, can I? Media guidelines deny me the right to speak the truth. Ironically, political correctness means we can only give fake news. Well, OK, let's see what I can say, shall we? Statistically, in London, the majority of knife crimes are carried out by non-white people, or people who identify themselves as white, you know, when they're not in therapy sessions apologising again for being white and straight and perhaps even male. Is that OK, for you, Mark? Have I fallen foul of any media guidelines so far?'

Mark Beckett loved and loathed his job with equal measure. He had a voice, an intelligent, smooth, empathetic voice, one polished at the finest public schools, thanks to affluent, bohemian parents who championed social equality, until it came to their son's education.

But he had a voice nonetheless, a sane voice in the

16

never-ending insanity. He saw himself as a counterbalance to the tabloid hysteria, the inflated xenophobia and those self-hating, invisible trolls. He offered an alternative to mainstream monsters like Margaret Jones.

He loathed her and her popularity. He was neither jealous nor insecure. A public-school education always bought confidence and security. He hated what her popularity represented. She was the acceptable mouthpiece of the seething majority, the closet racists who said one thing to the pollsters but ticked something else entirely at the ballot box. She had endorsed and encouraged a poisonous, vicious climate where nothing was off-limits. Every news cycle was open to manipulation and exploitation.

Even a dead Muslim kid was fair game.

Beckett sighed into the microphone.

'Margaret, I cannot believe you are conflating two entirely different issues here to score points with your unhinged fan base. What has the tragic death of a young man in Chinatown, which may or may not be a hate crime – unlike you, I prefer to wait for official confirmation – got to do with the racial profiles of knife victims on a council estate? You know, as well as I do, that these council estates are among the poorest in Britain, with people of colour predominantly making up the majorities because they are denied the socio-economic opportunities that other British citizens—'

'Oh for heavens sake, listen to yourself,' Jones interrupted. 'Why do they all come here, then? Why are they terrorising innocent families along the northern French coastline while they wait for an opportunity to jump on some poor sod's truck? Why do they not stay in France? Or Spain? Or Portugal? Why do they come here?'

'The kid came from Singapore, according to our sources. He came from one of the richest countries in the world. The last time I checked, Singapore hadn't been a war-torn country since 1942, when the British Empire essentially abandoned the island and left them to the Japanese. This kid was probably a student. This kid was probably making a better life for himself, at his own country's expense, putting money into our faltering education system. And you are surreptitiously playing your Islamophobia card again, to draw attention away from the fact that a political slogan was found beside the poor man, a political slogan that you won't say on here. Why won't you say it, Margaret?'

'Mark, I am not going to play your childish games on the air. You can play to your liberal gallery. I'll stick with the uncomfortable facts, if it's all the same to you. The boy's death is a tragedy, but the government's failure to tackle both immigration and knife crime—'

'According to our sources, and a photograph that this radio station has seen, one that we will not be sharing – believe it or not, we do have standards on this show – there was a prominent slogan, the name of a far-right movement, written on the wall near the victim. What did it say, Margaret?'

Jones looked up at the glass partition. Young faces. Different colours. She could see it in their eyes. Innocence. Idealism. Naivety. The hypocritical spoils of growing up in country towns and villages. They wouldn't help her. She was on her own. The story of her life.

'We are not going to give publicity to that mob,' she said.

'What did it say, Margaret?'

'We have an immigration crisis in this country, with young people, young men mostly, abusing our longstanding and genuine compassion for war refugees, sneaking into the country on lorries and boats to take advantage of our crumbling welfare system.'

'What did the slogan say, Margaret?'

Beckett already knew she was beaten. For Margaret Jones's followers, this killing had the skin colours the wrong way round.

'Make England Great Again,' he said, pausing for dramatic effect.

'Make England Great Again. That's what the slogan said, didn't it, Margaret? That's what our sources are telling us. That's what the photograph showed us. MEGA. Make England Great Again. That really messes with your narrative, doesn't it, Margaret? You can't denounce these racists and bigots and white supremacists, can you, Margaret? Not entirely. They make up half your support, don't they? They watch your TV spots in Russia and all those other bastions of tolerance and diversity. They fund your social media posts. You help their think tanks to dress up the racist rhetoric and make it more palatable for the masses. You share their content on Twitter.'

Jones pointed at Beckett. 'I've never shared anything from that group.'

'You have retweeted comments, unwittingly or otherwise, from members of Make England Great Again,' Beckett continued. 'You have been reluctant to criticise them publicly, either on our radio show or in your newspaper columns, and as far as I'm concerned, in these volatile times, we all have to pick a side. Otherwise, silence is complicity. And now a young Asian boy has died, allegedly beneath the slogan of a repugnant organisation that has been allowed to fester in the open wound that is our polarised society. Anyone who has half-heartedly agreed with the demented ramblings of Make England Great Again and their idiotic members, anyone who has shared, forwarded or endorsed xenophobic posts, videos or funny memes should seriously think about their actions. Are we seriously making England great again? Is this the behaviour of a great country? We'll take your calls after the break. You're listening to "Beckett and Jones for Breakfast" on London Call-In. News and sport coming up.'

Beckett sat back in his swivel chair and grinned at his incensed co-presenter. He was going to really enjoy their next few shows.

*

DCI Wickes wouldn't close his laptop. He wanted the tinny jingle of London Call-In to drift across the otherwise quiet office. No one spoke. Officers fiddled with their phones, refusing to look up, either at their superior officer or the dead man on the whiteboard.

'The kid isn't cold yet,' Wickes said. 'Someone around here has a big mouth.'

No one responded. There was nothing to say.

'So it's a hate crime. It's official.'

'We don't know that yet, sir,' DI Mistry piped up.

'Yes, we do. They just told us. Today it's on the radio. Tomorrow it's in the papers. The day after it's ranting on social media. Next week it's rioting. I'll have to liaise with Counterterrorism now. I suspect they'll take this one away from us. But in the meantime, this is our homicide. DI Mistry, you will run the investigation team. DC Devonshire, you will obviously assist.'

Mistry felt the envious eyes of the white men in the room. They still couldn't get past her skin colour. As always, she had to say what everyone else was thinking.

'Excuse me, sir,' she said. 'Is this another Asian face to pacify the Asian community? Are you giving me this because my skin tone matches the victim's?'

'No, because your skin tone doesn't match.'

The chief inspector smiled at his old protégé. He still admired that feisty mix of insecurity and arrogance among second-generation immigrants. Their eagerness to prove themselves made them the hardest-working coppers. But their cultural roots made them an asset among ethnic minorities.

Most of the time.

'The victim was a Singaporean Muslim. You are the daughter of Gujarati immigrants. So, no, Detective Inspector Mistry, I don't think you match your victim, OK?'

Mistry blushed. Her mentor had always been a kind and

fair man. He had always been better than this. She needed to be, too.

'No, sir, but it's what others will say,' she whispered, looking around the room.

'Then they come and see me, ' Wickes said, raising his voice. 'I haven't got time for petty office politics. You're in charge because the victim was Singaporean; that's the only real lead we have. We'll need to get in touch with family and friends, and you lived in Singapore. You know the place.'

PC Bishop looked up from his note-taking. 'You lived in Singapore?'

'Oh yeah,' Devonshire said. 'She was gonna marry one of 'em.'

CHAPTER 4

Stanley Low watched them shuffle into the auditorium, heads down, half asleep. Scrolling. Smartphones. Dumb students. He envied their innocence and hated their youth. Most of all, he was jealous. When he looked at them, he saw himself, in the same building, in a different decade, living a different life.

It was a life he barely remembered, before Tiger, before Ah Lian, before the killing started.

He saw the logo on the lectern, above the door, on the screen behind him and even on the professor's bloody tie.

LSE. White letters. Red backdrop.

The logo exuded pride. The London School of Economics, for the betterment of society. That's what it said on the glossy brochure. Low flicked the pages and thought about alternatives.

The London School of Economics, for the betterment of the moneyed class, the keepers of the capitalistic flag and the death of a Singaporean detective.

He knew he was being melodramatic. The school didn't break him. The place made him. He left London with a first-class degree. He also left behind the best years of his life.

He read the synopsis of the criminology course. *His* course. The scrawny Chinese student back in 1995 was now a study module.

Good luck with that.

Low had given up studying himself. In front of an LSE criminology class, he was a homecoming hero. In front of a mirror, he was unrecognisable.

As the criminology professor stood at the lectern, paying gushing tribute to a man he had never met, Low picked out two words in the course synopsis.

Mental health.

He had found his speech.

His mind was still racing when he heard the applause. He made his way to the stage, shook the hand of a still gushing professor in an ill-fitting suit, and stopped behind the lectern.

An audience of expectant faces waited. Criminology lecturers edged forward on their seats, beaming like proud parents. Low read those words again.

Mental health.

He took a deep breath. The silence screamed back at him. Those fizzing explosions in the brain: he could see the bastard things, leaping in front of him, mocking him.

He found himself in the packed auditorium, a smooth Chinese face, wide-eyed, sitting at the back, away from the spotlight, typically Asian. Low would focus on him, a link to the past and a chance to forget the self-loathing.

'Mental health,' Low stammered. 'Mental health. That's what it says in your course info here in the brochure. I'm reading the material here. "In your criminology course, you will consider the impact of criminal justice on different social groups, including those differentiated on the basis of their age, gender, socio-economic status, ethnicity, sexuality and mental health." That's great.'

Low hesitated, as if debating whether or not to continue.

'That's really useful. Let's talk about that first. I know you want to get to the famous cases, me going undercover for two years in an illegal betting syndicate, me bringing down gang

23

leaders, me solving high-profile, sensitive homicide cases that should've made me a hero, but instead somehow managed to piss off big business, the Singapore government and the Singapore Police Force itself, which is why I've been sent here to give you a motivational talk on criminology, but let's start with this bit about criminal justice in your syllabus.'

Low nodded towards the red-faced criminology lecturer, who turned away to check the mood of the audience. The tension was palpable.

'Yeah. Criminal justice. Let's look at something that has a direct bearing on your coursework, according to your syllabus here, something that will have a practical use in your studies. The impact of criminal justice on different social groups, including those differentiated on the basis of their age . . . I can help with that, as my guy was quite young . . . Gender . . . Well, he was male . . . Socio-economic status . . . He was mostly poor, unless a decent match-fixing scam came off . . . Ethnicity . . . He was Chinese, which doesn't really count because that's the majority race in Singapore. So he had the Chinese equivalent of white privilege, which was rather ironic, as he was eventually murdered by a white man.'

Students gasped. LSE staff fidgeted. Some whispered amongst themselves. The criminology professor started to rise from his seat. Low shook his head.

'No, no, don't worry. I'm not here to talk about his murder. It's that last bit in the syllabus that fascinates me. Consider the impact of criminal justice on mental health. That's something I think about every day; one particular case study, in fact.

'About ten years ago now, maybe more, I was tied to a chair in a rundown, empty shophouse in Singapore. I was working undercover. Another kid was tied to a chair beside me. Everyone called him Dragon Boy. He thought he was a gangster. Everyone else thought he was still waiting for puberty. Hence Dragon Boy, the little kid who thought he could. He was probably around your age. A teenager. He was an illegal bookie, an *ah long*, we call it in Singapore, a loan shark. He was nothing, really. We both worked for the syndicate boss, an old Chinese guy called Tiger.'

Excited mutterings spread through the audience. Low nodded.

'So you've obviously read my bio then. Yes. Tiger. Well, Tiger had tied us to a chair because he was convinced there was an informant within his organisation. We weren't really an organisation. We were a rabble of desperate Chinese men trying to make a living. But the word itself – syndicate – sounds much more impressive in the media, doesn't it? The Tiger Syndicate. So anyway, he started on Dragon Boy first, slicing his back with a *parang*. That's a huge knife, more a sword, really. Dragon Boy screamed, but never said a word. He was a loyal kid. He also wasn't the informant. I knew he wasn't. Because I was.'

Low waited for the audience to settle again.

'As you know, I was an undercover detective. The kid beside me had his back ripped apart because of me. But he never said a word. He protected me. So Tiger started on me.'

Low lifted his shirt and revealed the scars on his torso. As his speech was being filmed, the jagged pink flesh filled the large projector screen behind him. Students covered their mouths in shock.

'Two things saved my life that day. The first thing was simple logistics. Tiger's phone rang. There was a big game that night, a football match. He had a financial interest, so he had to leave. Just like that. He slashed two men and left them bleeding in their chairs. Why should he care? That was his job. But the second thing was, he never really believed I was the informant. Never. I was that good at lying. No, I was brilliant at lying. The best.

'So I sat there, saying nothing, as Tiger dished out his criminal justice on the screaming kid beside me, knowing that he was innocent and I was guilty.

'But I managed to keep Dragon Boy out of jail. That was my

25

criminal justice, my warped sense of loyalty to him. And a few years later, he became my informant. That was his warped sense of loyalty to me, I suppose. He protected me and I protected him. That was our relationship. Our code. But it didn't matter because a few years ago, he was stabbed to death. He was murdered trying to protect me.

'And now, thanks to Dragon Boy's death, and a million other things, my mental health is fucked. That's my criminal justice. That's my reward for a lifetime in crime. I can't sleep at night. I can't work during the day. And I can't get fired because of all my *wonderful achievements* with the Singapore Police Force. So they send me halfway around the world to talk to you lot. And here I am, the unofficial ambassador for fucked-up policemen. Any questions?'

No one raised a hand.

No one clapped.

No one spoke.

No one moved.

Low watched the Chinese student at the back of the auditorium. The kid looked dumbstruck. Low continued to scan the audience, eager to see a face that didn't belong to the bloodied, screaming Dragon Boy.

And then he found one. She was standing beside the exit.

Low thought he was hallucinating. She couldn't be there, surely.

The job had taken his soul a long time ago, but the face in the crowd had once stolen his heart.

CHAPTER 5

The George IV pub was the archetypal student pub, tucked away in central London, both chic and shabby. The cast-iron 'London School of Economics' name plate, taken from a British Rail train and hung over the bar, reminded every visitor of the pub's owners. The currency notes stuck to a pillar on the bar, coming from all over the world, underlined the international, affluent clientele and what the school was really all about.

Money.

Low's father had once sent his gifted son to the same place with the same intentions. A young, intelligent Singaporean prodigy was sent to London but never really returned.

Low took a seat beneath the bright, arched windows and watched her chat with the flirtatious barman. The kid had good skin, a hipster beard and a Eastern European accent, a reliable combination in a student pub. He was also in a safe metropolitan enclave. His accent would be considered exotic and worldly, rather than a threat to jobs and hospital waiting times.

Low figured the kid was where he wanted to be, flirting with an older, well-spoken Indian woman who was both pretty and professional, a classic cougar for a randy, underpaid barman.

That's what really bothered Low. She was still flawless. Age had actually improved her. Her teenage gawkiness had long since given way to confident elegance. The shy Indian girl on the Tube, shying away from the Friday-night revellers, hoping to get from one end of the District Line to the other without being called a *Paki* had vanished. She was a British-Indian woman, comfortable with the labels on both sides of the hyphen.

Low barely recognised the self-confidence, but her beauty was unmistakable. And it was killing him. And Low only had one way of dealing with pain.

'So what's it like being a brown face in Divided Britain, then?'

Detective Inspector Ramila Mistry ignored the belligerence and dumped the drinks on the varnished table.

'Do you remember this place?' she asked instead.

'Vaguely. Victorian pub. Still looks like the Flatiron Building from the outside. Still trying to be a Ye Olde London Pub on the inside. Still got the Hoare and Co. sign out front, one of the oldest businesses in London; still got the same people inside – merchants, bankers, wankers. Nothing changes.'

Mistry sipped her lemonade. 'Well, you certainly don't. Still trying to show off your intellect, giving me a potted history of a pub you've been in for five minutes. You don't have to try so hard. I still remember how clever you are.'

Low laughed loud enough to draw the attention of a table of economics students. Low's eyes told them to mind their business.

'Oh yeah, I'm a fucking genius,' he said, still looking at the students. 'I'm such a genius I get sent back here to inspire the trust-fund babies.'

'How are things back in Singapore?'

'Shit. I see you're married,' Low said, pointing at Mistry's wedding ring.

'Yeah, seven years.'

'Good for you. Kids?'

Mistry smiled. 'Yeah. One.'

'Great. Terrific. That's the small talk done. What do you want?'

Mistry took a moment to fully absorb Low's anger. She didn't want to respond just yet. She needed to take stock of his dishevelled appearance. She had read all the stories and followed his biggest cases. The international match-fixing syndicate and the Tiger operation had made headlines all over the world. Singapore was considered the engine driving global football corruption and Low had once had his hands at the wheel, a covert operative posing as a foul-mouthed gangster.

He should've been killed.

Mistry had never understood how Low hadn't been exposed. But she did now.

He *was* a foul-mouthed gangster.

She was examining him, looking for traces of that smart-arsed Chinese kid from her criminology class, the sarcastic little sod who always made her laugh.

But he was gone.

Low was unshaven and unwashed. His eye bags were heavy. His face was puffy and weary. His thick hair was greying. A little of the old handsomeness was still in there when he smiled, but he rarely smiled.

'Why don't you just quit?' Mistry asked.

The question caught Low off guard. 'Where did that come from?'

'Well, you obviously hate the job.'

'And you love it?'

'Yes. I do.'

'Really? You love being an Indian policewoman in Britain? Now? Been called a Muslim bitch lately?'

'No, because it's not 1974 any more.'

'Wow, that almost sounded convincing.'

'And you sound like you've been reading the *Daily Mail*. Other online news sources are available.'

'No, but I can read an online forum. I bet every time some fuckwit shouts *"Allahu Akbar"* and starts running through a pub

29

with a knife, you shit yourself and think, "How many times am I gonna be told to fuck off back to my own country today?"'

'No, it makes a welcome change from the regular, run-of-the-mill teenage stabbings, and I can pass the case off to the terrorism units.'

'You don't think about the increasing racial divide here?'

'No, I think, "Thank God, I don't live in a country where the races are engineered and programmed and told where and how to live."'

'You sound like you've been reading the *Guardian*. Other online news sources are available.'

'Oh, I'm sorry. I forgot. The Singapore government isn't all-powerful any more, is it? Tell me, who sent you here again?'

Low sat back to savour the argument. Finally, he smiled.

'God, I've missed this,' he said, drinking his Coke. 'Have you?'

'No. Fuck off.'

Mistry's mutinous giggle betrayed her.

'Yeah,' Low said. 'So have I.'

Low leaned forward. 'Lincoln's Inn Fields is across the road, isn't it? The park?'

'You know it is.'

'We did a lot of criminology research in that park, didn't we?'

'No, we didn't.'

Low allowed the memories to play out for both of them.

'No, we didn't,' he said.

Mistry swirled the ice around in her glass. 'Anyway, I might need your help with something,' she said, not looking up.

'Of course you do. A happily married woman doesn't seek out a mental ex-boyfriend to discuss the shags they once had in a London park.'

'Yeah that,' Mistry said, pointing towards Low's forehead. 'I might need that.'

'What for?'

'I've got a dead Asian teenager. Stabbed.'

'Teenagers get stabbed every day in London.'

'He's not a gangster. He's a student. A King's College student from Singapore.'

Low realised he was suddenly sitting up straight. He felt the cogs turning.

'Singaporean student? Check his financial records. Gambling. Cards, maybe football betting, took money from *ah longs*, you know, loan sharks, lots of illegal gambling around here. Chinatown is across the road.'

'Yeah, that's where we found him.'

'Straightforward, then. There's not a Chinatown in the world without betting shophouses. They've run illegal books for decades in London. Plus you've got the regular casinos in Chinatown. Students, foreign workers, they all get involved. You know us Chinese. If we see two cockroaches crawling up a wall, we kill 'em and get back to betting on the football.'

'He wasn't Chinese. He was Indian.'

'Ah, that's different.'

'Yeah and his body was found beside graffiti that read "MEGA". Make England Great Again.'

'Was the graffiti fresh?'

'It was written in his blood.'

'Ah, that's fantastic. Now you have a case.'

'Yeah, but we've got no witnesses. No one is talking.'

'Of course not. It's Chinatown. *Wah lau*, eh? Cannot talk cock with police in Chinatown. Too *kiasi*. No chance. Besides, the *ah peks* will never talk to you; you will always be *ah pu neh neh* to them, right? You remember.'

'Yeah, that's what I need. A bit of your Singlish bollocks.'

'Not really, you need Hokkien, Mandarin and Cantonese, all thrown into a pot with maybe a dash of Singlish for authenticity. You need me.'

Mistry raised her hand. 'Just as an observer, maybe for a bit of translating, that's it. If I can clear it, of course.'

'I'm only here for a few days, although I could probably extend.'

'No, that's fine, just for preliminary inquiries.'

'Can I see the body first?'

'No.'

'I need the scent.'

'No.'

'I can't investigate a murder case without it.'

'You're not investigating a murder case.'

'No I'm not, not unless I see the body first.'

Mistry sighed. Low looked well-leathered, almost beaten. But he still had that manic swagger, the arrogance that had guided her through her first year of criminology.

They used to be a couple of Asian kids from public housing estates, which was all they had in common back then. They had nothing in common now. Mistry knew the risk she was taking.

'Will you just stand back and observe?'

'Of course.'

'You won't interfere with the body in any way?'

'I'm a policeman, not a pervert.'

'You won't upset the other officers?'

'I'll do my best.'

'Stanley.'

'Yes, yes, I promise.'

Mistry took one more opportunity to study the battered but brilliant man. She calculated the odds. Low was a risk worth taking. Just.

'OK, but only if I get clearance from my DCI,' she said.

Low was already on his feet. 'Fantastic,' he said, downing the rest of his Coke. 'Let's go and say hello to your corpse.'

CHAPTER 6

Low was struck by the charming façade. The Westminster Public Mortuary was an elegant Victorian house with an arched entrance and timber window frames. He had never seen such a tasteful staging area for dead people. The mortuary at the Singapore General Hospital was buried in a grey, functional building. Even in death, Londoners and Singaporeans had to hang around in a mortuary that befitted their surroundings. One corpse got heritage and architectural elegance. The other got an ugly, utilitarian box.

DI Mistry led Low towards a stainless-steel table and pulled back the sheet. In any country, the murdered always looked the same. Bloody. Bloated. Pained.

'This is Mohamed Kamal,' Mistry said. 'Twenty-two years old. So handsome. Such a waste.'

Low found himself agreeing. Being confronted by a dead Singaporean was hardly a new experience, but Low felt a sudden pang of empathy.

His fellow countryman didn't deserve to die alone, in such fear, in a foreign country.

Mistry pointed at Kamal's legs. 'He was obviously quite fit – well-defined calves for an Asian student. Maybe a cyclist, or even a courier, food delivery, around Chinatown, they've all got the delivery apps now.'

'No, he's got small scars on his shins and around his knees, nothing serious, nothing you'd get from a bike fall. He's top half is mostly slim, but he's got a slight potbelly there, which is not enough gym and too much *nasi padang*, a red-meat, high-fat, halal diet. He was Indian. He was a social footballer, midfielder, stocky, low centre of gravity. Can check the local students and Asian teams.'

Low shivered. He never got used to a mortuary's temperature. He was Singaporean.

'What about the two stab wounds?'

'Same weapon, obviously, both in the back, just a long blade, nothing distinct about the knife. Could have been bought in any supermarket. Most of the kids in London are carrying them.'

'Most of the dark-skinned kids,' Low corrected, peering at the puncture wounds either side of Kamal's spine. 'No need to be PC with me. I've seen the stats. This doesn't happen in a vacuum.'

'What's that got to do with anything?'

'Nothing.'

'Then why say it?'

'No reason.'

'Everything you say has a reason. It's why you're still single.'

Low looked up. 'Very good. That's why you're a detective.'

'Why did you bring up the crime stats?'

'I don't know why you'd want this life, Asian kids killing each other.'

'His killer wasn't Asian. His killer was racist.'

'Racists aren't Asian? We both know that's not true.'

'Oh for fuck's sake, Stanley, that was over twenty years ago.'

'Am I interrupting something?'

Low turned and faced a tall white man, dressed in scrubs and adjusting his hairnet. He was younger than Low, and blessed with the complexion and confidence that come with being a white man raised in a better Essex suburb in the 1980s. His trim frame came from an annual gym membership that was actually utilised.

He stood the other side of Kamal's body.

'Who are you? The pathologist?'

'No, this is my partner, DC Devonshire,' Mistry said.

Detective Constable Tom Devonshire held out his hand, above Kamal's exposed stomach. 'Call me Tom,' he said.

The two men shook hands. Devonshire had a firmer grip and an eagerness to impress the older Chinese policeman.

'Hello, Tom. I'm DI Low.'

Devonshire looked embarrassed. 'Er, I thought you were just an observer, right? Don't get me wrong. You're a legend. DI Mistry has told us all about you. But you're just helping us out, right?'

'I'm helping DI Mistry because she asked me,' Low said.

Devonshire raised his hands. 'Hey, that's great. You're Singaporean. He was Singaporean. You could really help us with, like, your cultural connections.'

'Cultural connections? Where did you learn that? In your metropolitan police cultural classes? He was an Indian Muslim. I'm a Chinese bastard. Apart from eating satay, I've probably got more in common with you than him. And we've got nothing in common.'

'Why is he here?'

'Because I asked him to be here, all right?' Mistry said, realising she was speaking too loudly across a dead body. 'He'll give us a different pair of eyes. This is a sensitive case and Wickes wants a quick result.'

'Wickes? Isn't that a hardware shop in England?'

'DCI Wickes. He's let me handle this team. He's the one who's let you observe.'

Devonshire pulled on his gloves. 'No, I think it's great he's here. We've learned so much already. The dead kid ate satay.'

Low gripped the side of the stainless-steel table. He was visualising too many different scenarios, all of which led to him punching the *ang moh*, and he couldn't do that. He couldn't lean across a dead Singaporean to smack a dreary Englishman. He knew that. But he could use him for batting practice.

'What have *you* got so far, Constable . . .Sorry, I've never heard of you, what's your name again?'

'I'm not a constable.'

'You look like one.'

Mistry rolled her eyes. 'Stanley.'

'Stanley?'

'Yes, DC Devonshire, his name is Stanley,' Mistry said. 'Grow up.'

'Yeah, DC Devonshire, grow up. Tell us what you've got on my Singaporean.'

'Look, I don't have to put up with this shit,' Devonshire said.

Mistry slapped the table. Kamal's stomach wobbled.

'I'm not waiting for you two to finish your dick-measuring. Tom, tell him what we've got.'

Devonshire looked at the two Asians on the other side of the table. One female. One male. She was beautiful. He was repugnant. Devonshire would always do as he was told. For her. He took out his phone and started reading.

'Singaporean student at King's College, was studying engineering.'

'Engineering makes sense, a safe choice for Singaporean parents, a guaranteed financial return on all that investment in his education.'

'*Parent*. Only one. Mother died a few years ago,' Devonshire said, not looking up from his phone. 'Father runs a food stall back in Singapore, selling per-rata?'

'*Prata*,' Mistry interrupted, correcting Devonshire's mispronunciation.

'Yeah, *prata*. He's a government scholar, shared a flat with two

36

other students, both Malaysian, both Indian Muslim. The tech team are going through their laptops and phones, going through Kamal's phone as well, checking radicalised groups within the campus, possible cells.'

'Why?' Low enquired. 'You've got no evidence of radicalisation.'

'He's from a reasonably poor background. His father was a street cook and he was relying on Singapore government handouts. Yet he had a few quid on him and a few hundred in a bank account, which he had put in himself, wasn't wired from his skint dad in Singapore. And he wasn't working. We've checked with his friends and other students. So where did he get his money from?'

'They're lying,' Low said. 'There's never been a Singaporean Muslim terrorist. Second, his father wasn't a street cook, whatever that is – he was a hawker, a dignified, respected job with a steady income. And third, he was a government scholar. Government scholars are not generally radicalised. Brainwashed by their government to be civil servants, certainly, but not to be standing outside pop concerts in suicide vests. All of which means he had a job, somewhere around Chinatown. Paid in cash. Like every other menial job in Chinatown. There's no other reason for a Muslim boy to be in Chinatown, not enough cheap halal food. Find a place with South-East Asian food, Malaysian, Indonesian, anything halal, a place that sold *prata* or *dosai.*'

'Why?' Mistry asked.

'His dad is a widower working on a *prata* stall. Labour-intensive. Long hours. Can't afford too many extra hands. So his son helped him. Filial piety.'

'Filial what?'

'Look it up,' snapped Low, losing patience with Devonshire's ignorance. 'Find a local restaurant selling South-East Asian food and you'll find where he worked.'

Mistry was enjoying Low's channelled anger and Devonshire's repressed frustration.

'OK then, get uniform to double-check all the restaurants and cafés around Chinatown,' she said.

Devonshire glared at his senior officer. 'Do you know how many there are?'

'Yes.'

'Just because of what Low said?'

'Yes.'

'Can I say something here, Inspector Mistry?'

'No you can't, DC Devonshire. Just call them.'

Devonshire thought about doing something he knew his career might later regret. Instead he headed for the door.

'Wah, you really give face to your boss, ah. I'm impressed,' Low said. 'You want her job, is it?'

Devonshire stopped at the door.

'No, I want to sleep with my wife tonight. So go fuck yourself.'

He tapped his touchpad. The St George's Cross appeared on screen.

White and red-blooded. His England. His DNA. His way of life.

Others in the movement wanted the more obvious flag, the Union Jack, a tokenistic gesture to appease the mainstream media, the red tops, and the other right-wing supporters masquerading as tolerant multiculturalists to appease advertisers.

Britain was beyond saving, he thought, as the white capital letters filled the horizontal red line of the cross. Only one country was worth saving now.

Make England Great Again.

No more compromises. No more concessions to indecisive neighbours. The motherland was the last hope. The other countries wanted external alliances with outsiders, forever droning on about borders, trading agreements and dying languages. Collectively they were lost causes, no less foreign than the sovereignty-stealing hordes beyond the English Channel.

One country had to go it alone. Again. History stood poised, ready to repeat itself.

Initially, the MEGA leaders were apprehensive about the St George's flag. But England *was* the Union Jack, particularly to the rest of the world. That was the point. The country had carried the kingdom for centuries, economically and culturally. They queued up at Calais to get into England, not Scotland. Britain wasn't great. England was. From an economic standpoint, it was an incontestable fact, so they might as well make it a political one. Other alt-right movements pandered to followers across the island's flimsy borders, but the time for pandering was done. England was being diluted and defiled.

His England.

His hometown.

Every face was foreign.

They were everywhere, pouring through every pus-filled abscess they could find at his shopping centre, his old school, his bus and Tube, his doctor's waiting room and his place in every queue, stealing his space and spending his money.

He saw the future in the past.

Unlike the others, he actually read. They were self-medicated. He was self-educated. The Greeks. The Romans. The Silk Road. The Celts. The Anglo-Saxons and the Scandinavians. The American Revolution. The Industrial Revolution. The movement of peoples, a million Dick Whittingtons looking for work, advantages and privileges, history repeating itself over and over again in every chapter, in every book; he read them all.

But now it was different. The social weakness of his people had become the invaders' financial strength. London's streets were paved with welfare gold. England was paying not only for its own success, but also for the failures of tin-pot African dictators and religious nutcases in the Middle East. They came not to work, but to survive. He actually understood that. Unlike the Neanderthals in the movement, he recognised a refugee's thinking, the human need to get away at any cost, and be anything other than a victim. Of course he did. He understood misery, but he had learned to become the master of his own oppression.

They had to do the same.

He tapped his touchpad again and watched the incendiary language fill the screen. Simple words for the simple-minded.

Fake news. Ban the burqa. Gender-neutral toilets. Grooming gangs. Foreign aid. Muslim gangs. London stabbings. Jihadi killings. Refugee Britain. Poverty Britain. Foreign Britain.

We are foreigners in our own country.

We are being silenced by our own media.

We are being ignored by our own government.

But we will not be ignored.

We will not be silenced.

We will take our country back.

We will Make England Great Again.

The political slogans were crap. He knew that. That's why they worked.

He wouldn't Photoshop the images. Not any more. He would give the snowflakes no angle, no comeback, not now. Besides, there were more than enough online images from northern France, Turkey and Syria to give him what he wanted.

The movement would approve of the video and particularly its timing.

The dead kid in Chinatown would bring out the hipster beards with their whiny university educations and middle-class guilt, but only in the short term. Once the snowflakes melted away, as they always did, the racial retaliations would begin in earnest. He was prepared. History was on his side.

The movement finally had its Archduke Franz Ferdinand. The fuse was lit.

One stabbed Singaporean was finally going to make England great again.

CHAPTER 7

Hawker Heaven's schizophrenic menu amused Low. The restaurant's confusing fusion of dishes did just enough to appeal to day trippers who didn't know any better.

But Low did know better.

He was from Singapore, the real Hawker Heaven, not a pale imitation in London that was neither here nor there. Even the garish sign above the restaurant betrayed the chef's identity crisis. The letters were gold and the background red, obviously the lucky colours for superstitious diners obsessed with prosperity.

But the words almost made Low laugh out loud.

Hawker Heaven. The best Singapore and Malaysia cuisine in London.

The two countries rarely agreed on anything, let alone a menu. The competing dishes were a clash of cuisines. Hainanese chicken rice and *nasi padang*. Penang *laksa* and Peking duck. Dim sum and *dosai*. Singapore noodles and prawn balls. Low was still waiting for a London cook to tell him what a Singaporean noodle was. They didn't exist in Singapore.

Nor did the menu. It was a cynical mix of Chinese nostalgia

and fortune-cookie culture for tourists, but it made money. Nothing else mattered.

'Feeling nostalgic?' DI Mistry asked, locking her car.

'You're kidding, right? You don't remember what real hawker food tasted like.'

'It was a long time ago, wasn't it?' DC Devonshire snapped, walking around the back of the car.

'Yeah, I get it, you're married,' Low retorted. 'Maybe you should wear a sign, in case I forget.'

'Maybe you should shut up,' Mistry said.

The three of them looked through the window. The place was small and quiet, caught between lunchtime tourists and early theatregoers.

'I'll give you this, Stanley,' Devonshire said. 'You got this one right.'

'It's Detective Inspector Low.'

'Not here it isn't.'

Mistry stopped at the door. 'It's raining and I'm tired. What did they say?'

Devonshire checked his phone notes. 'Kamal was spotted on CCTV in the street going in and out of here a few times a week, carrying bags, presumably doing local deliveries. We're on Gerrard Street, on the edge of Chinatown, but an easy walk from where his body was discovered. The job probably helped with the homesickness.'

'Yeah, good work, a Muslim working in Chinatown, with non-halal food everywhere and a casino at the end of the street. He must have felt right at home,' Low said.

'He was here because of this,' Low continued, pointing at the menu. 'They've got *prata* on this ridiculous menu. He could cook it properly and the Chinese can't. Come on.'

Mistry and Devonshire followed their foreign observer into the restaurant.

*

Zhang Wei sat across from the police detectives. He brushed a couple of salt grains off the table. Old habits. Growing up in Penang, he watched his parents maintain the cleanest *laksa* stall in one of the shittiest streets. Penang had always been the unlucky city. The British went to Penang before Singapore, but ended up preferring Singapore's strategic location and deep-water port. Penang became the crumbling colony that the British forgot. So did everyone else. A predominantly Chinese island in Malay-controlled Malaysia, Penang had always managed to not quite fit in.

Zhang Wei's parents had always insisted they were the unlucky race living on an unlucky island in an unlucky country. He grew tired of the defeatism and decided to make his own luck. The best young *laksa* chef in Penang left to become another Asian fusion cook in London.

But he still kept the cleanest tables. Just like his parents. The name above his restaurant meant everything to him. In the bustling madness of Chinatown, he would always maintain a quiet corner of Hawker Heaven.

'I like the name of the place. Makes me feel nostalgic,' Low lied.

Zhang Wei smiled at a fellow Chinese face. 'You're Malaysian?'

'Come on, ah, you been in London for too long. This accent Malaysian, meh?'

'Ah, you're Singaporean.'

Devonshire, sitting between Low and Mistry, felt like mayonnaise in a brown-bread sandwich. He watched the two Chinese men with genuine interest.

'You can tell he's Singaporean just from that? He could be from anywhere.'

'Singlish,' Mistry muttered, eager to move on. 'He's laying it on like treacle. Now, Mr Zhang, how long have you worked here?'

'Don't work. *Own*. I own the place.'

Zhang Wei smoothened the apron across his inflated stomach, the proud, physical embodiment of Chinese affluence. Scrawny men once pulled trishaws and ran errands for plump, self-satisfied men. Zhang Wei was now one of the plump, self-satisfied men.

'You grew up poor, right?'

Zhang Wei didn't understand the Chinese copper's question.

'My dad was a taxi driver, all day long to the airport, taking *ang mohs* like this one,' Low said, pointing at Devonshire.

'What about you?'

'Hawker stall. Georgetown.'

'Ah, hence the name.'

'Yah.'

'Family stall.'

Zhang Wei nodded. 'Three generation. I was the third. My dad made the best *laksa* in Penang. And then he taught me. And I made the best *laksa* in Malaysia.'

Low laughed politely. 'But you left?'

'No choice. Asian currency crisis. Ringgit weak. Tourists stopped coming. Less expats in Georgetown. Killed the business. Killed my father.'

Low leaned towards Zhang Wei. 'He, er . . .'

'No, no, no. We're Chinese. Not cowards. Heart attack. November 1997. I come here in early 1998. Chinese New Year. The Year of the Tiger. Just me and my wife. I wash dishes at the casino. Five years later, I work here. Ten years later, I buy here. In memory of my father.'

Zhang Wei pointed at a photograph behind the counter. A Chinese family. Working. Sweating. Sepia-tinted. Fading.

'Was that the *laksa* stall?'

'Yeah, Georgetown, behind a big bank built by the British.'

'That's great, but we really must get to the reason for our visit,' Devonshire said.

'That is the reason, isn't it, Zhang?'

The Hakwer Heaven proprietor didn't understand the scruffy detective's sudden change in tone.

'What?'

'That photograph. The name of the place. Your dead father. The tidy tables and the stone lions, the work ethic and the weird menu; this is all about your pride. Your filial piety. Making your dead father proud.'

Mistry grabbed Low's thigh under the table. 'I think what my colleague is trying to say is ...'

'He knows what I'm trying to say. He's a liar. He lied to the PC Plods when they first showed him a photograph of his dead cook. He lied to himself when his dead cook didn't turn up for work. And he kept lying to himself when his dead cook turned up in the news and the Chinatown grapevine started to shit itself. You wanted what all Chinese want – Singaporeans, Malaysians, all of us. You want calm exteriors. You want to be left alone to make your money. That's who we really are, right? We're not loud and drunk like the *ang mohs*, or loud and Bollywood like the Indians, or loud and arty-farty like the Malays; we're quiet. Respected. And rich. We want our little corner of Hawker Heaven, our nest egg, our *hong bao*, our money, especially our generation, eh? We're not like China's new money. We don't work for pink Ferraris. We work for pride, for our parents, for self-esteem. And your dead cook fucked everything up, didn't he?'

Zhang Wei said nothing. He fiddled with the last salt grain left on the table, one tiny rebel against his daily cause.

'How do you know he worked here?' he said, struggling to get the words out.

'CCTV footage,' Devonshire replied.

'We have Asian students come here every day, same time, especially the South-East Asians.'

'Do they stay for seven or eight hours?' Devonshire asked.

'He made your *prata*, right?' Mistry said.

'I made the *prata*,' Zhang Wei insisted.

'Yeah, you did, because you're a great cook,' Low said. 'But you wasn't a great *prata* cook, not as good as him, not when it came to *prata*. The dough. The oil. The flipping, the line between too dry and too oily, too flaky and too soggy; it's a line that even you can't see. Only he could, because he saw it every day, with his father, just like you and your father with the *laksa* curry, so you swallowed your Penang pride and you brought in the Singaporean kid to make your *prata*, right?'

'Yeah.'

'And you paid him off the books?'

Zhang Wei just played with the salt grain, so Low repeated the question.

'Yeah, it was easier.'

'And cheaper.'

'It was for both of us. He was some government scholar, supposed to be studying all the time, not supposed to be moonlighting at different jobs.'

'Did you ever see him with anyone else? Did he have any enemies or argue with a customer?' Mistry asked.

'No. He was actually a good boy,' said Zhang Wei, 'a good worker.'

Zhang Wei felt his throat tighten, which surprised him.

Low leaned across the spotless table.

'What do you mean jobs?'

Everyone looked at Low.

'You said jobs? Why did you say jobs?'

'I don't understand the question,' said Zhang Wei.

'You said jobs. You were very clear about that. You added the plural. There were times when you dropped the plural, when there should've been one because there are no plurals in

47

Chinese and our "England not so *powderful*", right? We drop our plurals. But you didn't.'

'I don't know.'

'Yes, you do. Where else was he working?'

'He was just a student. I got lots of students here.'

'Ah good, we can check the taxes paid on their work, then. Did you declare their wages? Are they on the books? Shall we bring in your accountant? Do you want to be charged in court? Do you want us to take this place down? That photo. Your father. Those memories. Do you want us to burn it all down? Because we will. Because you turned your back on a dead Singaporean, and I'll speak to my old *kakis* in Chinatown and make your life a fucking misery.'

'Charles Dickens,' Zhang Wei whispered.

'Who?'

'The pub, behind Leicester Square. He worked there.'

Mistry and Devonshire looked at each other.

'Are you sure?' Mistry asked.

'Yeah.'

Devonshire prodded the table with his forefinger. 'Mohamed Kamal worked at the Charles Dickens pub, off Leicester Square?' he said.

'Yeah.'

'What's the big deal?' Low asked.

Zhang Wei flicked the grain of salt away. 'They're asking because they know it's one of *their* pubs.'

Low was thoroughly confused now. 'Whose pubs?'

'I sent him over there,' Zhang Wei said, ignoring the question.

'But why there?' Mistry asked.

'Because they would've smashed in my windows if I didn't. So I pay them. Or I give them free food. Or I give them my staff. I do as I'm told. We all do.'

Zhang Wei ignored the tear rolling down his cheek.

Mistry handed him a tissue from the box on the table. She patted his hand.

'You could've come to us,' she said.

Zhang Wei forced a laugh. 'Nothing you can do any more. They want to take their country back.'

CHAPTER 8

The Charles Dickens was a new pub trying too hard to look like an old one. Everything was dark brown. The bar. The tables. The chairs. The ales. The overworked staff; almost everything was brown except the clientele. Low thought about the irony of Hawker Heaven and the Charles Dickens. Different colours, different worlds; one present, one stuck in the past.

The three detectives stood at the long, polished bar and called the barman over. He was tall, too tall for his job. The low height of the bar made him stoop.

'Yes, mate,' the barman looked only at DC Devonshire, the white face in the trio.

'I'll have a coffee. What do you want?'

'I don't want anything,' DI Mistry said.

'Tea for me,' said Low. 'A splash of milk, not too much. I don't like anything to be too white in here.'

Low leered at the lanky barman, who ignored him.

'Take a seat. I'll bring the drinks over,' he said, still looking at Devonshire.

'Can we also see the manager?' Mistry asked.

Low watched the barman's face. It was barely perceptible, but it was enough to give the young man away. Fear.

'Is there something wrong?' The barman asked.

'No, just this.'

Mistry flashed her warrant card. 'Just a routine inquiry.'

The barman threw a tea towel over his shoulder and walked off.

'You see that? Scared of the manager,' Low said, as they made their way to a table, one that faced both the bar and the pub's entrance.

'He should be. It's a MEGA pub,' Devonshire said.

'Yah, you keep saying that, but here in central London? It's all tourists and students, right?'

'Different place now,' Mistry said.

The barman returned and awkwardly took a pot of tea from his tray. Devonshire helped and reached for his coffee. A much shorter man appeared at the barman's shoulder. He had slicked-back hair with shaved sides around his ears. His impeccable grooming and slight tan suggested a sunbed rather than a recent holiday. He gently touched the barman's arm.

'Thanks,' he said kindly, watching the barman leave.

'I'm Paul Harvey, the manager,' he continued, shaking each detective's hand. 'George said you wanted a word with me. Shall I sit down?'

Mistry pointed at the last chair around their small table. 'Please. It's your pub.'

Harvey adjusted his shirt and took note of the different colours around the table.

'How can I help?'

Devonshire pushed a photograph of Mohamed Kamal across the table. 'Have you seen him before?'

Harvey peered at the photograph. 'Don't think so. Good-looking boy, though.'

'No, you answered too quickly,' Mistry said. 'Shall we start again?'

'I'm sorry?'

'No you're not. He worked here, didn't he? As recently as two weeks ago. Already checked the CCTV footage in the street. And we saw him coming in and out of here at least five times so far. We're still checking further back.'

Harvey had another look at the photograph. 'Well, he's young. He's our demographic. We've got half a dozen colleges within walking distance. Get students in here all the time.'

Devonshire took back the photograph. 'He's not your demographic. He's a Muslim. Muslims don't drink.'

'Christ, you'd be surprised. They say one thing and do another. I've seen them in here. After college. All pissed.'

'I don't see any in here now. In fact the only non-white faces I see are me and him,' Mistry said, nodding towards Low.

Harvey looked at the shabby Chinese bloke for the first time.

'How come he doesn't speak?' Harvey asked, suddenly wary of the silent one.

'I'm just an observer,' Low said, sipping from his cup. 'Nice tea.'

Devonshire appeared anxious. 'I'm getting fed up with this now. You're lying. We all know you're lying. So let's stop wasting time, eh?'

He tapped the photo. 'You know this kid because he was stabbed to death in Chinatown, just across the road from here. So you know him from that. You also know him because he was working here. You won't admit it because he was cash in hand. We get it. We don't care. We just want to know why you wanted a Muslim kid working in a pub owned by a far-right movement with confirmed links to white supremacy.'

'Hey, I'm not having that. This pub is owned by—'

'Yes, yes, we know who the franchise is, we know you've got pubs just like this one all over the country and you've got the cheap family-friendly menu, with proper British grub and kiddie meals and a quiet atmosphere, just like how good English pubs used to be, and we also know that behind closed doors you like to get together with your Nazi mates and reminisce about the good old days, when you could leave your front doors open and not get burgled because there were no darkies like her around.'

Harvey grinned.

'I don't think you can call her that. I think the correct term is . . .'

'My wife,' Devonshire interrupted. 'The correct term is my wife. But she doesn't get called that when your Make England Great Again muppets go marching, does she? No, she gets called a Muslim bitch and a Muslim whore.'

Mistry brushed her husband's pointing finger away from Harvey's face. 'Yes, I think he gets the point.'

'I don't know. I'm starting to like him now,' Low said. 'Let him carry on.'

Mistry glared at Low and then Harvey. 'Do you want us to check your books? Do you want us to speak to your part-time staff, past and present? Do you want a uniform presence, inside and outside the pub, whenever you have a lock-in for your little Hitler wank-fests?'

'No.'

'So I'll ask again. Why did you employ a teetotal Muslim to work in a pub that's popular with members of an Islamophobic organisation?'

Low thought about Mistry's question. It was a fair one. Mohamed Kamal and the Charles Dickens pub were all wrong for each other. Something was off. Low looked around the pub. Everything was knowingly fake and wilfully nostalgic, like a game of Minecraft for xenophobes, building blocks to an imperial past. Fake Edwardian tiles. Fake copperplate writing for menu specials. Fake candlestick holders for the wine lists. Fake stained windows. Fake leather armchairs. Fake heritage. Fake pub. Fake night out.

Fake was good. Fake was a warm security blanket for closet supremacists.

But Mohamed Kamal was real. He was a real face of real Britain, shattering the illusion, burying the myth. His presence alone destroyed the fake environment around him. And that could really put you off your beer.

In a pub where image was everything, Mohamed Kamal had the wrong one.

Image.

Make England Great Again.

It's all about image.

'Image,' Low muttered, almost to himself.

They all looked at him.

'That's why you had a brown face in a white place.'

'What?' Harvey said, genuinely unsettled.

'A brown face in a white place. It's obvious. You had to. You're the masters of reinvention. That's what you do. For centuries. You blend in. You make the abnormal look normal. You're not normal, of course. We all know that. You're monsters. But monsters scare us, especially when we see them in the mirror. If you look like monsters, then people can't agree with you. People can't agree with monsters, can they? Bad image again. So you have to make them feel better by changing your image. Same views, of course. They never change. Just a different image for different times. You evolve. Like religion. You adapt. It's Darwinism for racist dummies. You dress differently. No more shaved heads and swastika tattoos. Now it's smart haircuts and sharp suits. A turd is still a turd, but you're a polished turd now, a presentable turd for the public, for the media. So you take down the St George's Flag behind the bar. Too obvious. You don't have busts of Churchill on the bar. Too obvious. You can't have an entirely all-white staff in every one of your pubs. Too obvious. So you throw in one or two dark faces. You don't want them, but it looks better on TV. The image is more palatable. If you don't look like monsters, then the people who secretly agree with you won't feel like monsters. You made a brown face a PR gimmick. You brought Mohamed Kamal into the lion's den to make you look better and now he's dead. One of your lot killed him and that makes you an accessory before the fact.'

'No, it doesn't,' Harvey said.

'Yes, it will. I'll prove it as a point of principle.'

'What principle?'

'He was Singaporean. I'm Singaporean. And I don't like your haircut. So, last chance. Why did you employ him?'

Harvey looked down at the floor. 'He told me to,' he said.

Devonshire took out his notebook. 'Who told you to?'

Harvey peered up at the security camera inside the pub, capturing him, incriminating him.

'Can we do this off the record?'

'That depends,' Mistry said.

'On what?'

'On what you say. This is a murder investigation. We're not here to protect anyone.'

'That's not what you're asking me. I don't know anything about that. Really. I don't. I was as shocked as anyone else. You're asking about the kid's job.'

Mistry considered her options. 'If it's a worthwhile lead and we prove that you're not involved in the murder.'

'I'm not.'

'OK, get on with it.'

Harvey rubbed the back of his head. 'Does anyone want another drink?'

'Get on with it.'

'OK, I was told to hire him,' Harvey said quickly.

Mistry almost smiled at Low. Almost.

'Who by?'

'Is this still off the record?'

'Is the kid still dead?' Mistry snapped. 'Who by?'

'You're right, OK,' Harvey said, looking at Low. 'He said we've got to dilute our whiteness a bit, at rallies, at town hall

55

sessions, in our pubs, everywhere. He said the Republicans always brought out their black supporters at TV rallies in America. We had to do the same.'

'Mohamed Kamal wasn't black.'

'You know what I mean. We've got a big rally coming up in Bethnal Green. Lots of publicity and all that, so we needed non-white faces right across the board. We have to say that this is a issue of nationalism, not racism, and that non-whites supported us as well, just like black and Hispanic Republicans. I was told non-white faces were actually worth more to us in the long run.'

'Why Mohamed Kamal?' said Devonshire.

'He lived local, studied local. He was a student working nearby. Convenient.'

'He was given to you by the owner of Hawker Heaven, wasn't he? A part-exchange in return for protection that week?'

'I don't know anything about that.'

Devonshire looked up from his notepad. 'Don't lie to us now. We know how you pay for your marches and campaigns. It's the same reason why your pubs are never vandalised or robbed.'

Harvey started fidgeting. 'Look, I really don't know anything about that. I'm just a pub manager with a pregnant wife and a mortgage. You think I want this shit in my life? I don't ask what pub I get sent to. That's up to the brewery. That's up to *them*. And some of these old pub and brewery owners, they can be quite, you know, old-fashioned in their views.'

'Racist views.'

'No, not necessarily. Economic views. Christ, I might not agree, but how many truly multiracial pubs do you know? I know being white and working class in the twenty-first century is the worst thing in the world to be now, but we've kept British pubs in business for hundreds of years. Now pubs are dying and we're supposed to say that's all down to cheap booze at supermarkets? Yeah, right. Look deeper.'

'Do you want us to feel sorry for you?'

'No, I'm just telling you how it is. Pub owners want to preserve their clientele. They also want to be politically correct. Who knows? Who cares? It's up to them. They tell me I need an Asian potboy to collect glasses. So they give me an Asian potboy.'

'Was he ever here when the MEGA members had their meetings?' Mistry asked.

'Yeah, it's possible, I suppose.'

'So he could've heard something or looked at someone the wrong way.'

'I don't know. How could I know that?'

'Who told you to hire him?'

'I can't tell you that.'

'You can if you don't want to go to prison,' Low said.

Harvey made sure no one else was within earshot. He cupped his hand over his mouth, shielding his lips from the camera.

'Billy Evans,' he said.

The name silenced the table.

Mistry watched the dopey barman collect empty bottles from a nearby table and thought about the bitter indignities of life.

She wasn't the right gender, race or rank to take on Billy Evans.

They would almost certainly take the case away from her now.

CHAPTER 9

Billy Evans adjusted his headphones, relishing the tension in the studio. They watched him through the glass. Young producers. Fresh graduates. Interns. Snowflakes.

He could smell their hatred.

He thrived on it.

Hatred kept him relevant.

Hatred made him rich.

He ignored Mark Beckett ignoring him. The London Call-In host was another actor playing a part. Beckett was no different from Evans really. Beckett just happened to be on the other side of the spectrum. Wealthy boy. Liberal man. They were ten a penny. At least Margaret Jones wasn't a phoney. She had retained her council-estate Conservative values and her Midlands accent. Beckett had picked up a new one along the way. He'd found it somewhere between the Thames Estuary and an old Guy Ritchie movie.

Evans sat between them, enjoying their discomfort. Britain's divisive political climate had obviously thrown the two hosts together, the unhappiest of radio marriages. The male bleeding heart and the defiant female voice of intolerance, they even turned gender stereotypes upside down. For three hours every weekday morning, their distinct echo

chambers combined to make a racket like no other on breakfast radio.

And it was a racket.

London Call-In had never made so much money. Hatred was
big business.

Even Billy Evans recognised that he needed Beckett just as
much Jones. Opposites attract controversy. And controversy
paid for Evans's new home in an exclusive gated community
in Hampstead.

More faces gathered behind the glass panel. Arms up. Phones
ready. Evans was always good for viral clips. The commercials
ended. The studio mics lit up. Beckett raised his hand for silence.

'Welcome back to the London Call-In breakfast show with
me Mark Beckett and my co-host Margaret Jones.'

'I'm not your anything,' Jones interrupted.

Evans almost smiled, but remembered the phone cameras. He
had an attractive smile, but a meme could easily fix that.

'And we've started already,' Beckett continued. 'As regular listeners of this show will know, I didn't particularly want today's
guest to come on.'

'Oh for heaven's sake, Mark. You either want freedom of
speech or you don't. You believe in democracy, as long as it's a
democratic decision or opinion that you approve of. You champion freedom of speech and then you don't.'

'Look, Margaret, let's assume our audience aren't primary-
school kids for a moment. I don't want any demagogues on here,
left or right, whether they are half-baked fascists or misogynistic
fundamentalists. I believe that if we give them a voice, we give
them a platform. We give them legitimacy in the eyes of their
idiotic followers. Suddenly our guest isn't a far-right extremist
with nothing new to say, nothing that hasn't been heard in
London since the 1930s; he's the "guy off the radio". He's the
"guy off the TV". By being on this show, we give him more
credibility than his ludicrous politics deserve.'

'No, Mark, we have him on here because he is saying stuff that a lot of people living on housing estates, people who can't get a job, people who can't get their kid into the local school, people who can't get an appointment to see their doctor for three weeks privately believe. But they can't say it. They can't complain because for far too long now, radio stations like this one have overly self-censored. We've become too obsessed with what we can't say, rather than what we can say, and what's happened? We left a vacuum for men like Billy Evans to fill.'

Jones pointed at Evans, who sat with his arms folded, watching his hosts do the heavy lifting on his behalf.

'And this is the one occasion where I might agree with you,' Beckett said.

It was his turn to point at Evans.

'Mr Evans doesn't want to be on this radio show. He wants to be a martyr. He wants to be a victim of the brutish, self-serving Establishment. He wants to show that we are all part of some global conspiracy, presumably one controlled by Zionists, and one that wants to share wealth and power among ourselves. That's the only reason I've agreed to have Mr Evans on our show today.'

'Well, I for one, will be interested in what Mr Evans has to say, because whether you care to admit it or not, Mark, people are concerned about immigration in this country. I think you should be worried, not about what Mr Evans says, but the fact that he has a growing audience of people that want to hear him say it.'

'They'll get their chance after the break, when we'll hear from Mr Evans and take some of your calls. We're back after the news and sport.'

Beckett nodded towards the faces behind the panel. The microphone lights went off. A smooth celebrity voice filled the studio, telling listeners why they should consider changing their car insurance.

60

Evans's work was already done. And he hadn't said a word.

Jones received a producer's instructions through her headphones.

'Er, Billy, I know it's a delicate subject,' she said, leaning towards her guest. 'And we have to be very, very careful for obvious legal reasons, but would you be able to comment on the recent killing in Chinatown? It's being called a hate crime, because of that graffiti, you know.'

Evans scratched the stubble on his right cheek. 'Absolutely. That was terrible what happened to that poor boy.'

Detective Chief Inspector Charlie Wickes peered into the eyes of the leader of Britain's far-right political movement.

He muttered the words under his breath, as if reminding himself.

'Make England Great Again.'

At times, Wickes struggled to understand his country. He adored his family, worked hard and played by the rules. The kids were at university, tuition fees paid through his hard graft. No tax breaks. No handouts. The mortgage was done and retirement in his beloved back garden beckoned. But he wasn't sure what he was retiring to.

The smooth, angelic face of Billy Evans was becoming the face of a world he didn't understand. Evans held no elected position. He didn't even have a political party. But he was the most famous politician in Britain. A politician with no party, no history, no baggage, just opinions; he was the perfect rabble-rouser in the age of anti-intellectualism.

He was also a good-looking bugger. Housewives loved him. The husbands were easy. They always were. Getting the wives on side had been Evans's real masterstroke.

Wickes turned away from the whiteboard. His office was full with chattering policemen and women. Even coppers loved soap operas. This one had a dead Muslim foreigner with a direct connection to a polarising political leader. Wickes could've charged admission. There was so much to get through today.

First, he had to deal with the Chinese elephant in the room. Singapore's loss was Wickes's pain in the arse.

'Most of you have met him already, but this is Detective Inspector Stanley Low from Singapore,' Wickes said. 'He's been helping DI Mistry with any Singaporean lines of inquiry. And from her report, I gather he's been very helpful in giving us this Evans lead. Thank you.'

Wickes tapped the whiteboard. Low reciprocated with a slight nod of the head.

'However, we must tread carefully now. I've been in with the commander at SO15 for most of the morning. Naturally, Counterterrorism are watching and are increasingly involved. I can't help that. They want a quick result. They also want minimal fuss. Nothing political. A foreigner, even a highly decorated foreigner like Inspector Low, cannot be connected to this investigation. Foreign intervention in our domestic affairs is already keeping our data teams awake at night and if the media found out we had an inspector from China . . .'

'For Christ's sake, I'm Singaporean,' Low interrupted.

Wickes decided to pause before answering. He was well aware of Low's intellect.

'I know you are, Inspector,' Wickes said, lowering his voice. 'I know that Singapore is an independent city state and takes great pride in its multiculturalism. But I am also aware that they will not discriminate, out there. The same people who call my Indian officers "Pakis" will call you a '"Chink" and assume that you are an undercover operative for some surveillance organ back in China, with the aim of influencing our political agenda through our law-enforcement agencies.'

'That's ridiculous.'

'No, that's social media. Barack Obama was a Kenyan.

62

The London Mayor is a terrorist and you are working for the Chinese government. That's how it works.'

'He's right,' Mistry said.

'Yeah, it's for the best,' Devonshire added. 'You can go and give more inspirational talks to LSE students. I heard they were a big success.'

'Who's talking to you?'

'Enough. You see. That's exactly my point, Inspector. I know about your achievements. I also know why you are giving lectures at the London School of Economics instead of heading your own team back in Singapore. And we can't have that. Not here. Not now. So again, thank you for your help. And we all wish you a safe flight back to Singapore.'

'Ah, fuck it,' Low said, shoving his chair hard into a desk. 'Good luck trying to catch him without me.'

'We did solve crimes before you arrived, Stanley,' Devonshire said.

Low walked over to Devonshire's desk, leaning into his face, forcing the younger detective to instinctively recoil.

'It's Inspector fucking Low.'

'Like the Chief Inspector says, not in here it's not.'

Low admired Devonshire's response. The *ang moh* had balls. He could see the attraction. But he couldn't let him have the last word either.

'Yeah? Well, be quick with this one, otherwise you'll be scooping up more dead Asians. He'll kill plenty before you catch him, DC Dipshit.'

Wickes stood between Low and the seated Devonshire, sighing like an exasperated kindergarten teacher separating toddlers.

'Don't be escorted from the station,' he muttered. 'Leave with your dignity.'

Low took a step backwards, as if reeling from an unseen punch. His eyes found Mistry. She turned away.

'Ah, don't worry about that, Chief Inspector. My dignity left me years ago.'

In the London Call-In studio, Beckett rubbed his forehead in exasperation. He was aware of the omnipresent webcam. But he wasn't playing to the gallery. Not this time. He really didn't want to look up at the man on the other side of the desk. He didn't want to play with the devil, but he had to say something.

'Mr Evans,' he began.

'Call me Billy.'

'No, I'll call you Mr Evans. We're not friends. And I'm not personalising you. I'm not prepared to participate in this jocular narrative that you and your acolytes are trying to spin for the masses.'

'I'm just asking you to call me by my first name, Mark. I'm giving you respect.'

'I don't want your respect, Mr Evans. I want an explanation. I want to know why you think it is propitious to hold a rally now, at this extremely sensitive time, in a part of east London that is very fragile after a number of violent knife crimes across all races?'

The phone cameras behind the glass moved from right to left, like ruddy-cheeked faces at a tennis match. Evans waited for them to find him.

'There are two sides to every story, Mark,' he said.

'No, there was a Muslim victim in a Chinatown alley with the xenophobic slogan of your mob sprayed across the wall. That's the only story I'm interested in.'

Evans pulled his seat closer to the studio desk. 'But you're not, though, are you? You won't say that slogan because you know it isn't xenophobic. It's a passionate rallying cry for proud patriots.'

'I'm not giving you or your outfit any more publicity than I'm professionally obliged to.'

'But why can't you say the words? Make England Great Again. Why has it become a hate crime to love one's country?'

Beckett watched the camera phones find his perspiring face again. He realised he was gritting his teeth. 'Because it's already great. It was already great.'

He spat the words out, far too aggressively.

Jones almost caught herself smiling. She knew Beckett's idealistic naivety would catch him out. He might as well be living in Legoland.

'And this is where you look out of touch, Mark,' she said. 'Because have you been to the Midlands recently? Have you been to the North East? Have you stepped outside your little multicultural mews in a trendy London enclave? Have you seen the effects of our manufacturing decline? For many people, this is not great. We've got food banks and children living in poverty.'

'I know that,' Beckett said, his voice wobbling. 'Then blame the government for their incompetence, or the banking bailout or just blame the unregulated banking industry full-stop. Blame offshore tax havens, the oligarchs, the media barons and Westminster's addiction to dirty Russian money. Blame all of them for squirrelling their billions away from our social services. There's a long list to choose from. But tell me, please, how is holding a xenophobic rally just days after the death of poor Asian student going to make England great again? There. I've said your idiotic, reductive, racist slogan.'

'I resent the term "racist" and I also take issue with you connecting our rally to a young man's tragic death,' Evans said. 'I resent the inference. And I think your listeners will, too. Again, I offer my sincere condolences to the young man's family. And again, his death has nothing to do with our organisation and we are happy to cooperate with any investigation. I can't be held accountable for every violent act or piece of graffiti in the country. This has nothing to do with who we are. Listen to my speeches. Read our online material. You will not find anything racist. We call for stringent immigration measures, the kind that are implemented in most developed countries around the world, including Singapore, which I believe is where the poor man was from. So in that respect, you are right, Mark. We don't really want to make England great. We just want tougher border control, like everyone else. We want to be like Singapore again. We want to be like Australia again. We want to make England normal again.'

Beckett threw his pen on the desk.

'You want to make England white again. And you know as well as I do that this rally of yours will give you exactly what you want. It'll give your lobotomised followers an incitement to riot.

'This is London Call-In. We'll take your calls after the break.'

Evans had been denied a chance to respond, but he didn't need one.

He actually agreed with Beckett. The melting snowflake was right.

With a bit of luck, the rally would be an incitement to riot.

CHAPTER 10

The coppers stood in a line. Yellow vests. Helmets pulled down. Truncheons held high. Waiting.

They filled the path cutting through Altab Ali Park. The park had two sides. Just like East London.

They confronted the white faces, tattooed necks and St George's flags. In those blotchy, ruddy cheeks, they saw England's past dreaming of an Aryan future.

Singing. Wistfully. Belligerently.

'We want our country back.

We want our country back.

We want our country back.

We want our country back.'

The darker faces of England's present stood behind the coppers, wearing leather jackets and straggly beards. They saw a violent past repeating itself. Older, greying faces preached tolerance. Younger, snarling faces promised retaliation.

Singing. Angrily. Defiantly.

'Fuck Billy Evans.

Fuck Billy Evans.

Fuck Billy Evans.

Fuck Billy Evans.'

The man himself paused to absorb the glorious poison,

allowing the surrounding camera phones to compile his next viral clip. His men had chanted his name since his arrival, shaking his hand and slapping his shoulders as he'd made his way through an adoring crowd of devoted patriots.

They sang the right name, but got their sums wrong.

'There's only one Billy Evans,

One Billy Evans,

There's only one Billy Evans,

One Billy Evans.'

He knew that wasn't true. His job was to prove it. Beneath the tattoos and the crew cuts, everyone was Billy Evans here, but he was preaching to the converted. He wanted the Billy Evanses in hiding, those sitting at laptops, or on buses or inside office cubicles, wrapped in a fraying security blanket of suburban respectability. He had hooligans on tap. They sustained him. Protected him. But only the terrified souls cowering in their market towns and fading villages would make him. He needed them in the long term. He needed an incident.

'You hear that?' he said to dozens of phones, GoPro cameras and cheering men with lettered knuckles. 'I'm here today to hold a legitimate political rally, to exercise my right to free speech, to champion our country's sovereignty – and I get vicious abuse. I cannot even guarantee my own safety in my own city.'

Just a few feet away, PC Cook ignored Evans's irony as he battled to separate white and brown faces. Evans was the safest man in London right now. He had a small, devoted army between him and the rioters, a human shield of steroid-injected muscle dipped in fake tan. They even wore sunglasses on a gloomy day, just to underscore how hard they were. Evans also enjoyed the protection of the Territorial Support Group, a line of riot police stretching from one corner of the green square to another, paid by the taxpayer to maintain public order and babysit a bigot.

Evans was buffeted and safe.

Cook was the one at risk of getting his head kicked in.

'I wish he'd stop bloody talking,' Cook said, waving his truncheon in the air.

'He's just telling them what they want to hear. The trouble is, it works.'

PC Bishop ducked as a glass bottle filled with urine sailed through the air. A copper raised his shield. The bottle bounced off the shield without breaking. Instead, it mischievously rolled along the police line. Their polished boots were now covered in another man's stale piss.

'Just stand still,' Cook shouted. 'Stop pushing.'

He could feel the fists against his stab vest.

'You're wasting your time,' Bishop screamed back.

'By shouting at them?'

'By doing anything. Push back a bit, for the cameras, but don't do anything daft. Whatever we do, they'll beat the shit out of each other anyway.'

Evans watched the two halves of the park squeeze on its central pressure points. Altab Ali Park had been deliberately chosen. Its path had essentially cut the square into two green triangles, an ideal setting for two tribes to dig in and make a bit of a mess. The park was off Whitechapel Road, the home of multiculturalism and Jack the Ripper.

Fear and terror had always visited Whitechapel.

Evans surrounded himself with the usual familiar faces from the movement. Tall. Muscular. Imposing. Handpicked. They always did a job for Evans. Any job. No questions asked. True believers made the best subordinates. They didn't need to be paid. One of them handed Evans a megaphone. Another placed a discreet box on the grass. Evans wasn't very tall.

He raised a hand to silence one half of Altab Ali Park. He couldn't silence the other half and didn't particularly want to. He had cameras recording the abuse.

'I want to thank you all for coming today in such numbers,' he said. 'This is a difficult time for us. It has become politically incorrect to say we want to make our country great again.'

Evans paused for his followers' boos. And then he waited for the other half to reciprocate. He didn't have to wait long.

'Fuck Billy Evans.

Fuck Billy Evans.

Fuck Billy Evans.

Fuck Billy Evans.'

It was almost too easy.

He waved at them, which made them push against the police line, which made his followers push back, which caused bottles to be thrown and men to be punched. His minions recorded everything on their phones.

It really was too easy. Both sides dumb as fuck.

'No, no, no, this is a peaceful protest,' Evans insisted. 'We are here to denounce the tragic death in Chinatown and insist that anyone who uses our slogan to justify such a violent act goes against everything we believe in.'

Evans paused for the patronising applause. And then he waited for the other half to start booing the applause. And they did, obviously. Young students. Old hippies. Liberal whites. Conservative Asians. Outraged Muslims. They all came together, right on cue, to boo the death of a Muslim to score a political point.

'But at the same time, we cannot deny recent history,' Evans continued. 'Globalism has swamped our shores. Globalism has taken our jobs. Globalism has taken their problems and made them our problems, and we've had enough. And this is the bit that no one in the mainstream media wants to admit. We're fighting back. Not just here. Everywhere. Globalism is being met with a new populism. It's not far right. It's not even right wing. It's just populism, which is regular people wanting regular policies that protect their jobs, their homes and their families from foreign

70

cultures and attitudes that we didn't want or vote for. All we are trying to do is protect the native values of a great country. And if that's a crime, then, yes, I'm a criminal. In the same way that Winston Churchill was a criminal. I will not apologise for saying again and again that this is the greatest country in the world and we should do everything we can to keep it that way.'

Evans waited for the competing chants to begin.

'We want our country back.'

'Fuck Billy Evans.'

'We want our country back.'

'Fuck Billy Evans.'

It really was a wonderful war.

And then a middle-aged white man with red cheeks and no neck broke through the police line and head-butted a brown man with a scarf around his neck for calling him a 'wanker'.

And then two younger brown men kicked the white man until he went down, shielding his red cheeks with shovel-sized hands.

And then a dozen policemen turned to face the fracas and a sizable gap opened up along the path of Altab Ali Park.

And then there was chaos.

At the back of Altab Ali Park, DC Devonshire stood beneath a tree and yawned.

Beside him, DI Mistry spoke on the phone, covering her other ear with her hand in a futile effort to drown out the encroaching violence.

'No, you can't have cornflakes for dinner,' she said. 'What was that? No, Benjamin, you can't ...I don't care what Granddad said. You eat cornflakes for breakfast, not dinner ... No arguments. That's it. Eat a proper dinner and then you can have one hour of TV, OK? Right, I love you. I'll see you later. Bye.'

Mistry put the phone back in her bag and watched an over-weight man in a Union Jack spread his arms, a bottle of beer in each hand, another drunken messiah in the MEGA movement, and walk towards a goading crowd of Asian men.

He managed to throw one bottle. Before he took aim with the second, a police truncheon put him down.

Devonshire winced. 'Ooh, nice one, Cook,' he said. 'Did you see that?'

'Yeah,' Mistry lied, not bothering to look up.

'Do you think we should help?'

'No.'

'This one looks quite serious,' said Devonshire, ducking as a bottle flew overhead.

'So did the one in Birmingham. And Worcester. And Walsall. They never last long. Big men. Small dicks. All pissed. It'll be all over in ten minutes.'

'There are some of ours in there. Charing Cross. I can see Cook and Bishop.'

'Yep. And Bethnal Green,' said Mistry, tapping her phone. "And the riot units, which means there are dozens of places in London right now where they're not, where there are real crimes happening right now. They should be out there, not here. These twats can kill each other.'

'All of them? Half of them are – you know.'

Mistry looked up from her phone for the first time.

'What? My people? Is that what you were gonna say?'

'No.'

'So what does that mean? You're not my people? What does that make our son? What "people" does he belong to?'

'Jesus Christ, you want to do this here? You know what I mean. The other people are racist fuckwits.'

'And that means what? I'm with the fundamentalist fuckwits on the other side. Twats are twats. Come on.'

The detectives traversed the edge of the park. They walked closer to mothers pushing buggies. The locals went about their business while grown men fought for issues that mattered only to them. Mistry and Devonshire turned onto the path from the left side of Adler Street, approaching Evans and his minders from behind. Once they got within five metres of Evans, uniformed officers blocked their path. Mistry flashed her warrant card in the young man's face.

'It's getting quite violent, ma'am,' he said, separating an overweight pensioner from his projectile, which was wrapped in a Stella Artois label.

Mistry's glare was enough. The uniformed officer pushed his back into the crowd, parting a sea of spitting faces.

Devonshire jabbed a teenage tearaway between the ribs, poking at the kid's intercostal muscles, literally taking the wind out of his sails.

In response, the kid shoved Devonshire. 'Come on then,' he screamed. 'You shouldn't have brought *her* here, anyway.'

The kid poked Mistry in her back, just below her right shoulder. She spun around and kicked her young assailant in the balls. He dropped to the floor, a crumpled heap beneath his England flag.

'Now fuck off,' Mistry said.

The kid did as he was told.

'That was impressive.'

Mistry turned round to find herself nose to nose with the leader of the Make England Great Again movement.

'Billy Evans,' she said.

'I am. Did you like my speech?'

'No. We would like to talk to you.'

'Go ahead. We're all on camera. Nothing to hide here.'

'Not here.'

Mistry caught the whisper, but only just. She wasn't sure that she'd heard it right. Then it was louder, more than one person, a quiet chorus.

'*Muslim bitch.*'

73

'There's no need for that, chaps,' Evans said.

But the crowd were no longer interested in the white voice, only the brown face. *Female* face. Confident face. She was on their ever-shrinking turf, insulting their leader, kicking their men in the bollocks, mocking them, emasculating them.

She stood among them. Fearless.

And they couldn't have that.

'*Muslim bitch.*'

The volume increased as the numbers swelled. They surrounded the two detectives, but they only had eyes for her. A man with a red cross painted on his face stood between Devonshire and Mistry.

'Do you wanna be nicked?' Devonshire asked.

'Do you wanna fuck off?' the Man With the Red Cross said.

His fist landed just below Devonshire's heart, beside the sternum. The detective's breathlessness suggested he was going into cardiac arrest. He wasn't. But he was out of the picture, punished for being with *her*.

'*Muslim bitch.*'

Their chanting was low, primaeval and terrifying in its focus and control.

Uniformed officers were fighting their way through, but they would never get there in time. Mistry took a step towards her husband, but a bare-chested man grabbed her shoulders.

'I'd leave him alone if I were you, love.'

'Don't call me "love".'

Her gut punch was enough to stall Bare-Chested Man, but not enough to stop him. He rubbed his stomach, as if admiring her handiwork. His playful snarl was met with a sarcastic cheer from the crowd.

'Right, you're under arrest,' Mistry said.

'What? All of us?'

The voice belonged to Man With the Red Cross. He was at her ear, whispering.

'How are you gonna do that, darling?'

Man With the Red Cross almost tore her arm from its socket. He pinned it back. She couldn't move. They closed in. Sweaty, pink faces. Too drunk to care, too sober to miss.

The teenage tearaway was now on his feet, his balls back in place. He wanted his manhood back, too. He held a beer can over Mistry's head and poured. The crowd cheered.

'*Muslim bitch.*'

Devonshire reached out a hand but lacked the oxygen supply to do anything else. Uniformed officers were chopping their way through, but Mistry was at least another five or six cracked heads away.

Evans had already vanished. A born politician with an eye for violence and a nose for bad publicity, he had slinked away, lizard-like, to a waiting car.

He had left the protest in capable hands. They would do the rest.

Mistry noticed the blade.

The knife was held low, away from the cameras, lost in the crowd, beside his right thigh. He was right-handed, just like Mohamed Kamal's killer. The irony was almost funny. Kamal left Singapore for a better life. She once went to Singapore for a better life. It didn't work out for either of them.

Bare-Chested Man took a final step towards her. Raising his arm. Showing off the knife. A tattoo on his right bicep. An English rose. Mistry could never be an English rose. Not in his eyes.

'Sorry about this, love,' Bare-Chested Man whispered.

Mistry closed her eyes and waited for the floating dizziness that never came.

Instead there was noise. Confusion. Uncertainty. Panic.

She felt the hand in her face. Pushing hard. Knocking her to the ground. A sudden, sharp pain in her fingers caused her to scream involuntarily, embarrassingly. She opened her eyes.

There were white trainers and ankle socks. Running. Stamping. She pulled her fingers away and looked up.

He was wearing a dark hoodie. A skull scarf covered most of his face. The sunglasses took care of the rest.

Bare-Chested Man was already on the turf. Lights out.

Man With the Red Cross didn't expect to be confronted by a screaming skull. Not here. Not on his side of the park. Not today.

Man With the Red Cross couldn't move. An asset had become a liability. The packed crowd that had previously trapped Mistry now caged him.

The head-butt was swift and precise. Man With the Red Cross saw his own nose shatter. The sprayed blood filled his peripheral vision. He didn't go down. He was proud of that. He stayed on his feet long enough to hear a strange insult.

'Fuck you, *ang moh*,' Skull Face said.

Man With the Red Cross watched his attacker punch a hole through the protestors and disappear into White Church Lane.

And then a police truncheon put him to sleep.

CHAPTER 11

The Waffen-SS soldier gave him inspiration. He loved the simplicity of the artwork. One man. One request.

Toi aussi! Tes camarades t'attendent dans la division Française de la Waffen SS.

He had memorised the French years ago. It was the only French he'd ever learned.

You too! Your friends await you in the French Division of the Armed SS.

He wasn't like the others. He was smarter. That's why he only had one Nazi recruitment poster on his bedroom wall, unlike the others. They had the Leni Riefenstahl films and the anti-Semitic caricatures, but they all missed the point.

His World War II poster was the only one that truly understood the essence of propaganda. He knew what the poster was really trying to accomplish.

Artistically, the usual boxes were ticked. Handsome soldier. Piercing blue eyes. Angled text. Block capitals. Simplistic message. The poster was the same as any other from the period, except in one aspect.

The language was French, not German.

The Waffen-SS recruiter still pointed his finger out of

the poster, just like Uncle Sam. But he didn't want you. He wanted *them*. He wanted the others. The non-believers. The enemies.

He wanted foreigners to fight for the invader's cause. The Charlemagne Regiment was a group of French volunteers who signed up for the Waffen-SS. They joined their *enemies* in the Armed SS. That was the poster's true power. It turned enemies into friends. Black became white. White became black. That was the greatest triumph of the will. The enslaved joined forces with the enslavers. Voluntarily.

Propaganda in its purest form convinced rational people to sign up for despair only when all hope was lost.

His Nazi recruitment poster understood that. And so did he.

They would never make England great again while there was still any semblance of hope in society. Social change wasn't inevitable. History always needed a nudge.

And now he had the man with the skull face.

He had no idea who the protester was and he didn't care. Trivial details concern only trivial minds. Skull Face was an imposter. That's all that mattered. Skull Face was a dark-skinned invader attacking two English patriots. Skull Face was defending a woman. She was brown. So she had to be a Muslim woman. She *had* to be. Which made Skull Face a Muslim man, brutalising two native Englishmen.

He had watched Skull Face carry out the assault. He had felt Skull Face brush past him as the masked man made his way out of Altab Ali Park. He had considered intervening, but remembered his higher responsibilities.

He had filmed everything.

He tapped his touchpad as Skull Face turned towards the laptop screen. The image froze. It was horrifying. The hoodie. The sunglasses. The skull scarf. The violence. The unmistakable skin tone.

It was perfect.

Skull Face had no identity. Just a voice.

He pressed 'play' and Skull Face spat the words at his camera. 'Fuck you, *ang moh*.'

He had no idea what the foreign words meant. But that didn't matter. He would change them to suit the cause.

Like the handsome Nazi on the poster above his desk, he would find the right words to reach the other side.

DC Devonshire started recording. The interview room was grey and functional. Charing Cross Police Station had an elegant façade and a drab interior. Outside, the public saw warm and smiley. Insider, the suspects got cold and miserable. DCI Wickes sat beside Devonshire, his arms folded, barely present. He had been called in from his garden beds, poking around and pruning, trying to add a few bonus points to the estate agent's sales pitch. His kids had gone. The house was too big and exhausting for a retiring couple. The Wickeses intended to downsize, but bare-chested racists were getting in the way. The chief inspector shouldn't be staring at bare-chested men on a Saturday evening. He should be at home with his wife, scanning the property pages.

The seaside retirement bungalow was slipping from view.

He could only see the busted blood vessels of the grotesque caricature sitting across the table. Pub lock-ins and early-morning kebabs had ruined the bloke's complexion. A bad postcode and the wrong newspapers had done the rest.

'Let's get on with this,' Wickes said.

Devonshire cleared his throat. 'OK, this is Detective Constable Devonshire with Detective Chief Inspector Wickes. Also present is Police Constable Cook. Could you state your name for the recording, please?'

Bare-Chested Man sat back in his chair. His stomach wobbled.

'William Jarvis,' he said.

'And where do you currently reside, Mr Jarvis?'

'I live in a flat above the Elm Park Café, which I own, in The Broadway, near Elm Park station.'

'And would you like to put a shirt on, Mr Jarvis?'

'No, I would not. My shirt was left at the park and you didn't give me a chance to put it back on before shoving me in the back of your meat wagon.'

'That's because you tried to stab one of our officers.'

Jarvis looked at the young solicitor sitting beside him. The solicitor was barely out of university, wearing a suit that betrayed his meagre salary. The solicitor shook his head.

'No comment,' Jarvis said.

DCI Wickes leaned forward. 'Do you always take knives to political rallies?'

'No comment.'

'We already have eyewitness reports, from police officers and members of the public, who saw you holding a knife and preparing to attack.'

'I was one of them,' Devonshire said.

'No comment.'

'We also have camera footage. Everyone has cameras at these events now. In fact, I believe your leader, Billy Evans, insists on his disciples filming everything, right? Just in case he gets pushed around and needs a legal defence.'

'He's not my leader.'

'No, I'm sure. No one tells you what to do, right? No one tells you to attack Asian women. You can make that decision all by yourself, right?'

'Fuck off.'

'You're finished, Jarvis. You know that, right? I don't need a statement from you. I've got a dozen accounts from witnesses. I've got a dozen cameras showing you preparing to attack an unarmed police officer. And there was one other thing. What was it, DC Devonshire?'

'I'm not sure, sir. I can't quite remember.'

'Me neither. Oh yeah. That's it. When you were knocked out cold by the secret Samaritan, you still had the knife in your hand. And when you were lying on the floor, still knocked out, you still had the knife in your hand. And when we surrounded you, and prepared to handcuff you, guess what? You still had the knife in your hand. You tit.'

'And you're a much older man, Jarvis,' Devonshire added. 'And you attacked a police officer, one of our police officers, my boss and my ...So I will make sure you never see the outside again.'

Jarvis leered at the younger detective. 'Giving her one, was you?'

Devonshire felt Wickes's firm hand on his shoulder. Wickes smiled at the fat suspect.

'Only one of us is getting screwed here. The attempted murder of a police officer takes care of you. The actual murder of an Asian teenager makes whatever life you have left a real misery. I will personally see to it that you share a wing with multiracial inmates, seeing as you like to spend so much time with them. You will be among gang members of colour.'

'Is this where I'm supposed to shit myself?'

'No, of course not. You're a right hard case. I can see that. You're a café cook who likes to stab unarmed women. I'm sure they'll all shit themselves when they hear that you're coming.'

'I'll handle myself.'

'You won't.'

'You'll be dead by Christmas,' Devonshire said. 'No more visits from the long-suffering wife or your two daughters.'

Jarvis looked surprised.

'Yeah, we already have officers at your Elm Park Café. We haven't told your daughters that their heroic father tried to stab a woman. Your eldest is already at university, right?'

Devonshire read a note on his phone. 'Yep, she's studying

Gender and Sexuality Studies at University College London. You must be so proud, just up the road from where you killed that Asian kid. And think how proud she'll be, the feminism graduate, when she finds out her dad tried to stab a policewoman.'

'Yeah, yeah, yeah, you've got it all worked out, haven't you? Funny how you ain't mentioned my other daughter, have you? My fifteen-year-old. Got molested on the Tube, going up the escalator. Grabbing her arse. Trying to stick their phone cameras up her skirt. Her fucking school uniform. Three Indian boys. Oh hang on, I can't say that, can I? They might not be Indian. They might be Pakis. Or Syrians. Or Libyans. Or any other Middle Eastern khazi that we're taking them in from this week. They were not Indians. They were BAME kids. They were Black or Asian or minority ethnic kids, right? That's who they were. You know who told me that? You lot. When we went to the station, sitting there with a crying daughter and an angry wife, and I've got the Old Bill telling me not to call them Indians or Pakis, because they are generalisations that don't help anyone. They're groping my little girl's arse on an escalator and I've got to worry about calling them by their right name so no one is offended in the police report.'

'I'm sorry to hear about your daughter,' Wickes said.

'Are you? Are you sorry that my wife found her looking at suicide sites? Are you sorry that she won't take the Tube any more and my wife has to drop her off at school every day? Are you sorry that she crosses the road whenever she sees a dark face?'

'You know that not every Asian is a sex pest.'

'And you know that not every white man is a racist in his own country, but that's what it fucking feels like. Let me tell you something ridiculous. I stuck little Union Jack flags in every sausage during the World Cup and someone reported me to the council. Fucking reported. I ended up in the local paper over it. So I stuck St George's flags all over my café window because I was pissed off with the story in the paper and a load of Asian teenagers threw stones through my window. And what did you lot say? I'd antagonised *them* with the flags. Somehow, it was my fucking fault. Think about that. Think about what England has become. I stick the national flag of my country in the window of my property and I *deserve* to get my windows smashed.'

'So your only revenge is to stab an innocent woman?'

'I wasn't really going to stab her,' Jarvis said.

His solicitor raised a hand. Jarvis pushed it away.

'No, fuck off you. Be quiet. I was just trying to scare her. I'd seen her and this one,' Jarvis said, pointing at Devonshire. 'Getting stuck into the crowd. I saw her kick one of our boys in the bollocks and I thought, "Enough is enough."'

'So you'd stab her?'

'No, just shit her up a bit.'

'Like the kids with your café window.'

'Yeah . . .No . . .Just, like, fucking, you know, let 'em hear us, let 'em know we're still here, that we're not fucking going anywhere.'

'Women?'

'No, them lot.'

'Foreigners? She's not a—'

'Yeah, yeah, yeah, I know. She's not a foreigner. None of 'em are. They're all as British as me, right? Gave us curries and kebabs and all that. I've heard it all before. But they're not as British as me, are they? Not when you really strip it down. Because I wasn't raised in a culture that treated women like shit. I wasn't brought up to call girls like my daughter "white meat". I wasn't brought up to think it's all right to grab a woman's arse.'

'But it's OK to stab them?'

'Oh for fuck's sake, you know I was never gonna stab her.'

'But you were going to stab someone?'

'Yeah, probably, maybe. I don't know. Someone's got to do something, because you ain't doing nothing.'

'Is that why you stabbed Mohamed Kamal?'

'Oh, fuck off.'

CHAPTER 12

Low finally realised why Ramila Mistry's childhood street looked so different. The front gardens had gone. Cars had replaced lawns. Those little grass squares with rose bushes and clipped hedgerows were filled with concrete and paved drives. Residents preferred having car parks in front of their living rooms.

As a student, Low had always envied the front gardens and green patches that filled London's council estates. In Singapore, private gardens were reserved only for the wealthiest. Everyone else was stacked on top of each other, the Government's idea of utilitarian housing being a game of concrete Jenga.

But England was blessed with space.

Even the poorest people had front gardens, but they'd paved paradise to create space for Ford Fiestas.

But Mistry was different. She'd never had a front garden as a kid. She was the daughter of Indian Gujaratis. So she had a corner shop.

Low stood outside, slightly out of breath. The walk from the Tube station seemed further than he remembered. But little else had changed, apart from the shop sign. Mistry's Mini-Mart had morphed into another franchise subsidiary, but the concrete out front was still littered with today's newspaper supplements and yesterday's dog-shit stains.

Low was reluctant to step inside. Mistry's Mini-Mart had always been a happy place. The memories were warm. But the shop was no longer called Mistry's Mini-Mart and Low was no longer happy.

And then he saw her through the window. She gripped an attractive boy with dark, silky hair and light brown skin, the glowing offspring of a happy Eurasian marriage.

Low didn't want to disturb them, to contaminate them in any way. He knew what he was. But he had to say goodbye.

He hadn't before.

The door buzzed as Low entered and a CCTV camera light flashed above his head. There used to be a quaint bell that rang over the door, calling one of the Mistry family in from their living room behind the shop. But that was then.

A familiar, but weary face grinned at him.

'Bloody hell I don't believe it,' said the white-haired Indian, in a hybrid accent that was born in Ahmedabad but made in Dagenham.

'Hello, Dagenham Dave,' Low replied.

The two men shook hands across the counter. Ramila Mistry watched them as her son ran around her legs.

'I haven't heard "Dagenham Dave" for years,' Dhaval Mistry said.

'That's because your name is Dhaval, not Dave,' Ramila Mistry said.

'You see, Stanley, she's still the same.'

'Oh, I know.'

'It's her second-generation-immigrant thing, Stanley. I'm supposed to reconnect with my roots now, apparently.'

Low nodded at his elderly friend.

'Of course. You came over here with a name like Dhaval, but the locals called you Dave and that soon became Dagenham Dave, which meant they had pretty much accepted you as one of their own. But your daughter here says that's a bad thing, right? You've sold out your history, right? Of course, you also worked your balls off to put her through university and what happens? She comes back and tells you off for burying your proud heritage. Right or not?'

'Piss off,' Mistry said.

'Hey, he's still a smart bugger,' her father said.

Dhaval Mistry straightened the newspapers on his counter and turned the sweets around until all of the names on the wrappers faced the front; force of habit.

'How old are you now, Dave?' Low said, enjoying Mistry's discomfort. 'Sorry, Dhaval. Shouldn't you be retiring already?'

'And do what?'

Low pointed towards the little boy, who was now running around in circles, throwing his hands in the air and singing 'I Like to Move It'.

'Spend more time with the grandson.'

'Are you serious? I spend more time with this one than his parents. I'm his grandfather, grandmother, father, mother and bloody shopkeeper.'

Low looked at Mistry. 'Grandmother?'

She shrugged. 'Died three years ago. Pancreas.'

Low realised he was staring at the little boy, who was still singing and dancing around his mother.

'Shit. I'm sorry.'

Dhaval Mistry tided the lottery scratch cards. They didn't need tidying.

'Yeah, well, that's why I'll never retire, Stanley. I'm Asian. We don't retire, do we? We work until we drop and then we pass everything on to our children. She talks about family legacy. This bloody shop is my family legacy.'

'Dad, I don't want your shop. I'm a detective inspector and you still want me to sell Mars Bars and bog rolls.'

'You see, Stanley? Whatever happened to respecting your

87

Asian elders? I look after her and then she looks after me, eh? Remember that?'

'It's all gone, Dave. Filial piety. All gone. Same in Singapore.'

'She forgets. England is a nation of shopkeepers. And we are Gujaratis. We built a world of shopkeepers.'

'Yes, all right, Dad.'

'Yes, all right, Dad. She still thinks it's easy. I arrived here in 1974, Stanley. Do you know what these corner shops were like then? Rubbish. A waste of time. They sold stale bread and baked beans. We revolutionised the corner-shop business.'

Low smiled. He had always liked Mistry's father. 'Yeah, you did.'

'Yeah, we did,' Dhaval Mistry replied. 'And you know our secret? We just work harder than everybody else.'

'Same in Singapore. You lot have been trading there for centuries.'

Dhaval Mistry gestured enthusiastically towards his daughter. 'Ah, you see, you hear that? For centuries over there in Singapore, over here, everywhere. That's what we are. Gujaratis. Shopkeepers of the world.'

Low picked up a bar of fruit-and-nut chocolate. 'Yep, you've been overcharging us for this shit all over the world as well.'

'Get him out of here. Bloody Chinese, all the same,' Dhaval Mistry said, laughing.

'Eh, I'm not Chinese. I'm Singaporean.'

'Oh yeah, Chinese-Singaporean. They're even worse. Treat the Indians like shit.'

Low held out his hand. 'Look after yourself, Dagenham Dave.'

'And you, Stanley.'

They shook hands for a little too long, recalling the last time they were all together in the shop. Everyone was happy then. Older loved ones were still alive. And younger ones were alive with the prospect of being in love. Death and tragedy made it hard for anyone in the shop to be as happy as they once were.

But for a few seconds, they could at least pretend.

As Low followed Ramila Mistry to her car outside, her father picked up her son and the pair waved through the shop window.

Low waved the bar of fruit-and-nut chocolate back at them.

'Bloody hell, he never paid me for that,' Dhaval Mistry said. 'Cheap Chinese bastard.'

Mistry's car pulled away. Both father and son watched her bounce slowly over the speed bumps before disappearing from view.

'I always liked him,' Dhaval Mistry said to his giggling grandson. 'Smartest man I ever met. But I'm bloody glad he didn't marry your mother.'

Low and Mistry waited at the traffic lights. Low watched the faces trudge across the zebra crossing. They no longer matched. White wasn't the only colour on view any more. As teenagers, Low and Mistry had always been the odd ones out. Now they blended in. They were part of the crowd. The shops around them supported the new colour scheme.

'Pawnshops and pound shops,' Low said.

Mistry stopped tapping her steering wheel.

'What?'

'This is globalisation, right here, in one street.'

Low surveyed the street through Mistry's windscreen. 'Look on this side, boarded-up jewellers, pawnshops and pound shops, for those who were left behind. And you look at the other side. You've got property agents, too many of them, waiting to get those with enough money as far away as possible.'

'White flight.'

'What else? Why would they stay? Their culture's been swamped. Look at the shops. On this side, African fruit sellers and Caribbean hairdressers. Look at that one with huge photos of black people with Afros. It might as well be called "run for your life". And then on the other side, pubs, bookies and charity shops, for the poor ones left behind. Those who've given up, those who can't bear to look at faces like ours any more. Aliens. We're an invasion now, a full-on invasion. They can't stop it. They know they can't. So what do they do? They run to their homes. Terrified. Lock all the doors. Close all the curtains and wank over Billy Evans videos.'

'It's not people like us any more,' Mistry said. 'It's people like them.'

Two elderly Muslim women wearing hijabs shuffled across the zebra crossing pulling scruffy shopping trolleys.

'Yeah, they look really scary: a couple of half-dead aunties buying rice at Tesco. Please. It's not them. It's us.'

'What are you on about?'

'Your dad was right. It's the second generation, our generation. Or maybe not even us. We're still the bridging generation. It's the one after us, the third generation, the millennial kids. They're the problem. They don't want to work in corner shops like your parents, can't get access to higher education like us, but they won't keep quiet any more either. They've got a voice, on phones, online, everywhere. They want to fight back. They want respect. And that's not right. They don't get it. They're not playing by the rules.'

'What rules?'

'The rules of the silent migrant; your dad's rules. He had to let people call him Dagenham Dave and "Paki". He had to close one eye when arseholes spray-painted that racist shit on his shop window in the early eighties. You told me all about it. How the racism radicalised you. Made you want to fight back, be a copper. And you could. Sort of. You were that generation in the middle. The acceptable face of settled, compliant migration. But these poor bastards can't do that.

Indian, black, yellow and even white, they can't do that. They're victims of austerity. They're all fucked. So they take it out on each other. They don't play by the rules of the silent migrant. Like they do in Singapore. We've got Filipino maids and Bangladeshi drain cleaners, the poorest people doing the shittiest jobs, but they all still know their place. They shut the fuck up and do as they're told. That's the only way the house of cards stands up. But as soon as they find their voices, Singapore's finished. Everybody knows that. It'll be like this place. Look at it. You can't have shop signs written in Polish. You just can't. The natives won't have it. It's too scary. Too alien. They forgot the golden rule of the silent migrant. Do your shitty jobs and shut the fuck up.'

'So what's your solution, then? The Singapore way? All that artificial racial harmony shit? All the races standing together on "dress-up-like-a-minority" day?'

Low laughed.

'I'm not saying it's right. I'm saying it works.'

'Listen to you, a poster boy for a country that keeps trying to get rid of you.'

'I'm just saying, your dad got it right.'

'Oh yeah, he got it right,' Mistry snapped, accelerating quickly as the light turned green. 'Yeah, totally got it right. That shop has been burgled three times, at least three times that I remember. In the worst one, they tied up my parents. Held knives to their throats. Threatened to carve up their only daughter, me, who was sleeping upstairs. They've had "Pakis go home" sprayed across the window twice. When I was working behind the counter as a kid, we put up with serious racism at least once a month and casual, run-of-the-mill racism at least once a week. So yeah, my dad got it so fucking right.'

Low sighed.

'Never did lose that naivety, eh? We don't get to be right in a white country. We get to survive. That's all. That's as good as it's ever going to get for us. I told you that back then, but you wouldn't accept it.'

Mistry glanced over at the man she once loved, struggling to find him.

'How can you still function with all that shit swilling around inside? How do you get out of bed in the morning? Why would you even bother?'

'Why would you want to come back to this place when you'll never be fully treated as one of them? Why did you leave Singapore?'

'Ah, that one's easy. You were in Singapore.'

Mistry allowed the nasty, vicious dig to burrow its way deep, in the hope of poking through to whatever was left of Low's soul.

And then she said, 'Look, I've got a lot to do today. So I can drop you off at your hotel, but you'll have to make your own way to the airport.'

Mistry didn't think she was being particularly callous or cold. She had already made up her mind. There was nothing left of Low's soul.

CHAPTER 13

As soon as DC Devonshire spotted the St George's flag, he knew he was back to square one. The CCTV image was grainy, but the tattoo was unmistakable. Right bicep. An English rose. The artwork might as well have been a passport photo. It could only be him. White vest. Boxer shorts. Slippers. A sentimental, jingoistic badge of honour on his right arm, it was William Jarvis. Putting out the black bin bags. Surrounded by rubbish.

The time stamp cleared him. Less than an hour between Mohamed Kamal's time of death in Chinatown and Jarvis stepping out from his café in Elm Park, yawning and scratching his balls in the darkness, half asleep, too bleary-eyed, too far away, at least fifteen miles away from the murder scene.

He wasn't there. He didn't do it.

'Happy now?'

Sharon Jarvis peered over the detective's shoulder. Her black roots matched the rings beneath her eyes. The faded tan and blonde peroxide were the work of a proud woman still trying to impress a husband who'd stopped trying after the honeymoon. Her face was staunch and resolute, but let down by too many late nights waiting for him to come home, half hoping he didn't, just in case.

Whenever his team lost, so did she.

That was her life.

The pill had reached her childhood council estate all those years ago, but feminism hadn't. Not quite. There was still a gap, where men like William Jarvis could cling to his patriarchal values.

He was a proud father, a loving husband and a devoted patriot. His Facebook page said so. He was also an occasional wife beater, but nobody's perfect and he always provided for his family. He made sure to remind them of that on the Sunday mornings after the Saturday nights.

The Jarvises had a lovely semi-detached home in a better part of Essex and Sharon Jarvis had wearily accepted the trade-off.

That was her life.

But it would never be Victoria Jarvis's life.

Sharon gave her daughter a maternal squeeze as they returned to one of the café tables. Devonshire sat on the other side, moving the ketchup and vinegar bottles aside.

The café smelled of stale cigarettes and chip fat. Customers came in with one and left with the other. The walls were lined with autographed posters of old boxers and footballers, forgotten names trapped inside fading frames, local faces from the past, put up for customers reluctant to accept the present.

The café stank of nostalgia, a warm, comforting relic for those unable to cope with the unfamiliar world outside.

Devonshire examined the faces sitting at the tables around him. They were mostly older, entirely white and they all fitted in with their drab surroundings, except one.

Victoria Jarvis didn't belong in the café. She was young, attractive, educated and idealistic. Even her accent came from somewhere else, a fee-paying school in rural Essex, where they emphasised wider, double-fronted homes and narrower vowels, the things that mattered in Essex.

Devonshire watched Sharon Jarvis's obvious affection for her eldest daughter. The mother had clearly put all the family's eggs in one basket.

'Thanks for showing me the café's CCTV footage,' he said.

'You had a warrant. Didn't have much choice.'

'Mum, come on. He's only doing his job.'

'Is he? Where was he when you sister was getting molested? Or when they were smashing our windows?'

'Your husband did tell us about that and I'm sorry. Really. But you filed a police report, right?'

Sharon Jarvis picked away at a yolk stain on her apron. 'Waste of time.'

'Will my father be released today?' Victoria asked, eager to move the conversation along.

'No.'

Sharon Jarvis was clearly losing her patience. 'You've seen the video, right? He was here the whole bloody night.'

'He's being held for assaulting a police officer.'

'He told me on the phone. He didn't touch her.'

Victoria Jarvis looked horrified. 'Her?'

'You didn't tell your daughter, Mrs Jarvis?'

'I told her all she needed to know.'

'Dad hit a woman?'

'He didn't hit anyone, did he?'

Sharon Jarvis glared at the detective.

'I can't comment on an ongoing, separate investigation. I'm here to ask you about this man.'

Devonshire carefully laid out five photos across the café table with the care of a croupier dealing out hands of blackjack.

The photos showed Man With the Red Cross at the Altab Ali Park rally. Two photos caught him in the crowd, pushing against the police line. A third captured him on the floor, handcuffed and barely conscious. But the women focused on the other photos.

Victoria Jarvis used the tips of her fingers to gently pull them towards her. There was Man With the Red Cross grabbing an Asian woman's arm, pinning it to her back, spitting words at her face.

95

And there was William Jarvis.

Proud father.

Loving husband.

Devoted patriot.

Knife holder.

Woman hater.

Victoria Jarvis started crying.

'Oh my God.'

She covered her mouth.

But Sharon Jarvis said nothing. She bit her lip.

'You have no right to show these photos to my daughter,' she said.

'That police officer was assaulted, Mrs Jarvis. I have every right. Do you know who this is?'

Devonshire tapped the face of Man With the Red Cross.

'No, we don't. Do you?'

'Yes, we know. We have him in police custody. John Perry. Local tearaway from Canning Town, bit of a pisshead, stacks shelves at a supermarket and hates the world as a result. He still lives with his parents, which is where he was on the night of the murder. He's an idiot with a watertight alibi. I just want to know if this was a random attack, or this bloke likes to work with your husband to stab people of colour.'

Devonshire looked straight at the weeping daughter.

'*Women* of colour.'

'Well, I told you, we don't bloody know him,' Sharon Jarvis insisted. 'There's hundreds of 'em at those bloody events of his. All nutters.'

'And you don't mind your husband attending far-right rallies?'

'Have you seen him?'

'I don't understand.'

Sharon Jarvis almost laughed. The detective was obviously from a well-bred postcode.

'No, you wouldn't, would you?'

Victoria Jarvis was still staring at the photographs.

'He's holding a knife, Mum,' she mumbled.

'Yes he is,' Devonshire said, loudly enough to persuade a man in blue overalls to look up from the football reports at a nearby table.

'Oh come on, Victoria, you know what he's like. Always fancied himself as a hard nut.'

'With a woman, Mum? A fucking woman?'

Now every customer was peering over at the young, pretty brunette. She was still crying.

'Not just a woman,' Devonshire said, looking only at Victoria Jarvis. 'My wife. The mother of my five-year-old son. That's my wife there, Miss Jarvis. Can you see her? She's the one with her arm being pinned back. She's the one looking absolutely terrified because your father is about to stab her with that knife. Can you see that, Miss Jarvis? Can you take in all the elements of the photograph? Maybe you can study this photograph in one of your gender studies classes.'

No one spoke for a while.

'You should've spoken just to me,' Sharon Jarvis said. 'No need to speak to her about this stuff. She doesn't *understand*.'

'What, Mum? What don't I understand? It looks pretty straightforward to me.'

Victoria Jarvis wiped her eyes on the sleeve of her baggy jumper.

'Tell him,' she said softly.

'Tell him what?'

'You don't need to protect me any more, or my sister. Tell him.'

'Vicky, I don't know what you're going on about.'

'Oh for fuck's sake, Mum. The trips in the bathroom. The dropped glasses behind the counter. The black eyes after a night out. It's gotta stop now.'

Sharon Jarvis was furious with herself. They would both see her tears. Her mask was slipping.

'I don't . . .'

Her voice was cracking.

'I mean, I can't . . .'

Victoria Jarvis jabbed the photographs with her fingernails.

'It can stop now.'

'But what about you and your sister.'

'We'll be fine.'

'He never put a hand on you. Or your sister. I made sure of that. I always stood between . . .I never let him . . .'

They were both weeping now. Victoria Jarvis grabbed her mother's hand and held on tightly, as if she would never let go.

'I know, Mum. We both know.'

'Used to think it was my fault. You know what I'm like, a right mouthy cow.'

'It was never your fault.'

'I should've left him.'

'You were protecting us. And you did. But now you gotta protect yourself, Mum.'

Sharon Jarvis pointed at the photograph of Mistry's assault. 'And her. I'm really sorry what happened to her. How old did you say your boy was?'

Devonshire smiled. 'Five. Almost six.'

'Ah, that's a nice age.'

Sharon Jarvis stroked her daughter's long, brown hair. 'They really are lovely at that age.'

'Yeah, they are,' Devonshire said. 'His name is Benjamin.'

'Yeah.'

Sharon Jarvis kissed her daughter on the cheek. 'Isn't she lovely?'

'Yes, she is, Mrs Jarvis.'

Sharon Jarvis took a tissue from a box on the table and blew her nose loudly. She had wasted enough tears.

'No, I think you should call me Sharon. No more of this Mrs Jarvis rubbish. And I think I'd like to make a statement about my husband. Can I do that?'

'Yes, of course, Mrs Jarvis,' Devonshire said. 'Sorry, I mean Sharon.'

Sharon Jarvis still needed her daughter's final approval.

'You think I should do this?'

'You know I do.'

'Yeah. You're right. Fuck him.'

Devonshire took out his notepad and ignored the phone ringing in his pocket.

Mistry stood in the doorway of Low's cluttered hotel room, watching him pack. He was taking too long. He didn't want her to leave. She didn't want to stay.

Only one of them had moved on.

Her phone rang again. The caller ID flashed 'TOM'. Again. Detective Constable Tom Devonshire. Her underling. Her husband. Her excuse.

'Look, I've really got to go,' she said.

'Then go,' Low mumbled.

'Don't be like that.'

'Like what?'

'A child.'

Mistry switched the phone to silent so the device beeped instead, as if carrying out a petty act of defiance.

'Someone's popular.'

'No, someone's busy.'

Mistry's phone beeped again.

'Just check your bloody phone,' Low snapped. 'We can do the awkward goodbye after.'

Mistry clicked on the link sent from her husband. She was directed to a YouTube video clip.

Mistry was suddenly watching herself. The camera appeared

to be following her, an easy and obvious target. She was a brown woman. She was two for the price of one.

And then Man With the Red Cross entered the frame, snarling, grabbing and screaming in her ear. The screaming was distant and tinny, but it still reached Low on the other side of the hotel room. He stopped packing. The familiar, shrieking pain of a woman he probably still loved pulled him across the room.

'Shit, someone took a video of it,' Low said.

'Shut up.'

They watched the rest of the video together in silence. Low winced as Man With the Red Cross yanked Mistry's arm, but the cheering was worse. Middle-aged white men surrounded the abused woman and did nothing. They cheered instead. They made monkey noises and Nazi salutes.

And then William Jarvis appeared from the left side of the frame, the hard nut with a knife, ready to bravely stab a terrified, incapacitated woman.

Again, the crowd did nothing, except make room. Even plastic Nazis needed *Lebensraum* to carry out their work. Jarvis stepped forward and then there was chaos. Bodies hit the ground. The footage shook and blurred as everyone in the crowd struggled to stay upright. But the phone-camera operator regained focus just in time to capture the agent of carnage.

The Samaritan with the skull face appeared.

The camera operator's arm reached out to grab him, but Skull Face swivelled and pushed his attacker hard in the chest. As the phone camera started to fall away, there was just enough time and distance to pick up the audio.

'*Allahu akbar*,' the Samaritan with the skull face shouted at the screen.

The image froze.

A caption appeared beneath Skull Face.

THIS IS MODERN ENGLAND.

The snippet was replayed.

'*Allahu akbar*,' the Samaritan with the skull face screamed a second time.

THIS IS WHAT WE HAVE BECOME.

The Samaritan with the skull face was magnified, blown up until only the scarf, hoodie and dark glasses covered Mistry's phone screen.

'*Allahu akbar*,' he screamed again.

THIS IS WHAT WE MUST FIGHT.

THIS IS A WAR THAT THEY STARTED.

THIS IS A WAR THAT WE WILL FINISH.

The Samaritan with the skull face appeared for a fourth and final time, but only his mouth was visible.

'*Allahu akbar*.'

THEY HAVE TAKEN OUR COUNTRY.

BUT WE WILL TAKE IT BACK.

MAKE ENGLAND GREAT AGAIN.

The video ended with details of upcoming rallies and instructions for donations to the Make England Great Again movement, all printed beneath a fluttering St George's flag and a headshot of Billy Evans.

'Shit, I never heard what that bloke said. It was too noisy,' said Mistry. 'We're gonna get what they want now, a bloody race riot.'

'No, you won't. That video has been manipulated. He never said *Allahu akbar*.'

'How do you know?'

'Because he's me. Obviously.'

CHAPTER 14

Billy Evans faced two uniformed officers. One was white, the other black, naturally. Ebony and Ivory. Side by side in a police station. Even the staff at Charing Cross belonged in a nursery rhyme. From the outside, the elegant Victorian building, with its red bricks and iron lanterns, represented the best of British engineering, architecture and ingenuity, a time when it was genuinely great to be British. Inside the station, every room was painted in the same, united colours of political correctness. The left-wing media called it racial diversity, but their acolytes didn't share Evans's background. Where he came from, a non-white face meant he was about to lose his wallet. He knew it. And so did the black and white plods on the other side of the room. They followed new rules, but they were still Old Bill, walking the same streets, arresting the same dark-skinned faces.

They just couldn't say that.

But Billy Evans could.

He knew he wasn't the working-class hero that England wanted right now, but he was the working-class hero that real Englishmen needed. He was the political leader that his countrymen deserved and the snowflakes hated him for it. Because they still didn't get it.

The snowflakes' private-school educations gave them a private-school audience, but Evans had crossed the class divide. He had a comprehensive-school audience for credibility and private-school funding for cash. The chavs gave him muscle. Eton's old boys gave him secret donations. Both lamented a lost England.

As long as a white majority remained, Evans would always have the numbers.

He smiled at the white copper. He got nothing. He smiled at the black copper. The black copper laughed. He was the smarter one.

'How much longer have I got to wait, chaps?' Evans asked. 'I'm doing a video clip outside a fish and chip shop later, one of the last ones left in the area; heard it's being replaced with a halal takeaway. Terrible.'

The grey door opened and DCI Wickes struggled through, balancing a cup of tea and clutching a file. He dropped both onto the steel table as DC Devonshire joined him, sitting across from Evans. A large, rectangular recording device separated them.

'What's terrible?' DCI Wickes asked, fiddling with the recorder.

'Oh, you heard that? I'm appearing outside a fish and chip shop later, one of the oldest in east London; three generations of the same family have run the place. But business has plummeted since the mosque opened across the road. It's another slice of our culture that needs preserving.'

'What are you going as? A battered sausage?'

'No, Chief Inspector, I'll be utilising my democratic right to speak out against the subjugation of our native people by a foreign culture and a faith that goes against the fundamental rights and beliefs of our country.'

'Christ, Evans, do you read *Mein Kampf* every morning? Some big words in there for a bloke who left school at fifteen.

You've come a long way since you were delivering leaflets for the National Front.'

Evans tapped the recorder. 'Shall we get started?'

'Are you sure you don't want any legal representation?' Devonshire asked.

'Why? This is just a friendly chat, right? Assisting with your inquiries. It's not like I'm going to be charged with anything, is it?'

'Depends what you tell us,' Wickes replied gruffly, switching on the recorder. 'OK, Mr Evans, thanks for coming in today. Can you tell us first about what you witnessed at Altab Ali Park, where one of our officers was attacked?'

'Well, first of all, is she all right?'

'Just answer the question, please, Mr Evans.'

'Would it be all right if I sent her something, maybe to the station?'

Devonshire clenched and unclenched his fists beneath the table.

'Just answer the bloody question.'

Evans grinned at the younger detective. 'Ah, so she must be your wife. I'm really sorry, mate. I'm a married man, too, can't imagine what you're going through. Wish her all the best from me. That was terrible.'

'Terrible like a closing fish and chip shop or terrible like a woman being attacked by two of your party's members?'

'We're not a party, Chief Inspector. We're a movement.'

'My apologies. Now, what did you see?'

'Nothing. The park was rammed with people and I couldn't get close, let alone see. And as soon as it all kicked off, my people got me out of the park. Sorry.'

'Ah, yes, your people.'

Wickes took two blurred photos from his file and slid them towards Evans.

'Are these your people?'

Evans examined the photos for long enough to pretend he was interested. 'No, I'm sorry.'

'You've never seen these two before. For the recording, I'm showing Mr Evans photographs of William Jarvis and John Perry, taken from camera-phone footage of a political rally organised by his party – sorry, movement – Make England Great Again. You've really never seen them before? Jarvis is a large, bare-chested bloke with a distinct rose tattoo on his shoulder and John Perry is a much younger man with a red cross plastered across his face. They had pretty distinctive appearances at the rally, a bit hard to miss.'

'With all due respect, they are two gentlemen with England flags. They could be one of five thousand people who attend my rallies.'

'You haven't stood in a crowd of five thousand since Millwall had a decent FA Cup run.'

'That's a good line, Chief Inspector. I like that. But I've got no idea who they are. Is that it?'

'No.'

Devonshire opened a laptop and played the latest Make England Great Again video clip. He turned away from the screen when his wife appeared. Evans relished his discomfort.

'Again, I hope your wife makes a full recovery.'

'She's got nothing to recover from. She's fine.'

Wickes was eager to press on. 'Who made the video, Billy?'

'I've got no idea. I can't control every fanatic who posts something on YouTube. We've already released a statement denouncing the video.'

'But it hasn't been taken down.'

'I don't work for YouTube.'

'It's still on Facebook.'

'I don't work for Facebook either.'

'No, but I don't see you asking for the video to be taken down either.'

'That would make me a bit of a hypocrite, wouldn't it? You know how many times the media has tried to silence me or deny me my right of reply.'

The clip reached its denouement. The three men around the table watched the Samaritan with the skull scarf put down Jarvis and Perry.

'He's handy. I'll give him that,' Evans said.

'Who is he, Billy?'

Evans laughed incredulously. 'Hang on, you expect me to know the identity of a Muslim geezer who threatened Jihad on camera?'

'You want to light the fire, right? He's your accelerant.'

'Dear me, Chief Inspector, maybe *you* need the lawyer. You know I don't know who this bloke is. You know I wasn't there when your woman was attacked. And you know I haven't got a clue who the two Muppets are either.'

Devonshire almost admired Evans's in-born swagger. The little shit was stocky and square-jawed, with a short-back-and-sides haircut that was fashionable now for the first time since World War II. He had a certain football hooligan chic: good-looking in a tight jeans and white trainers kind of way.

'But without you there is no rally,' said Devonshire. 'Without your rally, there is no attack against one of our officers. We'll get some sort of incitement to riot charge somewhere.'

'For what exactly? For being popular? For telling the people something that they already believe?'

'You're a pound-shop fascist, one on every street corner.'

'No, I'm not and you know I'm not. That's what scares you, all of you,' Evans said, looking straight at the black copper. 'You know exactly what I'm saying. A while ago, there was a man who said what I'm saying now. He pointed out that since the 2008 economic crash, there's been low economic growth. Austerity measures everywhere. Cutbacks. Job losses. Dying towns. Just pound shops and betting shops. And then what happens? Nationalism rises. Populism rises. Globalisation starts to suffocate the working classes. Cheap foreign labour wipes them out. It looks like the elites betrayed us. They sold us out to foreign workers and refugees. They swamped us. They took our jobs and gave us more crime instead. They forced multicultural-ism upon us. Who voted for multiculturalism? No one. But we got it anyway. And now we're all poorer and angrier and living in fear in a home that doesn't look or feel like home any more. One man said all that. His name was Anders Breivik. And he said it after killing seventy-seven people in Norway. You know who's saying it now? Everyone. That's what you're all scared of. The message has gone from psychos to mainstream.'

'Yeah, well, you're neither,' Devonshire said.

'You know that's not true,' said Evans, looking around the room. 'Anyway, where's the other one?'

'What other one?'

'The Chinese one. Paul at the pub kept going on about him, said he was really flash and clever. Why didn't you let me meet your Chinese detective?'

For some reason, DI Mistry was temporarily trapped in the nostalgia of her own youth. She saw herself, walking home from Dagenham Heathway Station. She was eleven, maybe twelve, but certainly in the first year of secondary school.

She saw five of them, a few years older than Mistry. Two boys. Three girls. All white. The numbers were wrong, two snogging couples and the ugly, odd one out. The ugly one had dyed blonde hair and a hard face, all dressed up and no one to snog. They leaned against the railings, four kissing teenagers and a scowling outcast, the ugly one with the hard face, forever looking for a target.

Mistry was always a target.

'Oi, Paki, are you fucking staring at me?'

Even as a child, Mistry knew she wasn't staring and she wasn't a

'Paki' either, but it didn't matter. The ugly one with the hard face had already got what she'd wanted. Her friends were no longer snogging. They were staring at the brown girl, already hating her for antagonising their weird mate and interrupting their foreplay.

'Why are you staring at us?' the most handsome boy asked. 'Are you jealous?'

'No, I wasn't staring. I wasn't,' Mistry replied, struggling to get the words out.

The ugly one with the hard face stepped towards her.

'Yes, you fucking were, you Paki bitch.'

Mistry started running and never stopped, down Heathway Hill, past the greengrocer's on the corner, across the traffic lights and all the way home to Mistry's Mini-Mart, her family's cherished kingdom.

Naturally, she had lied to her parents about the red eyes and puffy cheeks. They had swapped their poverty-stricken homeland for utopia. They didn't want to hear about dyed-blonde girls and Paki-bashing. Every day in Britain was great.

But Mistry wouldn't forget.

She would fight back.

She would take down every of them, in the streets, the smart way, the legal way.

A pretty 'Paki' irritated ugly blondes who couldn't get laid.

But a pretty 'Paki' with a warrant card irritated everybody.

And now, an idiotic Asian, of all people, was about to ruin everything.

Detective Inspector Stanley Low of the Singapore Police Force made his way around the hotel bed and tried to explain himself.

But Mistry wasn't listening. She struggled to even hear him. She only heard teenagers telling her to 'fuck off home'.

She saw herself convincing DCI Wickes that a visiting detective from Singapore, an old university friend, might offer some cultural context and useful insight into the murdered Singaporean in Chinatown.

She saw the scandal of a foreign policeman playing vigilante at a far-right rally.

She saw the internal investigation, the inevitable police leak and her resignation or sacking, whichever was deemed the least damaging for her employers.

She saw herself back in her father's shop, playing the obsequious Asian and handing over twenty Marlboro to an underage customer to keep the peace.

She would be back in her box, the subservient Paki in a corner shop, restoring the social fabric, knowing her place, Making England Great Again.

'It's over,' she muttered.

'What is? The case?'

'Everything. I'll get fired for this.'

'Fired for what? You didn't even know I was there.'

'I asked you for help.'

'Yeah, with the case, not at the rally. I acted alone. Let them blame me. They usually do.'

'Oh for God's sake, stop with your martyr shit. You've diverted the investigation. Wickes will now use resources we don't have looking for a vigilante dressed like Skeletor, when the guy is already in our bloody office.'

'Well, at least you won't have far to look.'

Low recognised the blazing fury in Mistry's eyes. She wanted to punch him. Most people did.

'You think this is funny?'

'No.'

'Why did you do it? Why did you come back? Why?'

Low half turned away.

'I thought you would need help. I wasn't sure if the other guy was up to it?'

'The other guy? You mean my husband, a trained detective? You mean that guy?'

'Yeah.'

'You really do need help.'

'I get help.'

'Well, it's not bloody working.'

'That's why they sent me here.'

'To make a mess?'

'No, to get rid of me. My career is finished.'

'And now you've finished mine. Well done. Two-for-one special.'

'It's just a video. They'll be another one tomorrow. No one knows it's me.'

'I know.'

'Then keep it to yourself.'

'I can't do that. I can't bury all this shit like you do.'

'Yeah. That's why you left.'

'No, it wasn't.'

'You left because of my mental instability at a time when bipolar was barely understood and Asians saw any kind of depression as a form of weakness, not something you take home to meet your parents. I understood it then. I still do. No one's more ashamed of this shit than me.'

Mistry felt the rage slipping away.

'You think I'm that fickle? I'd leave just because you suffer from bipolar? I left because you were struggling to see right from wrong. You weren't just understanding. You were empathising. You were *becoming*.'

'It's basic criminal psychology, you know that.'

'No, no, no, even before then, you started hanging out with them, on your own time, socialising with them in Singapore, telling me how much fun they were.'

'I was learning about their behaviour.'

'You were morphing into them.'

'Well, what do you want me to say? That I channel this toxic shit in here,' Low said, jabbing his temple repeatedly with his forefinger. 'That I always expect the worst of humanity so I'm never disappointed? That I knew, categorically fucking knew, that you were walking into a bear trap at that Billy Evans rally, a bloody brown face in a white crowd? You might as well have worn a sign. I know that because I know them. And that's the real reason why you got in touch with me. You can resent me. You can fucking hate me. But you know, deep down, that I'm your best chance of catching him.'

Mistry sighed and sat on the bed.

'I followed you.'

Low looked confused for the first time.

'To the rally?'

'No, the night before I left you and went back to England.'

'In Singapore?'

'Yeah. I wanted to tell you something, surprise you. So I waited outside the old police academy for you to finish. You remember? It was near that Singapore polo place. But when I saw you, from across the road, you looked different. You were wearing these scruffy clothes. You didn't look like you. Everything was slightly off. So I followed you. You only walked a couple of streets to a place you'd taken me before to eat that peppery pork soup.'

Low started to feel dizzy.

'Balestier,' he mumbled, holding the back of a chair for support. 'It has the best *bak kut teh*. Pork-rib soup.'

'Yeah, pork-rib soup.' Mistry smiled at the memory. 'Delicious. Anyway, you met these guys outside a karaoke place. Little gangster types. You hugged them and some of the hostesses outside. Sex workers. But that didn't really bother me. And then you went inside. I started to head over and then this big Chinese bloke came through the door. His face was covered in blood. And then there was another one. Head wound. Blood everywhere. Both of them were lying on the pavement, groaning, barely moving. And then your new mates came out. Holding snooker cues. And then you.'

111

'I was undercover,' Low whispered.

'Undercover, my arse. You were still in the fucking police academy.'

'They were gangsters, bookies runners, working for Tiger, cheating him, ripping him off. My old *kakis* from school were trying to impress him.'

'And you?'

'I was studying them.'

'Bullshit. You were enjoying them. I saw you step around the big guy. You took this snooker cue and you smashed him in the ribs, over and over again. And I watched your face the whole time. And you had this look. It wasn't anger. It wasn't joy. It was *acceptance*. This was your place. This was where you belonged. And I saw it again, the other day in the pub, when you went to work on the manager. It's the only time you really come alive. So I left you there with your new gangster mates and didn't bother telling you that I was pregnant.'

Low heard the whizzing explosions. The colours were hypnotic, overwhelming.

'What?'

'Yeah, I was pregnant. And I went straight to the travel agent and booked the first flight home.'

'Pregnant?'

Low couldn't really see beyond the fireworks. He couldn't see anything except something small and shiny on the table.

'There was no way after that. I came back to England and had an abortion.'

Low was weakening, struggling to stand. He focused on the silver objects on the table. They were keys. Mistry's car keys. He picked them up and ran.

He didn't bother closing the door behind him.

And he didn't look back.

CHAPTER 15

Low revved the engine repeatedly, but he couldn't move. London's snarling traffic trapped him inside a stolen, unmarked police car.

He was surrounded.

Men and women in power suits juggled low-fat lattes and organic salads on the pavement beside him. Black cabs rolled along the Strand like ants on an ice-lolly stick. In his rear-view mirror, Low watched the bus driver reach for his horn. The high-pitched screeching sent the pigeons flapping towards a different street corner to shit on. The bus driver slapped the middle of his steering wheel over and over again, waiting for a reaction.

But he got nothing.

The low-fat latte and organic salad jugglers stopped and stared. So did the black cabs and the bike couriers and the other buses, backed up in the Strand.

They glared at the odd one out. The small car surrounded by London's biggest and bright icons.

The only one that wasn't red. The only car in the bus lane.

Low absorbed the relentless, deafening screeching. The bus horn almost drowned out the internal explosions. The racket was strangely reassuring. Rage met with rage, recognising and confronting each other, like kindred spirits.

Through his rear-view mirror, Low watched the bus driver lean out of his window.

He looked Indian.

Just like her.

Like their baby would've been. Half Indian. The good half. The pure half.

'Oi, dickhead, get out of the bloody bus lane.'

The accent was local. The bus driver was London born and bred. Second generation.

Just like her.

Low turned and smiled, surprising the bus driver. Clearly, the bus driver didn't anticipate such indifference to all that horn-honking. There were CCTV cameras everywhere. The bus driver had the right of way. He also had peer pressure to deal with. The bus lane was full of disapproving colleagues, but the mad Chinaman was in front of him, blocking his path. His obstacle. His responsibility.

He leaned further out of the window.

'Oi, mate, get out of the bus lane, yeah? This ain't China.'

Low laughed loudly. The outrage. The ignorance. The inad-vertent racism and the inevitable condescension towards anyone with a Chinese face, the bus driver had the complete package. Low toyed with the idea of asking the bus driver for directions to Covent Garden, but he revved the engine instead.

'I'm fucking Singaporean,' he screamed.

Suddenly he was overtaking the buses and squeezing past black cabs, mounting the kerb of the islands in the middle of the Strand, barely missing the traffic-light poles. He no longer saw irate drivers and terrified pedestrians. He blocked out every face except one.

He only saw her.

She had succeeded where they had all failed. The illegal

bookies, the syndicates, the puffed-up gangsters and weeping serial killers, the pimps and the politicians and even Tiger himself had all tried, but only she had killed him.

And now her car was his escape, his endgame. He didn't know where he was going. He didn't care. He had left everything behind in the hotel room with her. Everything. None of it mattered any more. He didn't need it. Low wouldn't be going back.

Tourists turned away from Trafalgar Square to trace the sound of the speeding car racing past them, taking the roundabout too fast, clearly out of control.

Mistry had once taken Low to visit Nelson's Column, that ironic symbol to the same imperialism that had once imprisoned their countries. Low had climbed onto one of the bronze lions and given the middle finger to Mistry's camera, a silly act of anti-colonialism. But Low didn't remember the bronze lions now. He didn't even see them.

He only saw her.

He understood her reasoning. Of course he did. He ruined lives, mostly criminal lives, but not exclusively. There was always collateral damage. He had given up on his life years ago, probably around the same time he used a snooker cue to smash a gangster's ribs, not to crack a case, but to impress Tiger. He wanted to ingratiate himself into the nastiest crime organisation in Asia because he could. That was reason enough. He was so good at being a bad guy, who cared if the lines occasionally blurred? No one in arse-covering Singapore did. He solved cases. He ticked boxes. He was the perfect civil servant with a serious mental illness, but no one discussed mental illness in Singapore, so he was just the perfect civil servant.

Until he wasn't. Then he was just a serious mental illness and easily discarded.

But she cared. She was the only one that cared. And she was the only one that saw through him. And he was fucked. So she ran away, straight to an abortion to ensure that only one life was ruined, rather than three.

Low wasn't angry with her, or even with himself any more. Rage was impossible to sustain. Only self-loathing truly endured.

He floored the accelerator and Mistry's car sped past Horse Guards Parade and too many statues of men on horseback fighting too many wars for empire, hubris and idiocy. They were blurred ghosts. They belonged in the past.

Like Low.

The work usually sustained him, but the puzzle was shattering and the pieces falling away. The rally video, *Allahu Akbar*, the Man With the Red Cross, Billy Evans, the manager in the pub, the poor, dead Singaporean, Mohamed Kamal, the kid who came to London to study and ended up stabbed, they were all disappearing. Low couldn't hold them together, couldn't see them.

Just as he couldn't really see the Monument to the Women of World War II until it was almost too late. Just as he couldn't really see the black cab as he swerved to miss the memorial. Just as he couldn't really see the security bollards as he dragged the steering wheel to his left to avoid the black cab. Just as he couldn't see the horrified faces of selfie-obsessed tourists as he ploughed into the security bollards.

He just saw her. And that was enough.

Low closed his eyes and waited for death's painless release.

'Put your hands where we can see them. Now.'

The voice was authoritative, but strangely muffled and apprehensive.

Low's first thought was succinct.

Blood.

He could taste his own blood. He obviously had a gash on his forehead. But he felt suffocated, as if wrapped in pillows.

Airbags.

His brain was working faster than his body. He still couldn't move or open his eyes. Besides, the airbag was warm, soft and comforting. The harsh outside world could wait for a few more seconds.

'I said, "Put your hands where we can see them."'

Low heard the distinct metallic sound of clicking and locking. He knew that sound.

Guns.

'You need to show us your hands, now.'

Us.

Plural.

Police.

Something wasn't right. Low's brain felt like melting ice cream on a hot car roof, but he still sensed that their timing was off. He hadn't passed out. He was sure of it. Only seconds had elapsed, a minute at the most. It was impossible. He had to find his voice.

'Wah, you got here fast,' he croaked.

'You need to sit up now.'

Slowly, Low opened his eyes and faced a semiautomatic weapon on the other side of the driver's window. The muzzle was ten centimetres from his right eyeball. Six officers surrounded the car, all armed, all a confusing mix of testosterone and terror.

Low raised his hands and flopped back in his seat.

'Are you armed?' The nearest officer shouted through the window.

Low shook his head.

'Are there any other weapons in the car?'

Low shook his head again.

'I need you to lift up your shirt, very slowly, now.'

Despite the raging headache, Low turned towards the officer, struggling to digest the madness around him.

He spotted the other, blurry images running towards him, glowing in the fading sunlight, uniformed men, semiautomatics raised. Same weapons. Same training. There were so many of them. Quick. Efficient. Relentless.

And then he recognised the road behind them. Familiar. Iconic. Protected. He couldn't make out the words on the street sign, but he didn't need to. The panic-stricken Parliamentary and Diplomatic Protection officers had already told him.

Downing Street.

An Asian man had crashed a stolen car near Downing Street. Death didn't seem such a bad idea now.

CHAPTER 16

Low welcomed the physical pain. Unlike regular people, he didn't have a problem with suffering. Discomfort gave him clarity. Pain was familiar. He understood every symptom. His forehead throbbed from the impact of the crash. The ringing in his ears persisted. He could still taste the blood on the back of his teeth. This stuff was a handy distraction. He didn't have to focus on the internal shit that would eventually re-emerge.

Low preferred the torturous pounding that burned across his forehead.

It stopped him thinking about deceitful Indian women and dead babies.

In the interrogation room, he followed a single bead of sweat as it rolled through DCI Wickes's receding hairline. The room wasn't particularly warm, but the small, claustrophobic setting was filled with anxious bodies waiting for explanations and wondering who might get fired, demoted or reprimanded first.

Low had surpassed himself this time.

He had alienated the police forces of two countries.

Through the window partition, he smiled at large men with long guns, dressed in black and ready for anything that a skinny, unarmed Chinese guy might come up with while handcuffed and naked, apart from a hooded surgical gown. The gown rubbed against Low's bare skin.

'Is that thing irritating you?'

DC Devonshire was enjoying Low's humiliation. The sooner this insufferable parasite was returned to Singapore, the better for every officer at Charing Cross, not to mention his wife and marriage.

'Only when it rubs against the cuts.'

'Is it rubbing against the cuts?'

'Yes.'

'Oh well.'

'*Wah lau*, you're loving this aren't you? Is this your little victory? You sitting there in your shirt and tie, me sitting here looking like a vanilla ice cream, you should really let it go.'

'What?'

'Coming second. She picked me first.'

'She dumped you first.'

'Does she ever talk about me? Does it ever bother you that you came second to a Chinaman?'

'Enough.'

Wickes's voice surprised officers on both sides of the glass partition. The genial chief inspector was shouting.

'Have you got any idea how much trouble you're in? How much trouble you've made for us?'

'I was a tourist finding my way around London. It was an accident.'

'Oh, piss off, Low. You were driving a stolen police car and crashed it opposite the prime minister's street.'

'I know. What are the odds, eh?'

'Do you think this is a joke?'

'How can it not be? Of all the streets in London, I lose control of the steering wheel there. That street is full of bloody monuments in the middle of the road.'

'It's being treated as a terrorist attack.'

'I was driving away from Downing Street, away from it, not towards it. I swerved to avoid the stupid memorial thing and clipped a bollard in an empty street. You've seen it on the CCTV, right? It looks like what it is, a bloody accident.'

'You're an Asian aiming a car at the prime minister's residence.'

'Well, I've got a shitty sense of direction then. And I'm not Asian. I'm Chinese-Singaporean.'

'What's the difference?'

'There's never been a terrorist attack committed by a Chinese-Singaporean. Jesus Christ. We don't make war. We make money.'

'Nobody else will see it that way. The camera phones and newspapers won't see it that way. And them outside won't see it that way. They wanna take you to Counterterrorism. They can detain you indefinitely as a terror suspect until a full investigation is carried out. The commander is considering his options now.'

Low nodded slowly. He saw the angle.

'He doesn't want me though, does he? Doesn't want the publicity. And you don't want to hand me over either. You can't. It's almost an admission of guilt. A car from your police station, taken from one of your officers by an overseas officer with no jurisdiction here, no authority, no warrant card, driving a police car, a foreigner, in this toxic climate. You'd be first to go. Devonshire here wouldn't be far behind and Ramila, bloody hell. So all we can do is actually stick to the truth: a Chinese-Singaporean tourist borrowed a car and lost control in Whitehall. And you convince your media to report it that way.'

'This isn't Singapore, Low.'

'No, it's not, because, ironically, I'd have no chance there. I'd already be finished. But there's more at stake here, right?'

'Why would I bury this for you?'

'Because you're a decent man, a good man. You're nothing

like me. You want to do the right thing. And you know that this is the right thing to do, even if it's wrong morally. This has to be an accident. Another terror plot risks violent protests, anarchy, beatings in the streets, hate crimes, more funding for Billy Evans and his stormtroopers, more crime elsewhere as your limited resources are stretched to breaking point dealing with the far right. And for what? For failing to suppress a terror plot that wasn't a terror plot? You wanna waste time and money on destroying me? What would be the point?'

'You took Ramila's car,' Devonshire said. 'You have potentially ruined her career, you little shit.'

'Only if you allow that to happen.'

'I've wasted enough time with you,' Wickes said, standing up quickly. 'Keep him here while I go upstairs.'

Wickes leaned into Low's face.

'And you're right, Low. I am a decent man, have been for thirty-odd years, since I started in uniform. I'm a bloody good copper. So is Mistry and everyone else at this station. So I will do what needs to be done, for them. Not you. Them. And when all this shit is over, I promise you that I will not retire until your life and career are ruined.'

Low leaned back in his chair.

'Ah, you can retire whenever you like then,' Low said. 'I ruined my life and career years ago.'

A cool evening breeze drifted across the Eden Hall veranda. The British High Commissioner made a point at every private event to take her leave from the drawing room just before sunset. She loved Singapore most at dusk. Obviously, her plush residence was temporary, but Eden Hall felt like home, particularly at sunset. For a few, fleeting moments, the sunset reminded her of caravan holidays in Sussex, a reminder of a distant world and how far she'd come. Her official residence looked down upon lush greenery. A former nutmeg plantation built partially on

122

the proceeds of the opium trade was now a quaint, tropical slice of colonialism, the very best of Britain at a time when the old country seemed utterly determined to do its very worst.

The British High Commissioner sipped her gin and tonic as a vibrant yellow bird swooped onto his manicured lawn.

'Oriole,' she muttered. 'So beautiful.'

'It's a black-naped oriole. You can tell from its yellow-and-black plumage. Can you see the black stripe across its face?'

The Minister joined the British High Commissioner on the veranda, standing beneath the elegant white plasterwork foliage that made the grand property look like an ostentatious wedding cake.

'Hello, Minister. Are you enjoying the food?'

'Very much so. Reminds me of my studies in the UK. Fish and chips, bangers and mash, very nostalgic.'

'Yes, the expats love it at these gatherings.'

'Excellent turnout.'

'It always is. Everyone wants a little taste of home now and then, right?'

'Is that why you're out here alone at your own party, taking in the green, green grass of home?'

'Just taking a breather. Lots of hands in there still to shake.'

She smiled as the Minister loosened his damn collar. Only the British would insist on formal suits at a cocktail evening in the tropics. Their proud stoicism determined their rigid sartorial choices, even in sweaty Singapore.

'Oh, look,' said the Minister, pulling a hankie from his breast pocket. 'Our friend has found his dinner, too.'

The oriole plucked away at the berry, ignoring the bright lights and the large stage being assembled on the lawn for an evening of pipe bands and interpretive dance.

'Typical Singaporean,' the minister said, gesturing towards the bird with his wine glass. 'Not interested in the show, only come for the *makan*.'

'Indeed.'

The British High Commissioner sipped her gin and tonic. She needed more ice.

'What about the untypical Singaporean?'

'The untypical Singaporean?'

They smiled politely at a group of British women tottering on their heels towards the outdoor bar.

'Yes. How do we treat his behaviour?'

'I'm not sure I follow. Evening, ladies.'

The Minister raised his glass as another group passed, watching the wealthiest members of Singapore's expatriate society queue for fish and chips.

'Did you see our alcohol advisory we did for British residents and visitors in Singapore?'

'No.'

'It was very successful, actually. We politely pointed out that though the British enjoy a drink, we must be careful to respect the laws and customs of Singapore and never forget that we are guests in your country.'

'That's most laudable.'

'We actually saw drunken arrests drop slightly as a result in Singapore, among the Brits at least.'

'Excellent. Look at the oriole attacking that berry. No matter where we are, native Singaporeans will always hunt down good food.'

'Oh yes.'

They were aware that more guests were taking their drinks onto the veranda. The dusky breeze was addictive in Singapore.

'So we're thinking of doing something similar in the UK. A gentle reminder of how our foreign guests should behave in our country.'

The minister chuckled. 'I don't think anyone's going to out-drink the British, do you? Maybe the Australians.'

'Other kinds of behaviour, like traffic violations.'

'Ah. I have to say, this is outstanding wine.'

'Some think we should be rather draconian, set an example. Others think we should consider the bigger picture, international relations and so on.'

The Minister admired the oriole's progress. 'Look at that. The berry's almost gone. Singaporeans always eat fast, you know. We don't have time. We don't have space. Eat fast or don't eat. It's a first-offence approach, right?'

'What? Oh yes, but it's not so much what the offence is, but where and how it takes place.'

'You see that oriole? You know how much of his habitat has been destroyed? Singapore has suffered from so much deforestation, but look at him. He *negotiates* his space. He deals with his tiny environment. He's pragmatic. He survives. No choice.'

'Negotiates?'

'Yes. He works with what he's got. What else can he do?'

'But he's made a bit of a mess of the lawn over there.'

'Small issue. Easy to repair, right?'

The Minister and the British High Commissioner paused for photographs with an elderly Eurasian couple. The Minister called over a waiter to replace their drinks.

'As long as he's not hurting anyone, you might as well leave him in your garden, right? It doesn't help anybody to make a fuss, does it?'

'What if he keeps making a mess?'

'Ah, that's different. Then you'll have to call in pest control.'

The waiter arrived with fresh drinks.

'But he belongs to you,' the British High Commissioner said.

'Yes, but it's your garden.'

'You don't want him back?'

'What for? I'm not British like you. I'm Singaporean. We don't have gardens.'

Standing in front of Eden Hall's imperious façade, they raised a toast towards Singapore's setting sun as the black-naped oriole finished its dinner.

DCI Wickes returned to the interrogation room and threw his phone on the table.

'Not surprisingly, our two governments are in agreement about you.'

'They both think I'm an arsehole,' Low said.

'Pretty much. You're more trouble than you're worth at this point. We need calm exteriors on both sides.'

'Sounds familiar.'

'You stay until this thing dies down. You can't leave the country, just in case it blows up. We take your passport, but you keep a low profile. Stay at your hotel. No more unwanted help or interference, no more university lectures, nothing.'

DC Devonshire made no attempt to hide his irritation.

'He's just going to get away with it?'

'Get away with what? He's an Asian tourist who lost control on a congested London road and had an accident.'

'That's a load of bollocks.'

'It's also the truth.'

'Not the whole truth.'

'And nothing but the truth,' Low whispered.

'Shut up, Low. You put my wife's career in jeopardy. She's the mother of my son.'

'Yes, I gathered that.'

'Fuck off.'

Devonshire returned to his boss. 'How are we gonna explain Ramila's car?'

'We're the only people who know. It's classified. We'll slap a gag order on it.'

'All to protect him?'

'To protect *us* – you and Ramila, the station, our bloody

126

reputation, both governments. None of us needs this right now. He's managed to piss off the lot in less than a week.'

Low looked uncomfortable for the first time.

'What about Ramila? What happens to her?' he said.

'None of your business,' Wickes said.

'It's my only business now. I don't give a shit about anything else. I took the car. My responsibility. Nothing to do with her.'

'Save it for your statement. We're done,' Wickes said.

He gestured towards his junior colleague to leave. The Englishmen stood, looking down at the pathetic Chinese copper beneath them.

'Ramila should not be punished for this,' Low whimpered.

'It's a bit late for this chivalry shit,' Devonshire said.

The two detectives made a point of slamming the door as they left, leaving Low to wallow in his self-loathing. He picked at the flakes of dried blood on his forehead and directed his festering hatred towards the inventor of airbags.

CHAPTER 17

Zhang Jun Li watched the video over and over again. She sat alone, in the dark, quietly weeping. She preferred to be alone. Her Confucianist father was no help and her mother was dead. The video kept her company. Nothing else mattered, certainly not her studies or the clichéd part-time family job downstairs. She hated being a cliché, a cardboard cut-out of a Chinese immigrant, the kind that typically didn't exist in England any more. But she still lived the *Upstairs, Downstairs* duality of the Chinese immigrant. Upstairs she was chained to the books, looking to her medical degree as an escape route from her shitty life downstairs, where she was the skivvy handing over prawn balls and curry sauce. Of course, she wasn't really, not in Chinatown. Her clientele were mostly the metropolitan elite, unadventurous Asian tourists and Chinese expats dragging their Western partners along for a taste of something authentic from home.

But she still felt like a cliché. The cook's daughter taking orders and washing dishes by day, and the studying paediatrician by night, diligently conforming to every Asian stereotype. No tiger mom around, but a tiger pup nonetheless, doing as she was told. She lived in London, but the Confucian patriarchy of Ancient China still ruled upstairs in Hawker Heaven.

But things changed.

First, she fell in love.

And then she felt hate like never before.

She couldn't get rid of the hate. But she could channel it.

Jun Li replayed the clip again, pausing after each of the child-like slogans flashed across the screen.

THIS IS MODERN ENGLAND.

THIS IS WHAT WE HAVE BECOME.

THIS IS WHAT WE MUST FIGHT.

THIS IS A WAR THAT THEY STARTED.

THIS IS A WAR THAT WE WILL FINISH.

THEY HAVE TAKEN OUR COUNTRY.

BUT WE WILL TAKE IT BACK.

MAKE ENGLAND GREAT AGAIN.

The last line actually made her laugh. Bizarrely, she thought of her parents, so happy together, holding hands on rare day trips to Southend. Their Penang roots always pulled them back to the seaside.

Their routine never changed. Dad tracked down every take-away and fish and chip shop along the seafront and took notes. Mum handed out the copper coins for the 2p machines. And the day ended with candyfloss and a lecture, usually on a bench facing the sea, always facing the sea.

Dad reiterated how lucky they were to swap Malaysia for England, how much more money they had made, how less corrupt their new government was and, most of all, how hard Jun Li had to work to make the most of her lucky privileges. And Mum always nodded and picked at the candyfloss.

For her parents, England was already great. No one had to remake the place.

But the makers of the video disagreed. They wanted to take their country back from the different, from the foreign, from people like her parents, from the love of her life.

And Jun Li was almost grateful. Their rage almost matched

hers. They gave her a target and a purpose. They enabled her hatred.

So she opened her Facebook page and made a promise to herself. She would not stop typing. No matter how much she cried.

In the darkness, Low closed his eyes in the vague hope of sleep that never came. He fumbled around on the bed until he found the bottle and swigged until his throat screamed in protest. He didn't even like vodka, but it was cheap and accessible in London and the lithium no longer worked. Back in Singapore, his shrink had predicted a change in behaviour once the medication kicked in.

And there was.

Low had pinned a suspect to the wall during an interrogation.

Vodka didn't improve his condition. Low couldn't drown his sorrows or drench the omnipresent fireworks. That was a lazy myth, propagated by those whose understanding of mental health came from movies and Oscar-baiting actors. Eventually the vodka would knock him out and leave him alone with his unwanted dreams. He didn't earn a reprieve from the horrors of his own mind, but at least everyone else did.

He ignored the ringing phone. The voice would either be British or Singaporean, but essentially saying the same thing. He already knew what he was.

But the text messaging surprised him. Low never sent or received texts. His impatient thinking was too fast for his thumbs.

The phone glowed in the gloomy hotel room as Low opened the text.

ANSWER YOUR FUCKING PHONE.

As soon as the ringing punctured the silence, Low did as he was told. He took a deep breath, as if trying to dredge up the vodka.

'Look, I'm sorry about—'

'I'm not interested,' DI Mistry interrupted. 'You've got a laptop there, right?'

'Yeah.'

'Then turn it on and go to the Make England Great Again Facebook page.'

Mistry didn't even say goodbye.

Wearing only boxer shorts, Low stumbled across the messy hotel room and found the desk lamp, which forced him to shield his eyes and cower like a cornered animal. His laptop was found beneath a pizza box. Low thought about eating the remaining slice, but reached for the vodka bottle instead. He slumped into a chair and scrolled through the Make England Great Again Facebook page, bypassing the latest clips of brown people attacking white people and fake stories about Muslims swamping council houses to find the post. Mistry didn't tell him what he was looking for.

She didn't have to.

Low found the post beneath a photo of a beautiful, smiley young couple. The girl was Chinese. The boy was Mohamed Kamal.

As Low started reading, he realised his hands were shaking.

Dear Racists at Make England Great Again,

You murdered my boyfriend, Mohamed Kamal. The happy couple in the photo is us, which was taken about a month before one of you stabbed him to death. I know most of your members won't understand what's going on in the photo, so let me explain. The photo shows a couple. A couple is two people who enjoy each other's company, rather than spending evenings alone, masturbating about the next white supremacist rally.

I don't know why one of your sheep murdered my boyfriend, beyond the usual reasons (can't get a decent job, can't get any

sex, can't get a life) and, honestly, I don't care. I'm trying to
focus on Kamal's life, rather than his death. So I'll just say this.

You won't win. Ever. You can post as many xenophobic
and Islamophobic videos as you like, but you won't win. You
won't get the race war you want. You won't all be martyrs for
the cause.

You see, my family came from Malaysia. We were a Chinese
minority in a Muslim-majority country and we weren't half as
scared as you lot in your White Inadequate Party. One idiot
shouts 'Allahu Akbar' at one of your rallies, and look at you.
You all shit yourselves and make a video. Someone shouts
'Allahu Akbar' in Malaysia and we all go back to breakfast.

So your video doesn't show your strength. It shows your
weakness. Your fear. How could I, or any other racial minority,
be scared of that video or scared of you?

So I choose not to be scared. I choose not to live in fear. I
choose not to be frightened of little Nazi crybabies who hide
behind their laptops and make puny little videos. So on behalf
of my dead boyfriend, I'd like to say 'Allahu Akbar'. And on
behalf of racial minorities everywhere, I'd like to say fuck you.

I'll stop there so you can go back to your sad wanking in your
box bedroom.

Zhang Jun Li

Low downed the dregs of the vodka bottle and watched
the likes and shares beneath Jun Li's post spin like the reels of
a jackpot machine. He scrolled through the comments. The
echo chambers yelled at each other. Every white man was a
racist. Every Muslim was a terrorist. Every post predicted or
promised violence.

Low couldn't stop the shaking.

His fingers struggled to stay on the touchpad.

He was both wide awake and slipping away, alive to the

possibilities of the girl's incendiary post and dead to the world around him. Low and Jun Li had unwittingly intensified the conflict. Their actions had fomented a hateful reaction. In protecting loved ones, they had unleashed the trolls. Jun Li had reacted to the video and the video was a reaction to Low's unwelcome heroics, saving a brown woman from red-faced men.

Low had done this.

Low had instigated a race war.

His behaviour. *His* fault. Again.

He couldn't see straight. The death threats danced across the screen. His mind was shutting down, an act of self-preservation or surrender, he could no longer tell. He could no longer think. He was drifting off towards a drunken stupor, the self-prescribed anaesthetic of vodka and bipolar denial. Rock bottom was on its way. He could see it coming.

But then, he thought he saw something else instead.

He saw Mohamed Kamal's killer.

CHAPTER 18

The comment was different. It was personal. Even Low's drunken eyes could see that. Back in Singapore, his stint in the technology department, another punishment for another indiscretion, gave him a crash course in online psychology. Basically, there were not many trolls and most of them were cowards. They were sufferers of Short-Arse Syndrome, the little guys who shouted the loudest, as if a higher volume gave them extra inches in the locker room. And they were pretty much the same in every country; easy to spot, even easier to dismiss.

Within an hour of Zhang Jun Li's post, the MEGA believers had already flooded the page with regurgitated bile about immigration, religious fundamentalism and the imminent demise of the white man's culture. There was nothing to see there. Bleating sheep wasn't a spectator sport.

But one comment leapt out from the vicious rhetoric. He wasn't raging. He wasn't even particularly racist. He was engaged and hypersensitive to Zhang's criticism.

His Facebook name was Charlemagne.

His low-key comment had been mostly missed in the thick fog of invective and hardly garnered any likes, but Low recognised a familiar character flaw. Every sentence was dipped in self-loathing.

Jun Li, I am genuinely sorry for your loss, but it's a very
simplistic and stereotypical description of our followers. Have
you ever wondered why we have so much support right now? If
we're all racists and wife beaters and football hooligans, spending
every hour of every day masturbating (and you do have a
worrying fixation with masturbating, which is understandable
at the moment – you're lonely), if we are all grunting, punching
Neanderthals, why is our movement growing? Why do 2
million people follow this page? That's one in every thirty Brits.
That means you pass one of us every day in the street. You
serve one of us in Hawker Heaven every day. Do we look and
behave the way you say? Or are we just trying to do what your
family did when they ran away from Malaysia? Preserve a better
life for ourselves? Your family didn't want to live in a country
dominated by Sharia law and nor do we. What is so wrong
with that? Your family didn't like what Malaysia had become.
We don't like what Britain has become. The only difference is
we choose to fight back. So I don't fit any of your stereotypes. I
just don't want to be a stranger in my own country. Like you.
So I chose to do something about it. Like you.

The post was too long and too rational for a troll and too
detailed for a bot. Charlemagne's sentiments were genuine. He
was a true believer. He mentioned Hawker Heaven, a specific
reference, one rarely highlighted in the media. He was detailed,
precise, almost clinical. He had also switched personal pronouns.

'You went from we to I,' Low said to an empty hotel room,
allowing his rambling to take shape, to channel the mania. 'All
the way through, you're part of the "we" until it really matters,
when it's time to make a real difference, to go beyond, when
the sheep must become a shepherd. All those on here ranting
and raving, they're part of the herd, but not you. You're an indi-
vidual. You're gonna stand out. You already do. You changed
tenses, right at the end. *Chose.* You chose to do something.

You've already done it. Everything else is speculation, but you've already done it. You're fighting back, proving that you still fit in, that you still matter, still count.'

Low opened another tab and searched 'Charlemagne'. He read a potted history of Charles the Great, a medieval emperor, King of the Franks, the Belgians, the French, the Dutch and western Germany. Charlemagne sought to bring all Germanic peoples together and convert his subjects to Christianity, which made sense. But he also united much of Western Europe, which didn't. The so-called father of Europe was a bizarre icon for an English nativist. No self-respecting MEGA follower named himself after a prominent European.

Low considered calling Mistry when a comment appeared beneath Charlemagne's post.

Zhang Jun Li had replied.

Spare me the civility, Charlemagne. You are not the one good egg in a rotten group. There is no defence for what you do, no justification for racist intolerance. Everything you say or do on behalf of your racist organisation is an incitement to riot. In fact, you are even worse than the scum on this website. At least they're honest. They're just fucking idiots. You try to explain your bigotry. Did Mummy not hug you enough when you were little? Don't try and intellectualise what you lot do. My boyfriend was a worth a million of you. You're nothing. A nobody.

Low had to get up. He paced around the hotel room, waiting for the inevitable. Through the window, he watched London's night owls plot their way home, arm in arm, feeling invincible, hunting down taxis and buses. They looked otherworldly. They were happy.

He returned to the laptop. 'Don't bite, don't bite,' he muttered.

But Charlemagne had already posted his reply.

Yes, it's easier to say I'm nothing, that I mean nothing, a monster, a beast, something you can dismiss as abnormal. I'm used to it. We're all used it. Political correctness has kept us in the shadows for decades. We lost our voice. If we didn't praise every new mosque or adore every Obama speech, we were racist, right? But it's never that simple, is it? Now, we've got our voice back and everyone's confused. We won't go quietly into the long goodnight. We want to be heard, too. And we're being heard, millions of us. I'm being heard. Again, I'm sorry for your loss, but you won't silence us any more. You won't silence me.

Low heard the screeching brakes of a distant bus, presumably stopping for a swaying pisshead on a zebra crossing. He tried to picture the drunk giving a V-sign to the perplexed bus driver, anything to stop the weariness from taking hold. Adrenaline had won the earlier battle, but the vodka was now winning the war. His droopy eyes started to close as he slumped towards the laptop.

'Don't reply, don't reply,' he mumbled.

Sleep's warm embrace was on its way. Low could feel it coming. But he mustered the last of his energy to jolt himself awake just in time to see Zhang's response.

And you'll never silence me, dickhead.

'Stop now, just stop now,' Low mumbled at the screen.
But Charlemagne's response swiftly followed.

Sticks and stones. In the end, actions always speak louder than words. As the great man once said, 'I like things to happen, and if they don't happen I like to make them happen.' See you soon.

Low threw on some clothes and was out of his room and running for the lift within minutes. He didn't bother to switch off his laptop, leaving the shrieking echo chambers to underline the futility of their existence.

CHAPTER 19

Low left the taxi in Wardour Street. He felt nauseous. His legs ached, threatening to buckle as he found the alleyway of Dansey Place. Familiar smells flooded his nostrils. Stale piss. Dim sum. Stagnant water. Yesterday's coriander, tomorrow's takeaways, he was in hawker heaven looking for Hawker Heaven. He had to hand it to old man Zhang. The name was obvious, but it worked. The Chinatown alleyway even had the smells to match.

Low passed stacked pallets once filled with cauliflowers and *bok choy*. Leaking pipes dripped against rapeseed oil drums, recreating the rhythms of every coffee shop in Singapore. He was practically at home, a little corner of Chinese utopia in every major city on the planet.

When the *ang moh* corporations annexed foreign shopping districts, it was called Starbucking. When the Chinese did pretty much the same, it was called culture.

Low noticed the tacky heritage symbol through the alleyway, swaying in the next street. Chinese lanterns. Hundreds. They snaked through every Chinatown street. Instant prosperity. The tourists needed them for selfies. The Chinese wanted them for the casinos. Luck and money were interchangeable in Chinatown.

Low's running gave way to a light jog. His laboured breathing echoed through the alleyway. He was alone, scared and torn between drunk and sober. He was both exhilarated and exhausted. His skull pounded against his skin, starved of oxygen, trying to escape.

He turned into Macclesfield Street and stopped. He felt dizzy. His legs shook. He spotted Hawker Heaven further along the street, its sign glowing red and gold through the bleak, cold air. Low was a hundred metres away, maybe less, maybe more. His bleary, bloodshot eyes were no longer helping him. He trudged towards the restaurant, at barely a light jog. He raised his lolloping head. Thirty metres. Getting closer. Deserted street. Almost. Some stragglers. Leaving casinos. Nights made. Nights ruined.

Twenty metres now, perhaps less, but Low was swaying. Hawker Heaven's gaudy letters skipped towards and then away from each other. He tapped the side of head. A readjustment. An improvement. Low soldiered on as the colours changed.

Hawker Heaven's red and yellow gave way to just yellow, a flickering, hypnotic yellow.

Flames.

Low was suddenly sprinting. Adrenaline took charge. His legs were working faster than his muddled mind. He ran towards the fire raging inside the restaurant. Tables collapsing. Chairs melting. Family photos burning. Memories disappearing.

Two people.

There were two people.

Both standing. Separated. One was locking the glass door from the front. One was screaming at the glass from behind. Low changed direction, fists clenched. He had a target. The jailor. Tall. Bald. Black coat. Black gloves. Leather boots. The jailor turned. His face: white, wrinkled, old.

Winston Churchill.

It was Winston Churchill.

Winston Churchill was marching towards him.

Low was confused, disoriented. He hesitated, not for long, but long enough. He heard his cheekbone shatter. A bone crunched just below his eye. His arms went up, but his legs had already surrendered. He was falling, away from Hawker Heaven, away from the fire, away from the screaming man behind the glass door. He heard the black leather boots scraping towards him. One found the middle of his spine. Low howled. His body arched and then crumpled. The black leather boots drifted away.

Screaming.

The screaming revived Low.

The screaming reminded Low of his guilt.

He couldn't pass out. Not yet. He hadn't earned it.

On his side, he lifted his left arm and dug his fingers into the tarmac. He pulled. Low's shattered cheekbone slid across his coat sleeve. The pain was overwhelming, but the screaming sustained him. He was getting closer.

As he reached the doorway of Hawker Heaven, Low dragged himself onto his hands and knees and pushed against the glass. The heat singed his fingertips.

On the other side of the door, the desperate screaming had given way to hopeless panic, the sound of a wounded soul reluctantly preparing for death.

'Stand back,' Low whimpered.

He rolled onto his back. His bruised spine shot an excruciating protest to his brain. He blinked away the tears in his eyes and ignored his body's determined efforts to shut him down. Self-loathing overcompensated for a defeated body.

He kicked against the glass door.

Nothing.

He heard the screams of the dying.

He kicked again.

Nothing.

He saw Ramila Mistry walking away from him.

He kicked again.

The glass cracked.

He saw Zhang Jun Li and Mohamed Kamal holding hands, together, smiling forever.

He kicked again.

The glass smashed.

He saw himself, lying alone in a hotel room with an empty vodka bottle.

He kicked again and again and again and again, until he was showered in broken glass.

Suddenly he was on his feet. No pain. Reaching out. Grabbing. Diving. Rolling. Coat off. Covering. Protecting. Sheltering. Saving.

Low fell to the ground, away from the fire. He was done.

A voice beside him coughed and crackled into life.

'Cannot. Cannot stop. She's upstairs. Jun Li. Please.'

Zhang Wei raised a blackened finger towards the timber-framed window above Hawker Heaven and then fell silent.

The bedroom belonged to Zhang's only daughter, his brave, beautiful, defiant young daughter.

The bedroom was on fire.

Low tried to move. Nothing. He heard the screaming again, but this time it was coming from within. His body had beaten him. His eyes betrayed him. Double vision. Two men in long black coats. Black leather boots. Walking towards him. Scary faces. White. Wrinkled. Old. Marching in unison. Ready to fight. On the beaches. On the landing grounds. Never surrender.

Never surrender.

Low resisted his loss of consciousness to the very end, long enough to briefly correct his double vision, long enough to see two men become one.

One man. White. Wrinkled. Old.

Winston Churchill stood over Low, tilting his face to examine the detective's bleeding cheekbone.

Winston Churchill giggled.

Winston Churchill raised a gloved hand to his own face.

And the last thing Low saw before passing out was Winston Churchill giving him a V for victory.

CHAPTER 20

The first thing Low heard was the beeping. It was slow, steady and strangely soothing.

His heart.

The hospital had done well to find it.

The numbness came next. Mild tingling. It was repetitive, but not painful. His cheek felt bloated. He raised a hand to touch his wounds, but a clattering clinking stopped him, the sound of metal against metal.

He was handcuffed. Obviously.

Foreigners who crash cars near the prime minister's residence and then turn up outside a terrorist attack still in progress are seldom trusted.

Low felt the crisp morning sunlight against his face. Buses, taxis and couriers competed to make the most noise outside his window. He was in a London hospital, on a low floor, hand-cuffed to the bed.

His university lecturing tour wasn't going particularly well.

He thought about opening his eyes, but there really wasn't much point. He already knew who was standing at the end of his bed.

'So you're awake, then?'

That voice. That had to be the first voice on the morning

after the shittiest night. It was an appropriate punishment. The anti-inflammatory drugs took care of his cheek and spine, but there were no painkillers capable of taking the edge off that voice.

'Yeah.'

'You had a busy day, didn't you?'

And there was the other voice. By her side. The love of his life stood beside the pain in his arse. Perfect.

Low opened his eyes. The private room didn't surprise him. *Calm exteriors*. But the absence of police uniforms did. DI Mistry and DC Devonshire were the only other people in the room. Neither had slept much. She had the dark rings. He had the dilated blood vessels. Both had crumpled clothes, either thrown on this morning or still worn from the night before.

Low detected the stale smoke. They had come straight from Hawker Heaven, straight from hell. The fire. The bedroom. The screaming. The silence.

Low tried to sit up, but fell back on his pillow.

'The girl,' he whispered.

Mistry leaned forward.

'What?'

'The girl. The daughter.'

'She's dead.'

Low appreciated the handcuffs. He wanted to tear out Devonshire's trachea.

She's dead. Just like that. The voice was cold and detached. There was no emotion because there was no connection. Devonshire wasn't there. He didn't see. He didn't hear.

'Fuck.'

'By the time the fire brigade turned up it was too late. At this stage, hopefully, it was probably smoke inhalation. Hopefully, she would've passed out before the fire took hold. Hopefully.'

Low heard the compassion in her voice. He was pleased. The job hadn't stolen her compassion, not yet.

'How do you know?'

Mistry and Devonshire looked at each other.

'It seems they were both asleep. He broke in through a side door and he . . .' Mistry hesitated. 'He poured petrol all over the restaurant, the staircase and then the bedroom doors. He left the rest of the petrol in the can outside her bedroom door. She was never going to get out.'

Low saw him, giggling, bending down, a V for victory.

'How did he know?'

'Well, the bedroom door was pink and covered with photos of Jun Li and Mohamed Kamal.'

Devonshire cleared his throat. 'It seems that Zhang Wei – the father – he woke up and broke though his door. In blind panic, he ran downstairs for a fire extinguisher and then got trapped. The fire engulfed the place. The cooking-oil drums hardly helped. He's got serious burns to his arms and legs, but he's survived, in shock, which is hardly surprising. He knows what happened. They had to sedate him. But he'll live, after, you know. You saved him.'

'It doesn't matter,' Low said. 'He's already dead. The Chinese and their children. One supports the other. Then they swap. Filial piety. He knows it was all for nothing now. When she died, he died.'

Low looked up at the ceiling. There was a crack in the plaster. Britain's austerity measures were everywhere. He waited for the question to come.

'How did you know?'

It came from Devonshire. Obviously. Mistry didn't need to ask.

'I saw him on Facebook.'

'On the MEGA pages? We're monitoring them and the Billy Evans pages.'

'It was beneath her post.'

'Zhang Jun Li? We've read all that, too. There were dozens

of death threats and "fuck off back to Chinas" – the site throws them up every day.'

'He didn't make a death threat. He did the opposite,' Low said, speaking slowly. 'He felt offended. Sensitive. Defensive. And then he turned passive-aggressive, as if justifying what needed to be done and what would be done in the future. He was rationalising the behaviour of Make England Great Again, but then he switched to himself. He was rationalising his behaviour, his actions to himself. It was about *his* actions. He wanted to show he was a man of action. He wanted to show *and* tell. He wasn't like the others. He wasn't another keyboard warrior. He was doing something about it. He was making a difference. He was doing what needed to be done. At first, I just thought he was involved with those videos maybe and then his tone, his mood, everything, it all shifted.'

'Why?'

'She criticised him. She *emasculated* him. That's the worst thing you can do to this lot, the biggest red rag. Don't take away their manhood. Whether it's women's equality or a black superhero, don't make them look inferior. They're no longer the dominant gender. They're certainly not the dominant class. In fact, the other classes laugh at them on TV. Now they're at risk of no longer being the dominant race. That's too much. And then what? A young, educated Chinese woman comes along and tells him how worthless he is, how insignificant he is, in his own country, on his own Facebook page. There's nowhere to go after that.'

Devonshire made no effort to hide his incredulity.

'Oh, leave off, Stanley. You got all that from a Facebook page?'

Mistry ignored her husband. She was already on her phone, scrolling through the comments beneath Zhang Jun Li's original post.

'I'm not saying I knew he was going to kill her. But I thought she might be in danger. Everyone knew where Hawker Heaven was. I just wanted to warn her. I knew he would respond.'

147

'Why?'

'Because I would've done exactly the same. When you hate yourself that much, you'll pretty much do anything.'

Mistry stopped scrolling.

'Charlemagne?'

Low nodded.

Mistry passed the phone to Devonshire.

'Get him traced.'

Devonshire read the exchange between Zhang Jun Li and Charlemagne. He stopped at Charlemagne's final post.

'Did you see this bit? "I like things to happen, and if they don't happen I like to make them happen." That sounds like a promise, a threat.'

'Or a quote,' Mistry said. 'I've heard that before.'

She cut and pasted the quote into a search engine. Hundreds of results instantly appeared.

'It is a famous quote,' she said.

'Winston Churchill?'

Mistry looked up at Low. 'Yeah. How do you know?'

'That's him. You're looking for Winston Churchill.'

The eerie face of Britain's World War II leader stretched across the grainy screen. Winston Churchill peered into the camera lens, his wrinkled features blocking out the background.

He gave a V for victory. Then he spray-painted the lens until it turned to black.

PC Bishop rewound the CCTV footage and paused on Churchill's face.

'That's from the camera in Macclesfield Street, sir, not far from Hawker Heaven. He must be bloody strong to climb up the pole to do that. Someone must have seen him.'

'At that time of the morning? I doubt it,' said DCI Wickes, standing over Bishop's shoulder. 'And even if they did, so what? It's Chinatown, Soho, Leicester Square – there are pissheads in fancy dress every night down there. What happens next?'

Bishop turned back to a bank of CCTV screens. He fiddled with the buttons on a panel in front of him.

'We catch him here just slipping out of Macclesfield Street and into Dansey Place,' Bishop said, pointing at a screen on his left. 'I mean, that's not far from where Kamal was killed. It's also a long alleyway with no CCTV. God knows why.'

'It's Chinatown,' Wickes said. 'They don't want prying eyes in their place of business. Selling their imported veg and God knows what else. We're struggling to maintain the CCTV cameras we've already got.'

'Spending too much money elsewhere,' Bishop said.

Wickes picked up the frustration in Bishop's voice. 'Yes, all right, carry on.'

Bishop wheeled his chair along and played another screen.

'We pick him up again here, in Wardour Street, his back to camera. He's put his helmet on in the alleyway. Jumps on that moped, parked illegally, but obviously wasn't there long.'

'Owner?'

'Yeah, it was stolen a couple of hours before,' PC Cook said, stepping forward. He read from his notes. 'We can't be sure of the exact time when it was stolen. The owner was asleep at the time.'

'Anything on the owner?'

Cook flipped a page in his notepad.

'No, nothing. Mobeen Singh. Nineteen years old. Dental student. Lives near Whittington Hospital.'

'North London? Doesn't sound like a gang member.'

'He's not. Got the moped for a part-time job, delivering takeaways.'

'Then what?'

Bishop returned to his screens. 'Then we pick him up at Albany Street a couple of times,' he said.

149

'He's heading towards north London,' Wickes said.

'Yeah, then glimpses of him through Camden Road, at different spots, here and here, heading towards Seven Sisters, but we lose him before the Holloway Road.'

'Probably where he stole the moped from. Maybe he lives there, but I doubt it. He probably just had a route worked out to get back. Too many side streets, no CCTV, easy to get into another vehicle. Check for the moped around there anyway, see if it was dumped. Go door to door with a description. Look, you're not going to catch him looking forwards, so go backwards.'

Cook peered up from his notepad. 'What do you mean, sir?'

'Don't bother trying to find him taking the mask off. Get him putting the mask on. Find the CCTV of him going to Chinatown. Show me this prat before he becomes Winston Churchill.'

Low was barely awake, but sensed his presence in the room.

'I'm so, so sorry,' Low said softly.

'You have no children?'

'No.'

'Then you don't know what you are sorry for.'

Low heard the squeaking before he saw him. Zhang Wei was in a wheelchair beside Low's bed. His arms and legs were heavily bandaged. The skin on his face was flecked with scratches and cuts, the price paid for Low smashing the glass door and saving his life.

Those scars might heal. Others never would.

'I tried to get up, to get inside. I couldn't.'

'I know. So did I.'

Zhang raised his bandaged hands as proof, trying to convince himself as much as Low.

'From her bedroom door. The skin melted on my hand. I saw it drip down the door. My own skin. Didn't care. But I knew

I was wasting my time. So I fetch the fire extinguisher, but I never got back.'

Zhang started weeping.

'I never got back.'

Low tried to pluck the right words from the air.

'She wouldn't have suffered.'

Suddenly, Zhang's eyes blazed. He pushed the wheelchair closer to Low's pillow whispering into the detective's ear.

'Don't talk like them, OK? No bullshit. She died in a fire. She was burned alive.'

'No, smoke inhalation would've put her to sleep first.'

'Is she dead? Did my daughter's body burn?'

Low didn't answer.

'So what difference does it make?'

'Nothing.'

'Yah. Nothing. It was all for nothing. Everything. I brought them here, you know. My idea. Come to Great Britain, I said. *Great* Britain. Better money, better education, better chance for my daughter. You know she was going to be a paediatrician? The first doctor in my family, a private hospital doctor some more, in the UK. My only child. A doctor at a private hospital.'

'I don't know what to say.'

'No. But you know what to do.'

Low peered into an empty vessel. Zhang had the lifeless eyes of a doll. They moved. They blinked. They functioned. But they were mechanical. The man had gone.

'I don't understand.'

'You know who he is, right?'

'No.'

'Then why were you there?'

'I wanted to speak to you and your daughter. Warn you.'

'Warn me about what?'

'I don't really know.'

'Bullshit. You knew he was coming.'

'No. I didn't.'

'I know who you are. The Singaporean cop from last time.'

'Yeah, from last time.'

'The *kelong* one. Match-fixing. Undercover.'

'Yeah.'

'They brought you here to catch him, right? 'Cos the last one was Singaporean?'

'No. I'm here because—'

'I don't care. You catch him for me.'

'What?'

'You catch him for me. Those other ones, cannot. Too soft. Too . . .What's the word, ah? . . .Liberal.'

'It's not my . . .I mean . . .I'm going back after this.'

'So am I. *After.*'

'Look—'

'We know they won't catch him.'

'They are good police here. They will in the end.'

'OK, they catch him. Then how? A few years in prison, right? Cannot. I am Malaysian. You are Singaporean. We know what we are, right? That's why we have the death penalty and they don't.'

'You want revenge?'

'I want the same.'

'I'm a policeman.'

'But first you are Chinese. You are still the same as me. Family first. The *mat sallehs* have got their welfare and everything. They love everybody, even their dogs. They love dogs more than people. But for us, it's family. Only family. He took my little girl. You know what that means. In Singapore, in Malaysia, it's the same. You will do this for me.'

'Why?'

'Because you were there. And you didn't stop him. He burned her alive. He killed her because of the colour of her skin. *Our* skin.'

152

Low tried to heave himself up. The handcuffs stopped him. He slammed his hands against the rails on the sides of his bed. The clanking metal echoed around his hospital room.

His head flopped back against the pillow. Exhausted. Irritated. The crack in the ceiling was annoying him.

'How long have you stayed in Chinatown?' Low said.

'Twenty-one years.'

'Good. Then you'll know where I can get a gun.'

CHAPTER 21

Ah Lian bounced along the pavement. He always moved quickly, especially when he felt uncomfortable. This wasn't his world. He passed three-storey townhouses. Red bricks. White timber frames. Wealth oozed from every preserved pore. He checked the address, scribbled on a paper scrap. Mallord Street, Chelsea. He wasn't sure. The road seemed wrong. Quiet. Affluent. They would stand out, surely.

Ah Lian stood out.

He was a tattooed Chinese man among dog walkers and Land Rovers. As he passed a middle-aged couple, he pulled his hoodie tighter, which only made his unshaven, snarling face all the more incongruous.

He stopped in front an elegant archway. Its address was carved into the fine masonry. Tryon House. The varnished black door forced Ah Lian to catch a glimpse of his reflection. He looked old. The hoodie, stubble and faded jeans belonged on someone else. So did his haggard face. The lines revealed his age, but somehow hid his nagging fear. That was something, at least.

He checked the address a second time. First-floor apartment. Chen. The Boss. He took a deep breath, pushed the intercom and started bouncing again, waiting for the swagger to return. Hoping.

A voice crackled through the intercom.

'Yah?'

'Eh, it's Ah Lian, ah.'

'Who?'

'Ah Lian wha'. You know I'm coming or not?'

'OK.'

As the door buzzed open, Ah Lian thought about Tiger. He still missed him.

PC Bishop sipped his fourth cup of tea of the evening from the same, filthy polystyrene cup and returned to his bank of screens.

He was sick of this pointless job. He was sick of the sight of Winston Churchill.

He caught glimpses of that bloody mask from every screen as he worked his way backwards through time on the night of the Hawker Heaven fire.

He heard Churchill's voice now. Or maybe it was an actor's voice. Someone was always playing the old prime minister somewhere. In Britain's current age of isolationism, Churchill was still a comforting, reassuring voice.

Bishop watched Churchill on his stolen moped heading towards Hampstead Road.

We shall go on to the end.

Bishop slid his seat sideways to play another screen, where Churchill stopped at a traffic light in Camden Street, his surreal features barely poking through the helmet and wraparound glasses.

We shall fight with growing confidence.

Bishop played another screen. Churchill overtook a black cab in Holloway Road, making a point of keeping his head down in the darkness.

We shall defend our island.

On a fourth screen, Churchill's passed through Cromwell Avenue, obviously making his way towards Archway Road, and onto the Holloway Road. His helmet flashed white as it passed beneath each street light.

We shall never surrender.

Wait.

Bishop rewound the footage. Churchill's helmet continued to flash and fade as it passed beneath each street light, blurring the imagery. The CCTV camera was obviously quite a distance away. The moped was small and grainy, but Churchill's face, barely the size of a pinhead, was a slightly different colour.

Churchill wasn't wearing his mask.

Already on his feet, Bishop checked the timestamp and referred to a map of London on his cluttered desk. He felt the trickling sensation around his neck collar.

In CCTV terms, he was only seconds away from finding the man behind that bloody mask.

A gangly, bespectacled Chinese student led Ah Lian down a long, ornate hallway and into the living room. He never looked up from his phone. He was checking the latest football odds. He never spoke either.

The living room was modern, but sparse and messy. The smell of too many takeaways lingered. On a long sofa, two slim Chinese women giggled as they watched a South Korean boy band on a huge flat-screen TV.

The student slumped beside them and returned to his betting odds. All three ignored Ah Lian, who lingered in the doorway, unable to make sense of the bizarre setting. The grubby Chinese kids belonged in a crumbling Geylang shophouse back in Singapore, talking cock with the *ah bengs* and the chickens. But here they were, in a house borrowed from an interior-design magazine, in a street lifted from a Victorian drama.

'Eh, your place not bad ah, damn *shiok*.'

Ah Lian was trying too hard. The Singlish exposed him. His words sounded fake. Out of touch. He was a fading gangster trying to get down with the kids of white-collar crime. He was as old as his tattoos. Dried ink. Stale graffiti.

Naturally, the trio paid no attention to the weird Singaporean uncle in the doorway, the greasy, analogue *ah long* in their clean, digital world. They got back to business.

Counting money.

Pound notes were counted, wrapped and packed into supermarket bags. One girl counted. The other girl wrapped. And the guy packed the shopping bags. He kept an eye on his phone. They continued to giggle at the pretty boys and their co-ordinated dance steps on screen. Ah Lian couldn't count all the shopping bags in the room. There were too many.

'*Wah*, you rob bank, is it?'

One of the girls glared at the talkative gangster. He was annoying her now. She couldn't concentrate on the boy band's new song. She needed to memorise the foreign lyrics for a karaoke session later and the unwanted idiot wasn't helping.

Ah Lian heard a toilet flush. Instinctively, he clenched his fists. Old habit. The skinny betting addict noticed and smiled. Ah Lian spotted the smug adolescent grinning on the sofa and took a couple of steps further into the living room.

There were footsteps behind him. Getting closer. Heavy. Bare feet. Polished floor. The Asian way. The man behind him was both large and traditional, born in Asia, not England, where everyone wore shoes and socks indoors, even in the summer. Peasants. No respect.

'You Ah Lian?'

Ah Lian turned to face a fat Chinese man in his late twenties, wearing nothing but curry-stained Bermuda shorts. No tattoos. Just skin, too much skin for a man to be taken seriously. Too much time spent in front of a laptop, checking the latest odds, reading betting markets, making electronic transfers, cleaning cash.

'Yah, you Chen, is it?'

The fat man ignored the question, flopping into an armchair like an obese slug, facing the sofa, checking his cash-counting minions.

'What do you want?'

The accent was almost neutral, perhaps even educated, but certainly privileged and distinctly Chinese. He was made in the People's Republic of China, a smug PRC raised among the ruling elite.

Ah Lian couldn't stand still. He was on his toes, jittery, performing.

'He never told you, ah? Fuck, that guy ah, damn *guai lan*.'

The girls on the sofa laughed. Ah Lian leered back at them.

'*Wah, chio bu* everywhere.'

Now they all laughed, except Ah Lian. He was aware that he was sweating. He felt naked. Exposed. A phoney.

The fat man used the back of his hand to drag saliva away from the corner of his mouth.

'What are you talking about?'

'Wha'? Just talk cock, you know.'

The fat man sat back. His flesh wobbled. 'No. I don't know.'

'*Ka ni na*,' Ah Lian whispered.

'Car knee what? Just speak English, man.'

The girls laughed.

'*Chee bye*, this is English, wha''

'No, it's not. You want to speak in Mandarin?'

'Cannot. My Chinese half past six.'

'Why are you telling me the time? He's a fucking idiot, this guy.'

'Eh, balls to you, PRC bastard.'

Ah Lian wasn't aware that he was stepping towards the armchair.

'Calm down,' the fat man said softly.

The other three stopped counting their money.

'Fuck you, lah, calm down,' Ah Lian said, moving faster

across the living room. 'You PRC bastards all the same. Come to Singapore, take our job, now finish already, all PRC. Now, London. Same. I tell you ah, really *buay tahan*. Gimme a gun or don't gimme a gun, heck care, lah, but don't fuck with me, OK?'

The fat man smiled at the bizarre gangster.

'Oh, we'll give you a gun.'

The fat man pulled a revolver from the side of the armchair. Ah Lian heard the distinct, familiar sound of guns being cocked behind him. The three dopey-looking cash-counters were no longer watching TV or fiddling with their phones. They were taking aim at Ah Lian's forehead.

Ah Lian instinctively raised his hands and stepped backwards, doing the maths. Four guns. Four idiots. No chance.

'Whoa, whoa, whoa, come on, ah,' he said.

The fat man heaved himself out of the armchair.

'Who are you?' he said.

'Ah Lian, ah. They told you right? In Chinatown.'

'Chinatown what? You not from Chinatown.'

The fat man pushed the muzzle into the bridge of Ah Lian's nose as the two men played out an impromptu dance across the living room. The fat man took a step forward. Ah Lian took a step back. The fat man led the way, the lord of the dance, until they ran out of space.

Ah Lian felt the cold plaster of the living-room wall against his clammy skin. The fat man pressed harder.

'I'm from Singapore. They told you, right? Last time. I work for Tiger.'

'Tiger what? Tiger beer?'

'Tiger. Fucking Tiger. In Singapore. Everyone knew Tiger last time.'

The fat man turned to his underlings on the sofa. Their guns were still held high, but they were clearly flagging. Boredom was taking hold. They wanted to return to their screens.

'You know a Tiger?'

The other three shrugged their ignorance, as instructed.

'We don't know a Tiger.'

'It's the fucking truth.'

'Bullshit. I don't know a Tiger from Singapore,' the fat man said. 'But I do know a Detective Inspector Stanley Low from Singapore.'

CHAPTER 22

Low turned his head to the side. The girls were already losing interest, half watching the cherubic South Koreans on TV. The bespectacled boy still had his gun trained on Low's chest area. A novice. He'd hit the fat man first.

Seconds passed. Low felt his fear dissipate. The fireworks faded. The fat man wasn't going to shoot him, not in this expensive apartment, presumably rented. Not in Chelsea. You can't drag a dead Chinese detective along the streets of Chelsea. It was the wrong postcode.

'Why haven't you shot me? What are you waiting for?'

The sudden change in accent confused the fat man. Ah Lian had vanished, leaving behind a different man with a different body shape. Low was more upright, less hunched and monkey-like. He was no longer fidgeting. He wasn't even moving, just monitoring faces, taking stock of the mood in the room. Low liked Ah Lian. He loved the gangster's impulses. But he was a distraction. Low lost focus whenever Ah Lian was around.

'So now you are the Singaporean policeman?'

'Only if you are Chen.'

Chen lowered the gun, but didn't step away, not yet. He had to be sure.

'I'm Chen.'

'Then I'm Low. Now that's settled, we can stop fucking around and your bookie can make me a cup of tea.'

Chen edged away, falling back into his armchair. Low followed, sitting on an armchair across from Chen, as if preparing for an uneasy political summit. The teenage cash-counters and a sofa stacked with shopping bags sat between them.

'Go and make him tea.'

The bespectacled bookie registered his displeasure. He hesitated.

'Go on,' Chen ordered.

Reluctantly, the younger man dragged his weary body away from the sofa like a hormonal teenager. 'What do you want?'

'Milk and one sugar. The best thing about England is the tea. Everything is bloody Lipton's in Singapore. You ever have Lipton's tea?'

No one was interested in the question.

'Shit tea. But no choice: it's got a monopoly, a bit like you in Chelsea.'

Low gestured towards the Tesco plastic bags filled with £50 notes. He waited for the stroppy one to leave the living room, still studying the betting odds on his phone, the gun held limply against his leg.

Low noticed a whiteboard propped up against an antique cabinet with the weekend's matches scribbled in marker pen.

'Is that why you picked Chelsea?'

'What?'

'For the football.'

'No. There's a casino near here. Very quiet, owned by Genting.'

'Ah, Genting. Malaysian. So Asia controls the casinos around here now.'

'Asia controls everything around here now.'

'I can see,' Low said, pointing at the plastic bags. 'Eastern Europe?'

'Albania.'

'Of course. They take all the risk, right? Smuggling. Dealing. Whatever. They fail. You don't care. They succeed. They come to you. The tea boy out there keeps an eye on the banks. Interest rates. Exchange rates. The pretty girls here with the cute *siew mais* do the pick ups in car parks. They get caught. You don't care. Plenty of hostesses in Soho. They succeed. You and your China backers get paid. Everyone closes one eye in London. They need your investment, no matter where it comes from. Low risk. High return. No exposure.'

'That's the Chinese way.'

'Calm exteriors.'

'You guys have been doing it for years.'

'Yeah, but Singapore is smarter than that. We don't hide in a Chelsea apartment. We hide in plain sight. We do our washing in Marina Bay, in front of the whole world.'

'Singapore does it right.'

'Singapore doesn't have a soul.'

'Best way.'

Both men smiled at each other. Low was starting to like Chen. The fat man had a frankness about his criminality that was almost refreshing in the current climate.

The sulky one returned with the tea, shoving a chipped mug into Low's hand.

'Thanks, man. Hey, no biscuits, ah?'

Chen leaned across the armchair, resting on his flabby arm.

'Why the Ah Lian thing?'

Low sipped his tea.

'Why the "gun in my face" thing?'

'I didn't know what you were doing.'

'I didn't know what I was walking into. Ah Lian helps.'

'So does this.'

Chen pulled out the revolver again. On closer inspection, Low realised it was a Taurus 905, easily concealed, but heavier

163

than a Smith & Wesson. Being a smaller gun, there were only five rounds. At close range, one was usually enough.

'You didn't show any fear,' Chen said, resting the revolver on his thigh.

'I didn't need to. The gun isn't loaded. You didn't hold it like a loaded gun. Too light. That told me two things. One, you hadn't held as many guns as me. You've hardly held any guns. And two, you tried a bluff that you knew you couldn't see through. Their guns might have been loaded. I don't know. Couldn't see. But yours wasn't. You panicked. The gun should've been your last resort, not your first. You folded too quickly. So I knew what you were.'

'What's that?'

Low sipped his tea again, raising his cup to the petulant bookie.

'Nice tea,' Low said, before returning to Chen. 'An amateur. That's what you are.'

'Fuck you. Do you know how much money is in this room?'

'Oh, I don't know. Millions and millions and millions, I suppose. Those plastic bags might as well be one giant erection. You were showing off. You knew who I was, but you didn't hide the bags because you wanted to show me what a big man you are. But you're not really, and that's fine. I don't need a big man. I just need a gun and you'll do for that. You're an accountant for men I'll never meet, men I used to work for, men who've probably told you what I'm capable of. They told you I'm a reckless, fucked-up Chinaman with no interest in life or death and no purpose beyond following an unbending moral code, right? Which is why I'll turn a blind eye to the money laundering, your empty guns and your frankly embarrassing attempts to look like a boss. I'll just take your gun with the bullets that you're gonna give me and leave you to play gangster with yourself.'

'You're still a policeman. Why would I give a gun to a policeman?'

'Because I'm not a policeman. Not here. And because you're not giving me a gun, your bosses are. You don't have a say in the matter. These racist pricks are bad for business. Make England Great Again makes Chinatown poor again. Those immigration raids, the ones that pacify right-wing voters, they're hurting all of you,' Low said, pointing at the cash-counters on the sofa.

'And your couriers here won't be around if the Government starts cancelling student visas and foreign work visas to pacify a right-wing electorate – and they will. They'll do anything to stay in power. And no visas means people smuggling. And that means stuffing Vietnamese in the backs of trucks again. And your bosses don't want that, not to collect drug money in a Tesco car park. It's not worth it. These far-right bastards are messing things up for anyone who doesn't have a white face. And now they're actually killing you. They're burning down your legitimate businesses in Chinatown. They're forcing the police to stick their noses into your world, and your bosses can't have that. I could lie and say it's a Chinese revenge thing. An eye for an eye and all that shit. But we both know that's not true. In the end, it's always about the one true Chinese philosophy. Money. If our racist killer keeps killing Asians, you can't be left alone to make your money.'

Low emptied his cup.

'I have to say that was a lovely cup of tea. Just the right blend of milk and sugar,' he said, carefully placing the cup on the hardwood floor. 'Now, do as you're told and give me that fucking gun.'

CHAPTER 23

A pasty-faced intern hurried into the radio studio. He was aware that he was sweating. He was also aware of all the wide-eyed faces watching him through the glass partition. They had less than two minutes. There was an ad about car insurance, then one about travel insurance for the elderly. London Call-In listeners were all terrified of being deprived of something.

The intern dropped a laptop in front of Mark Beckett. The laptop clattered against the radio host's skinny flat white, spilling coffee on Beckett's headphone cables. Across the table, Margaret Jones pushed her microphone aside to get a better view.

'You've knocked your coffee there,' she said, grinning.

'Yeah, thanks, Margaret.'

The intern pulled open the laptop. A producer tapped on the glass partition and pointed at the digital clock.

'We're back on after this ad,' Jones said.

'I know that.'

'You won't make it.'

'I will if you stop interrupting.'

The producer's voice drifted through their headphones. 'Thirty seconds.'

'OK, you better go,' Beckett said, ushering the intern away.

'Twenty seconds.'

Beckett scanned the horrific material on the screen.

'You're out of time,' Jones declared.

'No, I'm not,' Beckett said, smiling back at his breakfast co-host. 'I know you'd like me to be, though.'

'I'm not worried.'

'You haven't seen the video.'

'Five seconds.'

The microphones lit up. Behind the glass partition the panting intern enjoyed the high-fives from grateful producers. His internship was looking promising. He had gone to the right schools.

Beckett raised an arm for silence, force of habit, a reflex left over from the cheap, cluttered studios of community radio. But he co-hosted the most popular and divisive talkback show in Britain. Beckett and Jones were the only people inside the studio, the only voices required. They spoke for the two halves of a divided audience.

'And welcome back to London Call-In. You're listening to the number-one breakfast show, with me Mark Beckett and Margaret Jones. Now, I want to discuss something that Margaret clearly doesn't.'

Jones dragged the microphone towards her chin, a fist away from the face, as always, the consummate professional and the best rabble-rouser in the business.

'No, I don't want to discuss it because I don't want to give publicity to these people.'

'But you don't have any choice any more, do you Margaret? You encouraged these cretins to crawl out of whatever rock they'd be hiding under for the last ten or fifteen years, shielding their eyes from the blinding glare of political correctness.'

'You don't half talk some pretentious twaddle.'

'You gave them a platform, via their various far-right factions masquerading as mainstream political parties. You pandered to the darkest dregs of humanity with your incendiary comments on immigration, the EU and the apparent threat to our so-called way of life, and now they've taken your baton and run with it, you're in denial.'

'I'm not in denial about anything.'

'You're in denial about filth like this. Now, listeners, I'm going to play you a clip from the latest Make England Great Again video, uploaded less than an hour ago, while we were on air. I know you can't see it, but just listen to the language.'

Beckett nodded towards the faces behind the glass partition. Beckett tapped his laptop, which was linked to surround-sound speakers. The YouTube clip began. Its narration echoed around the studio.

A montage of Hawker Heaven photographs drifted across the screen. The Chinatown scenes were happy, sunny and full of tourists.

'This was England before.'

The narrator's voice was slow, deep and robotic after being run through a digital processor. Identification was obviously impossible.

'This is England now.'

Hawker Heaven was on fire and then a smouldering ruin.

'This is not the England we want. This is not the England we remember.'

There were photos of an idyllic England, an almost mythical England. Every park and playground was green and sunny and filled with white families. Children ate ice creams on sandy beaches. Grandparents snoozed in deckchairs. Parents queued for fish and chips. They were picture postcards from the 1970s, PhotoShopped interpretations of whitewashed childhoods. It was England's social history, filtered through a Ladybird storybook.

'That was our England then.'

'This is England now.'

Bloodied men fought at Altab Ali Park. Muslim men tore up

St George's flags. Women screamed. Children ran. The images got faster, blurring and merging. Islamic preachers. Grooming gangs. Mosque marches. Polish layabouts. Refugees. Rubber dinghies. Stadium bombs. Street battles. Police truncheons. Skull Face. *Allahu Akbar.* Brown-faced mayors. Skull Face. Making the connection. Brown-faced mayors and brown-faced skulls, same colour, same religion, same people, no distinction. *Allahu Akbar.* Brown-faced mayors. White-faced anger. Red-faced victims. Invaded. Surrounded. Trapped. Running. Everyone was running. Running away. Chased away. No longer welcome. No longer a home. Keep on running. Screaming. Bleeding. Dying.

'This is not who we want to be,' the metallic voice droned over the footage. 'We are ready to take our country back. Whatever it takes. Make England Great Again.'

The St George's Flag fluttered across the screen, until Beckett slammed the laptop shut, a tad melodramatically, but he was aware of the studio webcam. There were viral YouTube clips to edit after the show.

'Now I know you can't see the video,' Beckett began, speaking slowly, ready to build to his characteristic crescendo. 'But you don't really need to, do you? You've got the bombastic sound effects. You've got the pithy, fascist slogans in a voice that sounds like E.T. He was obsessed with going home as well, wasn't he? But this is really where we are now, Margaret, isn't it? Your army of columnists and tub-thumping shock jocks have made this Goebbels-like Nazi propaganda an everyday occurrence.'

Jones felt like a cornered stray, which was her happy place. A cornered stray has only one response to an unwarranted attack.

'Mark, I think your comments are downright bloody disgusting,' Jones began, playing up the Birmingham accent to appeal to the man on the street, whoever he was. She hadn't gone anywhere near the man on the street since secondary school.

'Firstly, you already know that this outrageous video has nothing to do with Make England Great Again or Billy Evans, who has already publicly denounced the video on social media. And I think it's disingenuous to link my well-documented comments on our antiquated immigration policy with every random nutter.'

'Oh, here we go. Here comes the lone-nut theory. They all operate in a vacuum, don't they Margaret? They're all just angry young men. But who made them angry?'

'No, I'm not going to play games with you here. I'm not giving this nutcase any justification or explanation on radio and if you attempt to somehow blame me or connect me in some way to this video, then me and you are gonna have a very serious problem.'

'I never wanted Billy Evans on this show. You did. I never wanted to discuss his rabble on this show. You did. I never wanted to upload these toxic clips onto our website, but the station did.'

'Because people want to see them, Mark. Why are people listening to this stuff?'

'For the same reason people used to watch public executions in the town square. Shall we bring those back as well?'

'Look, let's put your flowery imagery to one side and focus on the real issues, shall we?'

'That the mainstream media has legitimised fascistic language in everyday life?'

'The same mainstream media that pays your huge mortgage.'

'It's a small townhouse.'

'In a posh postcode. What's the difference? You're out of touch with the mood out there and you attack me with your snowflake clichés because you don't understand why my columns are so popular. You don't understand why these videos are so popular.'

'No, I don't. I really don't. But I can take a stand. I can

say that this nauseating video from that racist mob will be the last clip I'll ever play. And I'll never mention those thugs and their so-called movement on this radio station again. I'm willing to call a spade a spade, Margaret. Racist pond scum is racist pond scum. Are you willing to say the same? Or do you fear alienating the people who pay *your* mortgage? What do you think out there? Let us know. We'll take your calls after the break.'

The producers gave a thumbs-up through the glass partition. The mic lights went off.

'You're such a wanker,' Jones muttered.

'Bollocks.'

Beckett threw off his headphones, knocking over his Amnesty International mug and spilling the rest of his skinny flat white across the desk.

Behind the glass partition, the intern grabbed a box of tissues. As he dashed into the studio to clean up the coffee puddle, he decided against the full-time gig.

Low had made space for only three things on the grubby desk in his hotel room. Laptop. Pizza box. Gun.

Nothing else mattered.

Low grabbed a slice, allowing the melted mozzarella to dribble down his chin and onto the floor, the latest contribution to his growing collection of carpet stains.

He was still wearing the blue hoodie, covering most of his face. He wasn't cold. He was just more comfortable in Ah Lian's clothes.

On his laptop he replayed the latest MEGA clip over and over again. The Skull Face footage didn't particularly bother him. That guy was someone else, just doing his job, defending *her*. No regrets. No remorse. None.

The *Allahu Akbar* dubbing was the problem. The vocal manipulation served its purpose. It woke up the face-painted

171

fools, but it also woke up Zhang Jun Li. The crude Islamophobia had offended a young woman's sweet soul.

It angered her.

It empowered her.

It killed her.

Low watched Hawker Heaven burn. The flames. The fallout. He watched the images flash across his screen, dozens of them, from all angles, from all perspectives and agendas. Everyone had a camera now. Everyone was a journalist. Everyone was a police officer. But for Low, less was always more. A journalist's eye was different from that of a pathologist or a police officer. They were trained to see different things. The general public were even worse: too much adrenaline and not enough objectivity. They panicked. Their hands shook. No focus.

But one shot in the montage was different.

It was focused, revealing everything and nothing. The shocking scene of Hawker Heaven burning matched the one scorched into Low's skull, but not quite. The flames were lower, climbing through the chair legs, but not quite reaching the tabletops. Hawker Heaven was ablaze, but not yet engulfed.

And there was no one in the picture. Zhang Wei wasn't in the frame. He hadn't run downstairs yet, in search of the fire extinguisher that he was destined never to find.

Low hadn't arrived either. No one had. The fire had barely started. And yet the photo was crisp, clear and focused.

Low rummaged through dirty socks and loose change on the hotel bed until he found his phone. He waited for the inevitable beep.

'Look, I know you're not allowed to talk to me, or you don't want to talk to me, or whatever. But you've got to get tech to work on that new video. Examine the first photo of the fire. He took it. Winston Churchill.'

CHAPTER 24

Beckett read through the producer's list of callers on hold. Usual suspects. Too many foreigners in the town centre waited on line one. Middle-class student was ready to blame his grandparents' generation for their selfishness on line two. Little Englander seemed poised to burst a blood vessel over Europe's hegemony on line three. And liberal snowflake agreed with Beckett's views, for the most part, but didn't approve of his constant badgering of Margaret Jones, which bordered on sexist mansplaining. He was ready to explain why on line four.

Beckett had been warned before about his condescending tone, which always sounded worse opposite a female voice. Line four offered a friendly chance to redress the balance with little chance of collateral damage. Plus, nothing irritated Jones more than whiny liberals playing the chivalrous knight and leaping to her defence. She didn't need help from anyone, whatever the political persuasion.

Either way, Beckett couldn't lose. He checked the name and opened line four to 3 million listeners.

'Hello, Leonard from Westminster, you're through to London Call-In. And I believe you want to take me to task for the way I speak to Margaret.'

The pause was too long.

In a regular conversation, such a gap was awkward. On live radio, it was commercial suicide. Radio silences were called dead air for a reason. They killed careers.

Beckett fixed his gaze on the producers through the glass partition. Wasted calls made him appear ridiculous, especially on the studio webcam.

Beckett tried again.

'Hello, Leonard, you there? No? Well, let's go to Sue in Ramsgate and—'

'I'VE KILLED TWO. YOU WILL BE NUMBER THREE.'

The booming voice succeeded where thousands of others had failed across two decades.

The voice silenced forty-year-old liberal host Mark Beckett.

The voice silenced fifty-year-old conservative commentator Margaret Jones.

The voice silenced every staff member inside the London Call-In station.

The voice silenced 3 million listeners.

The voice wasn't human.

It was robotic. It was deep, growly and processed.

It was the voice of the Make England Great Again videos; the voice that implored a nation to do whatever was necessary to take the country back.

It was the voice that reached a tolerant society's most secret, intolerant prejudices.

And Beckett had no response for it. Nothing. When presented with such inhumane hatred, he had no weapon in his academic arsenal. He just had words. Meaningless words. Redundant knowledge. Boring facts. Balanced analysis. Reasoned argument. No point. No value. No hope. Like all liberals, he was a man of peace up against a voice of war. In that regard, he really was a snowflake.

He melted.

The dead air was deafening.

'Hello, Mark Beckett, are you there? Or shall I go to Sue in Ramsgate?'

The robotic voice was mocking Beckett now, underscoring his impotence. His terror.

Jones smiled at Beckett, sympathetic now, perhaps even empathetic, aware on this occasion that she had won the coin-toss. Heads I win. Tails you get the death threat. That was the nature of their populist business. They incited verbal riots every morning over breakfast. Hate mail and hollow threats were guarantees of a decent Christmas bonus, vitriolic proof of a job well done.

But no one had ever promised to kill either of them live on air before.

Until now.

Beckett had broken through that particular glass ceiling. His publicist's job was done until the end of the year, perhaps with the pick of reality TV shows to choose from. Beckett could now dance on ice, sing on a charity single or eat kangaroos' testicles in the jungle. All he had to do was stay alive.

Of course, if Beckett turned down the reality-TV offers, Jones was available on standby, as long as she maintained her public profile in the meantime.

'Yes, we're still here, Leonard,' she said, speaking quickly into her microphone, surprising everyone on both sides of the glass partition, including herself.

'It's all right if I call you Leonard?'

'I don't want to talk to you,' the voice said.

'Well, Leonard, you can't make threats against a colleague and then expect him to talk to you,' Jones replied, almost maternally.

She had seen enough crime dramas to know that she had to keep him talking. Her publicist would be grateful for that later.

'You didn't call me racist pond scum. He did.'

'When did I call you racist pond scum, Leonard?'

175

Suddenly Beckett was back in the room. He was alive to his responsibilities. He was also aware of the new faces staring at him through the glass partition, speaking frantically into phones, calling every emergency number they could think of, panicking.

Beckett could panic later. He wobbled briefly. Anyone in his position would've done the same. That voice. Cold. Artificial. Terrifying. It was a shock, no doubt. But Beckett was buggered if he was going to let the kind of fool he railed against on his show ruin his day, let alone his career. He had been working his entire life for this moment: idealism against ignorance. He had to win.

'We can't maintain these uncomfortable silences Leonard, otherwise they'll kick us both off the air. When did I call you racist pond scum, Leonard?'

'After the video ...When you ...'

Beckett sighed into his beloved microphone. He truly loved his job.

'Look Leonard, I get it. You've listened to our show every day. You've probably punched the radio, thrown things at it, pulled out your earphones, done everything you can to get my liberal drivel out of your head. And you've probably sat there dreaming about this moment a million times, like my favourite movie character Rupert Pupkin. When you finally speak to me, you're gonna tell me this and you're gonna tell me that. You've probably practised it, said it in front of the mirror while you're shaving your own head. You're gonna put me straight once and for all for calling out your grotesque lot for what you really are. Well, this is it, Leonard. This is your chance. I'm here. Get it off your chest.'

Beckett raised his palm to the glass partition, ignoring the tapping at the window and the fingers being dragged across necks. No one was cutting him off.

'Listen, Leonard, they're going to shut us off. You've made

176

a serious threat against me on air, Leonard. That's a crime. Official protocol must kick in now. I won't even have Billy Evans on my show again. I don't want to speak to the monkey or the organ grinder, but I'll let you speak now. Only now.'

'I'm not scum.'

The robotic voice was softer, as if faltering.

'You're referring to the video clip. Yes, I think it appealed to pond scum. I think I also called the propaganda "toxic". I think it is. It's trying to spread hate. It's trying to create tension and violence between races. It promotes division rather than inclusivity. I think that's toxic.'

'Loving your country is toxic?'

'No.'

'Loving how England used to be is toxic?'

'No. But I love it just as much now. I love its diversity.'

'You live in a middle-class bubble.'

'No, I live in north London, a place that's—'

'I know where you live.'

Jones heard herself gasp on air. Now it was Beckett's turn to placate his colleague. He raised a thumb in the air.

'Is that some sort of threat, Leonard? Is this where I'm supposed to be scared?'

'Are you scared, Mark Beckett of Camden Town?'

'Yeah, that's right Leonard, Camden Town. I'll give the entire address on air if you like, because I trust our policing services, our multi-ethnic and multiracial policing services to do whatever is necessary. I trust my lovely Indian neighbours on one side and the Jewish neighbours on the other to keep an eye out for me, along with the Polish window cleaner and the Romanian *Big Issue* seller at the top of the street. They're all a bit of a Neighbourhood Watch service for me and I trust each and every one of them. Now, I know all these people upset you, Leonard – perhaps you feel they're taking away your job, your home, your money or your wife, I don't know. But it's them, not you, that's making this country even greater than it always was.'

'You are not as smart as you think you are.'

'You don't know what I think.'

'You don't know what it's like to feel a stranger in your own country.'

'No, you're right. I don't. Because I've never felt like a stranger here.'

'But you make fun of people who do.'

'So what are you going to do, Leonard? Really, I want to know. What's your logic here? On behalf of white people – because I'm taking a leap here and guessing that I'm taking to a fellow Caucasian – on behalf of white people who feel like strangers, you're going to kill a white man? That's your grand plan? How will you square that circle with your mates at the next Nazi rally? I get the Muslim thing, the refugee thing. I mean, it's idiotic, but I get it. But white against white? It's war with your own kind now?'

'Only those who stand in our way. Like Charlemagne. Like you.'

Beckett allowed the dead air to fill his eardrums. He didn't fill the silence. For the first time he found a radio host's biggest phobia soothing. He blocked out the blurry commotion on the other side of the glass partition and concentrated on removing his headphones. The task was slow and arduous, but worthwhile.

The headphones hid his shaking hands.

Beckett then received a call from a female detective at Charing Cross Police Station, who instructed him to stay at the studio until armed officers arrived.

CHAPTER 25

DCI Wickes waited for his major investigation team to fill the room and thought about his back garden. It was almost planting season. Wickes's wife wanted more rose bushes, but the thorns drove him mad during pruning. Besides, too many rose bushes turned the place into an old pensioner's garden.

Wickes wasn't a pensioner. Not quite.

But he felt so old this morning.

Wickes didn't agree with his generation's swing towards isolationism. Thirty years with the Met had made him a staunch believer in community, open dialogues and shared values. He had scooped up whatever was left of murdered teenagers in racially segregated ghettos too many times.

Walls never worked.

But he understood a pensioner's vulnerability. The first sign of getting old wasn't increasing thoughts of mortality, but the awareness of one's vulnerability. That was the one thing Wickes had in common with his generation. He had never felt so vulnerable, so exposed in a society he struggled to understand.

He had almost fifty blank faces in front of him, waiting for their senior investigating officer to lift flagging morale. But Wickes had no solution for the problem on the whiteboard behind him. No real leads. No obvious clues. No understanding. That's what really bothered him. He didn't understand these killings.

Judging by the men and women in front of him, he wasn't alone.

'OK, morning everyone, let's get going. The press want a statement about Mark Beckett. I've sent Mistry to the radio station to collect statements and then collect Beckett. Naturally, he doesn't want police protection. The pillock thinks we can all join arms in Hyde Park and sing Bob Marley songs.'

Wickes appreciated the polite titters. He was a popular leader at Charing Cross.

'Tech is working on the voice. It's obviously the same voice as the videos, or the same software at least, which is probably all that can be confirmed at the moment. But Beckett playing to the gallery did do us a favour in that regard. They're tracing the call now. It was a landline. If it's from a house, it pinpoints his location too specifically. So I'm guessing it'll be a phone box and we have a lot more CCTV cameras than we do phone boxes, so that'll help. Danny, tell me you got something with the moped. You've been on the bloody cameras long enough.'

PC Bishop made his way to the whiteboard. He pointed at a blown-up map of central and north London.

'Yes, sir. As you can see here, I've tracked his rough journey to and from Hawker Heaven, from where he stole the moped in the Islington, Hornsey area to where he parked it near Dansey Place.'

Bishop moved over to a dozen A4-sized black-and-white CCTV images of a masked man on a moped.

'This is every half-decent CCTV image I could get so far. As you can see, long coat, black gloves, crash helmet, goggles and gloves don't tell us much.'

'Except he was sweating,' a voice interrupted.

'Yeah, apart from that. But I did find one other image, sir, taken from near the Holloway Road, the first image of him after he nicked the moped.'

Bishop unfolded an A3-sized black-and-white CCTV image and pinned it to the whiteboard. Everyone else in the room leaned forward. Wickes squinted.

'What am I looking at here, Danny?'

'That's him, sir. That's him just before he put on the Winston Churchill mask. I found him.'

Wickes stepped away from the whiteboard and tilted his head. Both sides. Every angle.

'Is this a Rorschach test?'

'A what, sir?'

'I can't see bugger all.'

Laughter filled the room. The other officers were relieved to hear their boss confirm what everyone else was thinking.

Bishop tapped the image, hoping that his arm hid the blushing.

'It's him on the moped, sir. There's the coat, the helmet and there's his face. This was the best shot picked up on CCTV.'

'From where? Scotland?'

'Yeah, it's probably from at least six hundred metres away.'

'And that's the best we have? In the middle of London? We've got more cameras than David bloody Bailey.'

Bishop peered down at his polished size 10s.

'They are not all switched on, sir. Cutbacks. I checked. We keep them there to reassure the public.'

'Jesus Christ.'

'Islington are helping me, checking their database, going door to door in that area. It's a step forward, sir.'

'How?'

'We've at least confirmed he's an IC1 male.'

'A white bloke?'

'With what looks like dark brown hair.'

'A white bloke with dark brown hair?'

'Yes, sir.'

Wickes ignored the giggling in the room.

'Well, that's handy. I thought we were looking for a blonde Indian woman with a slight limp. Sit down, Bishop.'

Bishop ducked as the scrunched-up paper balls headed his way.

'Piss off, the lot of you.'

Wickes wasn't annoyed. He appreciated the levity.

'OK, Tom, tell me you've got more than a white blur with dark hair.'

DC Devonshire checked his notes.

'Yeah, the Charlemagne thing. He mentioned him twice, if we're assuming it's the same person. Once at the end of the radio call and on the Facebook exchange with Zhang Jun Li. That was his Facebook name. Charlemagne. It's a weird one. Charlemagne came from northern Europe, maybe Belgium or Germany, and conquered most of Europe. An emperor. Autocrat. So that could be the attraction. But he was also known as King of the Franks. The Franks were the early French, but they came from Germany originally. So work that one out. He was Mr Europe, remembered for bringing much of Europe together. I mean, the complete opposite of Winston Churchill and his big wartime speeches.'

'It could mean anything. Don't waste time with Wikipedia. Call someone at the British Museum or one of the local universities. Give me more than a bloody Google search. Tech could do some Charlemagne checks online, but that's needles and haystacks. Scour the Billy Evans pages. See where else Charlemagne pops up, if he does. And even then, he'll have all sorts of VPNs before he posts anything.'

PC Cook hurried into the room, waving a laptop in the air.

'Oh, look,' said Wickes. 'It's peace in our time.'

'We've traced the call,' Cook said, connecting his laptop to the projector screen. 'And we've traced him, his exact position. And he's seriously taking the piss out of us now.'

Cook spoke quickly as he fiddled with projector cables.

'The call was easy to trace. He wanted us to trace it. Landline. Phone box. Stayed online for ages. It wasn't even an obscure phone box, either. It was this one.'

The most photographed red phone box in Britain appeared on the projector screen. Cook hit pause.

'Bloody hell,' Wickes said. 'That's the one in – you know.'

'Yep. Great George Street. They've got a few red phone boxes there, all in a row, all for tourists, because they give you two London icons in one shot, the red phone box with Big Ben and Parliament in the background.'

'But there'd be CCTV everywhere. He'd know that,' Devonshire said.

'Yeah, he wanted that. Watch.'

On the CCTV footage a tall, hunched man wearing both a hoodie and a long coat opened the door to the phone box.

'He goes in and turns his back to us,' Cook said, providing commentary, unable to contain his excitement. 'He already knows where the camera is. He's already checked the area, maybe earlier in the day, maybe before. We're checking the other tapes now. So far, we've just got him walking up to the phone box, head down, hoodie down, sunglasses on, impossible to make a clear ID. It's early in the morning, cold, after the civil servants have started but before the tourist buses arrive, reasonably quiet and gloomy. And this is the smart part. It's raining. Drizzle. That shitty English fine rain.'

Wickes nodded his approval, for both his junior officer's insight and his prime suspect.

'Yeah, that's very good. Nobody looks up from the pavement.'

'Maybe it was coincidence, maybe not,' Cook said. 'But watch this bit.'

The long-coated figure lifted the phone above his head, as if threatening to smash it against the wall.

'We've checked the timing. That's when Beckett goes into his rant. But then he stops. He seems to calm down. He listens again. Always hunched over. Head down. Inconspicuous. And then he finishes – watch – puts the phone down gently, looks outside on both sides, always looking down, maybe looking for feet, anyone in the way. And then watch, this CCTV camera is about ten metres away from the phone box, in Great George Street. Watch what he does next.'

The hunched figure in the long black coat and hoodie shuffled slowly towards the CCTV camera. Head down. He stood beneath the camera and waited, still peering down at the pavement, as if undecided.

And then he removed his sunglasses, pulled off the hoodie and looked straight into the lens.

With Big Ben over his shoulder, Winston Churchill gave his customary V for victory.

CHAPTER 26

The sudden bang sent people in all directions. DI Mistry's squad went for their pistols, all dropping to a crouch, their anti-terror training distilled into instinct. Reporters, photographers and curious onlookers ducked and covered their heads. Even London's omnipresent pigeons took flight.

But Mark Beckett didn't move. He was surprised at his inaction. He felt no fear. He didn't feel anything one way or the other. He recognised dread and panic every time a script vanished or a caller dropped out as his radio microphone lit up. He enjoyed a crisis with every breakfast show.

But he had never been shot before. That was a new experience. So mind and body weren't sure how to react. They were playing catch-up. There was no precedent for being shot, nothing in the radio host's training manual about being the target of a murderous fascist. He took a deep breath and waited.

But the Indian woman beside him had memorised a more relevant training manual. Mistry tackled Beckett in the chest. His shoulder met the grey, cold pavement of London's South Bank before he'd exhaled.

He was pinned to the floor. This officer was assertive, attractive. Beckett couldn't move. He wasn't entirely sure that he wanted to.

'Inspector—'

'Shut up,' Mistry hissed, reaching for her gun.

'A taxi,' a voice said, drifting towards Blackfriars Bridge.

'It was a taxi,' said another, the embarrassment unmistakable.

'Get him up,' shouted a third voice, clearly irritated.

Mistry dragged Beckett to his feet and holstered her weapon.

'OK, get him to the car,' she said. 'And tell the photographers to piss off.'

'I'm almost disappointed,' Beckett said, dusting off his jeans and sweat-stained black jacket. 'There are worse places to get shot than here: Waterloo Bridge over there, Oxo Tower behind us, hell of a way to go.'

Mistry grabbed Beckett's arm just above the elbow and led him along Hatfields, towards a fleet of waiting cars.

'I actually like your radio show,' she said. 'But this machismo really isn't you.'

'It's not, is it?'

'No.'

'I think I'll stop talking.'

'I think it's best.'

Mistry pushed the radio host into the back of an unmarked car and checked that they would be boxed in on both sides. Hatfields was home to a number of radio and media companies, so Beckett's murder threat was a busman's holiday for the reporters working in the same street. They stepped outside the front door to get tomorrow's front-page photos. The slammed taxi door had already given them a double-page spread of gun-drawn coppers and terrified strangers cowering in terror.

Journalists were always a pain, but not an unwelcome one in this instance.

There were just too many of them in a confined space on the South Bank, too many eyeballs to escape a positive ID.

But Mistry surveyed the street one more time. She was the daughter of a shopkeeper. She always double-checked the figures. Five cars. Two lead. Two follow. Busy street. Heavy traffic. A bonus. Sitting ducks all round. They would have sirens to thread London's needles. He would not.

Mistry was satisfied.

'Ramila.'

And then she wasn't.

'Ramila.'

No one called her Ramila here. She was DI Mistry, guv'nor, boss or ma'am among the older uniforms, but not Ramila. Only DCI Wickes called his favourite protégé by her given name, but only in certain situations and never in public.

Besides, DCI Wickes wasn't here.

'Ramila.'

And he shouldn't have been here either.

Mistry closed her eyes and thought about her husband and young son and the life she had carefully cultivated. And then she returned to a past life that just wouldn't leave her alone.

'You've got five minutes.'

Mistry didn't bother with pleasantries. She didn't offer him a drink. She didn't ask him how he was. She didn't need to. Low's physical deterioration stood out like a sore Chinaman in a pretentious bar for theatre thespians. The Old Vic's imperious façade poked through the gaps in the pub's window. The theatre was a celebrated pioneer trying to recapture former glories in a changing environment with different tastes. Low knew the feeling. At least the Old Vic was a listed building. No one in government was going to protect him.

Mistry's fury was easy to project. She despised this man. Her sympathy was much harder to hide. She had once loved him and he was visibly spiralling. He was unwashed and unchanged. His jeans and jacket were covered in last night's carbs and calories. And yet he was smiling at her.

'What?' she asked.

'What do you mean?'

'The stupid smile.'

'I always liked your feistiness. No one talks to me like you. Not in Singapore. Too much face-saving.'

'I don't care.'

Low raised his blotchy arms. They were still covered in the cuts and burns from Hawker Heaven. The swelling in his left cheek had gone down since the hospital, but the bruising had spread. Half his face looked like a mouldy grape. The other half looked like it hadn't slept for a week.

'OK, fine, five minutes.'

'If that.'

'Did you get my message about the video?'

'Yes.'

'And?'

'And what?'

Mistry pushed the cutlery aside.

'You think you're the only one to work out that he's probably making the videos? Of course he is.'

'Then follow the videos.'

'We are following the fucking videos,' Mistry shouted.

A waiter appeared at the table, keen to lower the volume.

'Would you like to see our wine list?' he asked.

His accent was somewhere between France and pretentious.

'No, I wouldn't,' Mistry snapped.

'Would you like to order a drink?'

'No.'

The waiter cleared his throat.

'Well, you have been sitting here for quite a while.'

'We like the service here. Now sod off.'

The waiter wasn't having that, even if she was Indian and pretty and the kind of clientele that the bar owners coveted.

'I might have to ask you to leave, madam.'

'And I might have to arrest you for wasting police time.'

Mistry produced her warrant card. The waiter backed away, bowing as he went.

Low lifted an empty glass on his table.

'Well, a glass of water would've been nice.'

Mistry caught herself smiling.

'Oh, fuck off, Stanley.'

'Look, I'm sorry about your car. You know I am. I was shocked and stupid. And you were right. You always were.'

Low tapped his forehead, avoiding eye contact.

'What I've got up here. I know it doesn't make me marriage material.'

'No, really.'

'It just makes me wrong, wrong with you, wrong in social situations, wrong in bloody restaurants, everything.'

'Do you have a point?'

Now Low's head was up, peering into Mistry's eyes. 'But it makes me do one thing right. I can cut everything else off. I can live in here,' he said, tapping his forehead again. 'And I don't come out again until I see what's right in front of me. Like him over there.'

Low pointed at the waiter, delivering a basket of multigrain breads to another table. 'I see him and that ridiculous accent. No one in France has that accent. No one has a French accent like that, except on TV, when English actors show that they are French by speaking English in a French accent that no French person ever actually uses. But we have come to accept that. We want Hercule Poirot because it sounds intelligent and travelled and cultured and everything that we're not, British or Asian. We don't have an English accent as sophisticated as that. So he exaggerates it for the theatre crowd. He lays on the garlic and the 'haw-hee-haw' for the day-trippers. He does it for the tips and probably hates himself for it, a performing foreigner, a French caricature. Every day he plays Inspector Clouseau for pocket change. He plays up to every patronising stereotype of the effete, moustache-twirling Frenchman just to amuse his ignorant English customers. That's what I see.'

'I just see a waiter.'

'No, you don't. Don't pretend you're just another bobby on the beat. You're not. If you were, you wouldn't have left me in Singapore.'

'No, I left you because you were beating up gangsters with snooker cues.'

'Fine. You win. I don't care. But you know I'm right about Winston Churchill. He's making the videos. Get tech to trace him.'

'We are. He's using VPNs. Every teenager has one. Makes him untraceable.'

'Well, then, go after the party members. The Make England mob, get them in, *tekan* them. Billy Evans knows who makes the videos.'

'There are hundreds of them.'

'Bring him in. Whack the bastard.'

'We can't detain them without trial like you. We need probable cause.'

'On terrorism charges, you can.'

'Who? Detain who?'

Low rubbed the back of his head. 'I can get you what you need.'

'No you bloody won't. We will get him through Beckett.'

'*Aiyoh*, talk cock, sing song. You think he's gonna kill a white guy? It doesn't fit. He can't justify that. Not up here.'

Low tapped his head again.

'He can't rationalise a white guy. A white guy makes the whole crusade meaningless, makes him worthless. He wants to impress the white guys, wants Billy Evans to praise him, not denounce him. He wants to be one of them. That's why she had to go. She mocked his masculinity, questioned his manhood, pressed all the wrong buttons. He had no intention of killing her. None. But he had to prove it wasn't all for nothing. And she put him down. She emasculated him, remember.'

'Have you heard Beckett's show? He emasculates men like this guy every day. He attacked him directly, too, publicly, on air. Honestly, I'm surprised someone hasn't petrol-bombed his house already.'

'Someone might, but not our guy. He doesn't see Beckett as a real threat. Not like Zhang Jun Li. She was a threat. She was out-spoken, a woman, an Asian woman defending an Asian Muslim man. It was too much. A white bloke talking cock on the radio is nothing. Guardian columnists do that every morning. No big deal. They're used to the left-wing putdowns. They almost crave the criticism, allows them to play up the martyrdom, outcasts in their own country and all that. In truth, they need Beckett as much as he needs them. Our guy will not kill Beckett, OK? You are in more danger than a white male celebrity from Camden. You know I'm right about this. I'm wrong about everything else in life, yes, but not this. You've got to let me help you.'

'For fuck's sake, Stanley, I don't need your help. I never did. Maybe you and him both feel emasculated, eh? You're both wearing stupid bloody masks. Is that how you're gonna help? Bring back your Skull Face? Because it really helped our dead Chinese girl, didn't it?'

Mistry stopped to compose herself. She straightened the corner of the tablecloth. She saw Low flop backwards, as if reeling.

'If you really want to help me, just go home.'

'I can't. I made a promise.'

'To who?'

'Zhang Jun Li's family. Like you said. She burned to death because of me. I've got to live with that. And he's got to die for it.'

Mistry reached for Low's hand. She didn't hold it. She seized it.

191

'Don't do this. Don't force me to step between you and him.'

'You won't do that.'

'Really? Why? Because of you?

'No, because of your son. Your husband.'

Low pulled his hand away.

'You know that I've got nothing left to lose.'

CHAPTER 27

Standing in front of his beloved poster, he wanted to prove that he was ready.

Naked. Exposed. Flawless. Prepared.

The Waffen-SS soldier pointed at his chiselled body.

Toi aussi!
You too!
Tes camarades t'attendent,
Your friends await you,
Dans la division Française de la Waffen SS!
In the Make England Great Again Movement!

He knew that the Nazi propaganda poster was calling for French volunteers to join the French Division of the Armed SS. Only the details were different. In history, the message never changed. It was a call to arms, a call to convert, a call to inspire others to do the unthinkable.

He had to go into combat against his own kith and kin to rouse his own kith and kin. A race war had to be manipulated from within.

He had already ruled out making another video. Billy Evans

only denounced them in public, as did his simple-minded followers. Even they had to kowtow to the mainstream media's tokenistic nod towards political correctness, as if that was going to ever make a difference at the ballot box.

In private meetings, Evans and his inner circle knew that the MEGA movement needed a spark, a tipping point, a heinous crime of such unspeakable horror that would force the moderates in the middle to pick a side. Their real side, their true colours, their inner voice that spoke to them when no one else was listening, the one that told them to move away from dark faces on the London Underground, the one that instructed them to hate the headgear, the one that ordered them to run and hide in white suburbs, secretly hoping that someone would say the unsayable or do the unthinkable.

But they never would. Their childlike faith in humanity would always see them cling to the whimsical dreams of integration, tolerance and acceptance.

But some can never be accepted, under any circumstances.

Some can never be acceptable.

He knew that. And he was prepared to sacrifice himself to wake up the nation to the only possibility left. Force a divide. Then conquer.

On the computer desk beneath the Nazi poster, he had laid out everything he needed for the night's work, as if seeking the soldier's approval.

Mask. Gloves. Riding glasses. Knife.

He had bought the knife from a memorabilia site, under the name of Mr Leonard. It was a twelve-inch German dagger with an eagle spreading its wings across the blade's base, above the black handle. The dagger was more symbolic than effective, but he always remembered his father's words: a good workman never blamed his tools. The power to stab someone came from within, not from the weapon.

He held the vintage dagger in front of the soldier's face,

seeking approval. He was certain that the rosy-cheeked, blue-eyed young German was smiling back at him.

He had regretted not taking the knife to the Altab Ali rally and the Hawker Heaven thing. That Indian woman had embarrassed him at the rally. So had that bastard with the skull scarf. And the Chinese copper outside the fire. He could've used the knife with the Chinese copper. He wouldn't make that mistake again.

He had to get dressed, but he caught a reflection of himself in the framed poster. The polished glass allowed him to stand next to the SS soldier. Together. Same mindset. Same mission.

He admired his reflection and marvelled at the two men staring back at him. He held the pose. He had to leave soon to find the radio host, but there was still enough time.

DC Devonshire edged along the sofa. He wanted to be closer to his wife. DI Mistry ignored him. She wasn't in the mood for any attention.

'It's a nice home, Mr Beckett,' she said.

Mark Beckett allowed himself a smug glance around his living room. 'Thank you. Apparently, it used to be home to a couple of market traders from your neck of the woods.'

'Charing Cross?'

'No, the East End. I'm guessing from the accent.'

'Brown people didn't all grow up in Brick Lane, Mr Beckett. I grew up in Dagenham.'

'It's terrible what's happening there. Too much knife crime, not enough youth centres and racial integration. You see, the trouble is—'

'Yeah, you're not on the radio now,' Mistry said, running her hand through her long hair to hide her irritation.

Beckett sat back in a tatty, second-hand armchair that he'd bought in Camden Market.

'Sorry, force of habit. It's just that these issues mean so much to me.'

'I know they do,' Mistry said, reassuringly. 'And when you see a downtrodden, oppressed brown woman like me, your moral compass makes you duty-bound to defend me. I understand the middle-class guilt of the educated white man, really, I do. I live with one every day. But I don't need a lecture.'

Devonshire couldn't understand his wife's antagonism.

'Are you all right?'

'I'm fine. I'm just a little fed up with men trying to protect me today.'

'I really wasn't trying to patronise you,' Beckett insisted.

'No, he wasn't,' Devonshire agreed.

'Maybe not.'

Mistry reached for the tea on Beckett's antique coffee table. 'But I do really like your home, Mr Beckett. It's nice and spacious. In fact, it's spotless.'

'Childless,' Beckett said. 'And wife-less.'

'Yes, sorry about that,' Devonshire said.

'It's all right. It's funny, when you think about it. We struggled on regional radio for years. Didn't have a pot to piss in. Then I go viral overnight, my listenership goes through the roof and she goes off with the plasterer who did our conservatory. It's all a bit clichéd, really, isn't it? It turns out that I really do crave the spotlight and she really doesn't. She'd rather be with Tory-voting White Van Man from Maidstone.'

'I've never been to Maidstone,' Devonshire said, almost to himself.

'Why would you?'

'I don't even know what's in Maidstone.'

'My bloody wife.'

Mistry laughed. Beckett had a sense of humour. He also hadn't learned that women tend to resent being pigeonholed.

'I'm sure she's very worried,' Mistry said.

196

'She did call to see how I was, hours later of course. They don't listen to our radio show. Obviously. There's not enough football on it for *him*.'

'OK, Mr Beckett.'

'Call me Mark. Mr Beckett makes me think of the nuns, telling me off in the playground.'

'Mark, I've got to be honest. We don't really think he will come for you, at least not here.'

'That's reassuring.'

'He'd know we'd protect you,' Devonshire said. 'And we are. There will be a uniform presence, front and back, and we're here.'

'You won't be here forever.'

'No. And he'll know that. But we don't think he'll wait that long.'

'Oh fuck.'

Beckett swigged from a bottle of imported beer.

'So he won't kill me here in the short term because he knows you lot are here. So he'll kill me somewhere else in the short term because he can't wait. How did you work that one out?'

'The Hawker Heaven fire. He reacted the same night as the girl's Facebook post. He's impetuous, impatient and angry.'

'Jesus Christ, don't sugarcoat it, will you?'

Mistry fiddled with the corner of a cushion.

'But you are the best lead we have. With your help, we could coax him out.'

'You want me as bait? You want him to jump me in the street? He's not stupid.'

'No, but he's not rational either,' Devonshire said.

'Ah, that sounds even better. Let's set a trap for impetuous, impatient, angry and irrational Nazi killer who's publicly promised to kill me on air. Are you sure that's enough? Maybe I could ring a bell in the street and sing "Stand Up if you Hate Nazis".'

'It sounds shit. We know that,' Devonshire said. 'But we can end this now, with your help. We can provoke him. We can force him out.'

'How?'

Mistry took over.

'You're the voice of tolerant Britain. You antagonise the intolerant. So piss him off. Irritate him. *Emasculate* him.'

Low's voice had slipped into hers.

'It's a risk. But poor Zhang Jun Li brought him out onto the street with one Facebook exchange. Imagine what you could do on Twitter. Or even a live chat, a kind of press conference from your living room with us, or just me and you. Imagine that. The bearded liberal with the Asian policewoman, both mocking him, in front of a large audience, his own fan base.'

Devonshire had heard enough.

'OK, let's take a breather.'

The detective was already on his feet.

'Can I have a word outside, please, Inspector?'

He had parked the stolen moped at the other end of the street, beyond the range of the nearest CCTV camera. He was too far from the house to be seen, but close enough for his binoculars. He hadn't bothered with the mask just yet. He figured the helmet and wraparound goggles were enough. Besides, there wasn't a detailed description. He was just a tall white man in a long black coat going about his business on the drizzly streets of London.

On the pavements, no one looked up from their frozen feet. On trains and buses, no one looked up from their phones. And no one looked anyone in the eye any more. It just made life easier.

He knew he probably had a few hours. Stolen mopeds were commonplace, thanks to teenage gangs pinching them to hunt each other down. But the thefts still had to be reported.

He checked in with his binoculars. The images were too fuzzy. He adjusted the focus and realised he had been a tad too cautious. The lenses weren't quite powerful enough to cover the distance. He squinted and tried again. Better. Not perfect. But better. The image was still blurred, but he was pretty sure that the legs stepping out of the house belonged to a woman.

Devonshire followed his superior officer through the front gate of Beckett's house, nodding to the shivering police constable on duty.

'No one goes in or out until we get back,' he said. 'OK?'

The bored PC nodded back at the warm, well-dressed detective with the stunning, high-flying wife from Charing Cross. At least the detective smiled. His wife had a face like thunder. She was going to give it to her smarmy husband. They were going to have a row right in front of him, literally on the doorstep he'd been assigned to protect. He would have a story for the lads back at the station later.

'What do you want?'

Devonshire gestured towards the police constable pretending not to listen.

'Keep it down a bit.'

'Sod that. What do you want?'

'I don't want you to do press conferences with Beckett. It's too dangerous.'

For the second time today, Mistry wanted to punch a love-struck fool.

'Oh not again. How many men are gonna rush to my bloody rescue today? I don't need three men trying to protect me.'

Devonshire looked at his wife differently.

'Three men? Who's the other one?'

Mistry bit her bottom lip as she hesitated and then decided she was past caring.

'Who do you bloody think?'

'Ah, fuck, where?'

'Outside the radio station, on the South Bank.'

'Did anyone see you?'

'No, of course not.'

'What did he want?'

'The same as you, to swan in and rescue me, and I told him to piss off.'

'What did he say?'

'He said that we're probably wasting our time with Beckett.'

'Well, I can't stand the bastard, but we both know he's probably right.'

'Wickes wants us to babysit Beckett. So we babysit Beckett. We can make changes in the morning.'

'We don't both need to do it. You haven't seen Benjamin for days.'

Mistry rolled her eyes.

'Don't fucking guilt trip me now.'

'I'm not. But get a good night's sleep. Have breakfast with Benjamin and then we'll see Wickes in the morning at the debrief.'

Mistry almost went for her husband's hand, but spotted the eavesdropping uniform over his shoulder.

'I am bloody knackered.'

'I know. You look like shit.'

'Sod off.'

They smiled at each other.

'Go on. Go home. We'll Facetime together when you get in.'

'What are you gonna do?'

Devonshire looked up at the Camden townhouse. 'I'll spend the night with him, won't I? Karl Marx up there.'

Mistry rubbed Devonshire's arm. 'Be safe.'

'Always.'

Devonshire watched his wife until she turned the corner at the end of the road. And then he addressed the PC standing at the garden gate.

'You can stop bloody earwigging now. Fancy a cup of tea?'

*

He waited until he was positive that she was alone. He didn't expect dog walkers or joggers at such an ungodly hour. The commuters had reached home hours ago. The nearest pub was a couple of streets away and it wasn't quite chucking-out time. Besides, the weather didn't encourage a midweek piss-up.

He checked again.

No idle cars. No headlamps. No pedestrians. No residents wandering outside to separate recycling from regular rubbish. No cameras. No one was watching.

He pulled the mask from his coat pocket.

He heard his voice. He always did.

The Battle of Britain is about to begin.

He quickened his pace.

Upon this battle depends our own British life.

Head down. Mask on. Head up. Liberated. Ready.

We can stand up.

He was almost behind her now. Closing in. Sensing victory.

The life of the world may move forward.

He smelled her perfume. It was embracing, inviting and distracting. She smelled so nice, so beguiling. He almost wavered. Almost.

Let us therefore brace ourselves to our duties.

He noticed the small hairs running down the back of her neck. He reached out, just like he'd practised in front of the framed poster. The left hand took care of her mouth. Muting her voice. The dagger in the right hand touched her throat. Stealing her voice.

He took a moment to appreciate her terror.

This was his finest hour.

But he couldn't contain himself any longer.

'I probably shouldn't say this,' he said. 'But I'm a big fan of yours, Mrs Jones.'

CHAPTER 28

As a gloved hand pressed hard against her mouth, Margaret Jones blinked as she gazed at the street lamp above. The tears were for the bright lights. Not him. She wasn't going to cry for him. She rolled the saliva around her tongue and spat into his hand.

He pulled her away from the street lamp's glare, towards the darkness of a shop doorway. He needed to be quick.

'You fight back,' he said, rubbing Jones's saliva back across her face. 'Like me.'

'I'm nothing like you,' Jones hissed through a gap in his glove.

'Yes you are. That's why I've come for you, Margaret. Can I call you Margaret?'

She wouldn't speak.

'Thank you. You're defiant. Like me. You're willing to get your hands dirty. You know what we're trying to do. You also know that if I was going to kill you, you'd already be dead.'

He tapped the blade against her throat.

'But if you move or speak again, you'll only kill yourself. Where does he live?'

He removed his hand.

'No chance,' Jones said.

He sighed. She felt his warm air blow against her dyed blonde hair. She pictured a warm shower.

'We are on the same side.'

'I'm not a scumbag killer.'

He smiled. He truly admired this woman. She was a real working-class hero.

'But you speak for those who are.'

'Mark Beckett is a good man.'

'So is Daniel Jones, nineteen years old, politics student at Manchester University, staying in digs in Rusholme.'

'No.'

Now the tears were real. Jones had taken every job since leaving secondary school at sixteen, worked every hour and swallowed every principle to ensure a different life, a different class, for her son. It couldn't be for nothing.

'You can't. Please.'

'I found you. I'll find him.'

'You can't kill our own. You'll lose support. We all will.'

'So you won't tell me where he lives?'

He felt her tears dripping onto his glove. He nodded his approval and pulled his hands away.

'Good. You're not a hack. You see the bigger picture. You see what we're trying to do. Now I know. You'll write what's necessary when it's all over.'

Jones wiped her face.

'Thank you, thank you.'

She half turned and saw his grotesque, rubbery mask. Winston Churchill was looking up at the street lamp.

'No, thank you, Margaret. You gave our forgotten voices a platform. When it's all over, you need to remember that we could not have done it without you.'

Jones felt bold enough to turn and face him directly.

'Done what?'

'You'll see.'

The knife was back at her throat, stinging her skin.

'But I still need his exact address. Now. Or I will spare you and kill your son.'

Jones realised she had no choice. Beckett would understand that. She closed her eyes and waited for her hands to stop shaking.

She would need to start on her newspaper column soon.

Paul Harvey locked the main door and headed to the cellar behind the pub. All things considered, the Charles Dickens had enjoyed a good night. Day-tripping theatregoers and tourists didn't pay attention to London's politics and crime rates. They came for dinner and a show and a chance to visit a pub with an iconic face from Ye Olde London.

Tourists were like the men who really ran Harvey's pub. They wanted to live in London's past. They weren't interested in brown potboys getting stabbed in Chinatown. They didn't particularly care. It wasn't their world.

Harvey counted the barrels and climbed the cellar's staircase back to the street.

He didn't make it.

A boot sent him backwards. He landed on his back, wedged between two barrels. The searing pain in his left shoulder matched the throbbing, stabbing sensation in his back. He couldn't move.

A man made his way down the staircase, closing the cellar hatch to the street, shutting out the street lights. Harvey heard the footsteps coming towards him. He tensed. But it made no difference. A boot found his ribs. Harvey screamed.

'Do you have any fucking idea who owns this pub?'

'That's why I'm here.'

'Well, we ain't paying you. We've got geezers all over Britain. We've got Russians, Albanians. Who the fuck have you got?'

'I've got me.'

The cellar light came on unexpectedly, forcing Harvey to shield his face. His watery eyes couldn't make out the cloudy figure crouching beside him.

'Remember me?'

Harvey wiped his eyes.

'Oh fucking hell. You're that Chinese Old Bill.'

'Yeah, and you're that *ang moh* with no balls.'

Low grabbed Harvey's testicles. The pub manager howled in protest. Low squeezed harder. Harvey reached for a beer bottle on the barrel behind him. Low got there first, smashing the bottle against the brick cellar wall. Harvey summoned the last of his energy to throw a weak punch. Low brushed it aside and then brought his hand back quickly, slapping Harvey across the cheek. Harvey's resistance faltered. His strength dissipated. But Low held on.

'You know, in Hokkien, a Chinese dialect, your balls are *lum pah*. Can you say that?'

Harvey gripped the sides of the barrels, his fingernails scratching at the splintered wood. 'I'll have you fucking killed.'

'No you won't. Now say *lum pah*.'

Low squeezed again. Harvey's body stiffened.

'*Lum pah, lum pah*.'

'Very good. One of my favourite Hokkien expressions is *lum pah pah lan*. It literally means "the testicles hitting the penis". You see, that's what annoys me with the *ang mohs*. You all think the Chinese got no sense of humour, right or not? But where's an expression like *lum pah pah lan* in English? The testicles hitting the penis? Damn *shiok*, right?'

Harvey raised an arm in surrender.

'Don't "heil Hitler" me, not when I'm telling you my *lum pah* story. Anyway, *lum pah pah lan* basically means when your plan goes wrong or backfires, like, "Wah, that *ang moh* in the pub, try to go home, but then the *siao* policeman come. I tell you, ah, he damn *lum pah pah lan*." That's what you are now, *lum pah pah lan*. What are you?'

Harvey's tear-stained face was turning purple.

'*Lum pah pah lan*,' he mumbled.

'What was that?'

'*Lum pah pah lan*,' Harvey shouted.

'Very good.'

Low released his grip. Harvey rolled onto his side, clutching his groin.

'Now, tell me who makes your videos,' Low said, wiping his hands on Harvey's expensive suit jacket.

'What videos?'

'No, no, no time for bullshit now.'

Low pulled the revolver from his hoodie pocket. Harvey recoiled. His shoes scratched against the concrete as he tried to edge away from the Singaporean.

Low pushed the muzzle into Harvey's tender testicles.

'Tell me who edits the Make England Great Again videos or I'll blow your balls to Chinatown.'

Harvey started crying.

'Please. I'm just the bloke who runs the pub.'

Low leaned into Harvey's face. Their noses almost touched.

'"I'm just the bloke who runs the pub. I didn't see Mohamed Kamal get abused. I didn't see him disappear. I'm just the bloke who runs the Auschwitz tearooms. I didn't see the smoke from the chimneys." Fuck you. Silence is complicity. They can't operate without you. Who is he?'

Low pushed Chen's Taurus 905 deeper into Harvey's groin, almost lifting him off the ground.

'I don't fucking know,' Harvey shouted, raging against his own impotence.

'Well, that's a problem for both of us then, because you're my only connection. So if you tell me nothing, I've got nothing. But if I kill you, here, in a pub that they control, that's gotta flush the rats out of the sewer, right?'

'I can't tell you what I don't know.'

Low stepped away from the weeping pub manager. Harvey had a point.

'Yeah, killing you doesn't help me really, does it? Especially when you clearly don't know.'

Low slipped his gun inside his hoodie pocket.

'Exactly,' Harvey said. His relief was palpable.

'Yeah. All you can really do is tell me what you do know.'

Low stepped forward and stomped on Harvey's testicles. The pub manager wailed like a cat in heat.

'Tell me something.'

Low found Harvey's balls again. Harvey looked ready to throw up or pass out. Low wasn't entirely sure.

'Nothing?'

Low kicked again. The fireworks were back. He wallowed in the familiar, soothing, fizzing sensation that was taking hold. He was in control of being out of control, his special place that no one understood, not his employers, not the *ang mohs* and, most of all, not her.

He stomped again, allowing his boot to play the conduit, passing the pain from one tortured soul to another, convincing himself that he was working for the greater good, hoping that the bullshit would satisfy his ravaged conscience when sleep eluded him later. There really was no rest for the wicked.

'Tomorrow.'

The voice was fading, but it was enough to bring Low back into the room. He wasn't sure how long he'd been kicking Harvey.

'What?'

'Tomorrow night.'

'What about it?'

'Here, tomorrow night, after closing.'

'What?'

'They'll all be here.'

'The video guys?'

'Everyone. All the main ones, for a private party.'

'What for?'

'Celebration, private sponsors. Another million on Facebook or something.'

'Are you lying to me?'

'What the fuck do you think? I've got no bollocks left.'

Low wiped the sweat from his forehead.

'OK, you let me in tomorrow, through here, OK? If you tell them I'm coming, I'll kill you. If you warn anyone not to come, I'll kill you. You understand?'

Harvey spat a mouthful of blood. It splattered across a beer barrel.

'Yeah, but there'll be a lot of people here – the money people, the hidden ones. You need to be, like, you know, rational.'

'Rational? Do I look rational to you?'

Low answered his own question with a final stomp on Harvey's sensitive area.

CHAPTER 29

Margaret Jones waited for the microphone light. Her career had been leading to this moment. She had hosted breakfast shows before, but not for an audience of this size. This was the full English. Her father would've been so proud.

But she had opted for a different seat in the radio studio this morning, taking the guest's seat. She didn't want to face Mark Beckett's desk.

His seat. His microphone. His cup. His script notes. His life. Everything he had ever wanted was in their shared studio.

But he wasn't there.

The producer pointed at Jones through the glass partition. The digital clock on the wall, beneath the London Call-In logo, counted her down. She was seconds away from media history.

Her newspaper column had already made her viral. She was an international trend. Her radio broadcast would make her immortal.

The light turned red. Her show. Her time.

'Good morning, it's 6.01 a.m. and you're listening to me, Margaret Jones, on London Call-In, the country's leading talk-back radio station, where every conversation counts. But we must begin on a sombre note.'

She hesitated. There were so many eyeballs behind the glass panel, darting around like marbles on a coffee table.

'This is the first time I have presented this show alone. We have had stand-ins before and we had one yesterday, but I wanted to be alone on this show. I wanted to take a stand. Mark Beckett, the argumentative little sod, would expect nothing less. As you probably know, a masked man threatened me last night. A coward in a Winston Churchill mask held a knife to my throat and threatened to kill me. He threatened to kill my son. He thought the Churchill mask made him brave and patriotic, when of course it made him weak and idiotic. Churchill didn't hide. The British don't hide. And I won't hide. I am working with the authorities on catching this parasite and I've taken the necessary precautions to protect my family. But you know, in a warped way, when you have a knife tearing at the flesh on your neck, everything becomes clear. Your choices are simplified. You can either live or you can die. I chose to live. I fought back. I kicked him in the nuts and I escaped.'

On the other side of the glass participation, they cheered. An overeager intern waved a plastic Union Jack flag at Jones. She acknowledged their support.

'He wanted to kill me. And he wanted to kill Mark Beckett. He told me as much. He thinks we're a threat to his psychotic ambition. He wanted to silence our speech. He thinks being a patriotic Brit means denying us the very bloody thing that makes me proud to be British. And that's why he has no idea what that stupid mask means. Churchill fought for our freedom. He stood up to tyranny so we wouldn't have to live in chains. This clown thinks he can do it the other way round. Well, he can't. The first call I made was to the police. The second was to my son. And the third was to Mark Beckett. In all three calls, I demanded extra security and action. I don't always agree with Mark Beckett and he certainly doesn't always agree with me, but we're buggered if anyone is going to shut us up. And so we're going to do the very thing that this failed terrorist doesn't want us to do. We're going to co-host our radio show.'

Jones waited for the thumbs-up behind the glass partition.

'For those of you watching our live webcam feed, and judging by the numbers, there's a lot of you, both domestically and overseas, your screen is about to be cut in two.'

Jones opened her laptop to check the live feed. She saw herself on one half of the screen. On the other, Beckett waved back at her.

She wasn't overly impressed with his smiling and waving. He looked too pleased with himself, like a performing seal rather than a potential terrorism victim.

In his crowded living room, Beckett moved his laptop just enough to include the detective sitting beside him on the sofa. She was a woman. She was also Indian. She would drive his detractors up the wall. He could practically feel their insecurities dripping through his headphones, the seething pent-up rage of thousands of impotent middle-aged men forever looking for a scapegoat to kick.

Beckett had considered taking Jones and their audience on a tour of his living room first. Two uniformed officers stood in front of his bay window, peering through the net curtains. Another patrolled the bags of rubbish and stinging nettles in his back garden and a fourth protected his front door.

The working-class Asian woman had swapped with her middle-class white husband before breakfast. They made a cute couple, the archetypal viewers of Beckett's online rants. He had wanted to hear their views of his show over coffee and croissants, but the white one had wanted to get back to their kid.

And Beckett had changed his mind about the living-room tour. He had to retain a shred of privacy. Once this ordeal was over, he was back to his daily bigots threatening to brick his windows. He didn't need to provide a detailed list of his home contents on the most divisive radio show in Britain.

Besides, he had Detective Inspector Ramila Mistry for company. She was the wrong colour, the wrong gender and even the wrong intellect for the apoplectic. She was perfect.

'Morning, Margaret, how are you feeling?'

Beckett had spent much of last night and this morning discussing Jones's welfare and devising their show with her, but he had to play the game for the cameras.

'I've never been so angry in my bloody life,' Jones shouted through Beckett's headphones.

'So no change there, then. Look, I think it's important to point out that I was against you being in the studio this morning.'

'But I haven't listened to you for three years.'

'Exactly.'

'But seriously, Mark, this man made a threat against your life. He wanted me to disclose your location. I wouldn't do that. But you need to be very careful until the police catch him. As long as you are there, you are safe.'

Jones's voice had adopted a patronising tone that rankled. Beckett didn't want to be a prisoner in his own home. He was under orders. But he didn't have to like it.

'I am here, Margaret, because the police have insisted that it would be a strain on resources for them to be following me all over London. As they've suffered enough funding cuts in recent years and are struggling with rising crime rates, the last thing they need is to be chasing a metropolitan snowflake in and out of organic fruit and veg shops. I get that. But I don't want to play the victim here either. I'm not scared of pond scum. In fact, I'm more than happy to invite Winston and his puerile video makers into my home any time he likes. He knows I live in Camden Town. Well, I'm the house with the blue door, three houses down from the newsagents. Maybe I could stand on the step and wave him in off the street. Get on Google Maps, Winston, look for the road—'

'That's enough,' Mistry interrupted.

The detective inspector leaned across the yapping fool and closed his laptop. Before Beckett had a chance to speak, Mistry yanked off his headphones.

'Now shut up.'

As the uniformed officers giggled, Beckett watched what was left of his dignity fly across the living room with his headphones.

He laughed so loudly.

The radio show had exceeded his expectations.

That liberal. That charlatan. Humiliated. Ridiculed. *Emasculated.*

Now Mark Beckett understood. The sense of being outnumbered and overruled, in one's community, on national radio, his safe place, it was almost too good to be true.

He stared up at his beloved poster. His comrade pointed the way. Their vision was becoming an unstoppable reality. The Charlemagne Regiment was so profoundly ahead of its time, so prophetic. In the end, friends must convert enemies to prevail.

Convert them. Or kill them.

The genius lies in its simplicity.

No conflicted compassion and distracting talk of morality. Political correctness had thrown what was left of society into a cesspool filled with the unwanted and the impure. Men like Beckett believed in grey areas like children believed in unicorns. There were none. They didn't exist. It was black and white. Convert or kill. Take extreme measures to defeat extreme enemies.

Talking achieved nothing. Look at Mark Beckett. Look at Billy Evans. Making speeches and viral clips, increasing fan bases and building bigger echo chambers, but who else was really listening? What had really changed? They had dug in on both sides and not moved an inch, like the Allied forces at Bastogne. Someone had to go beyond. Someone had to do the most reprehensible thing imaginable and be inhumane to save humanity.

They had to kill their own.

Deep down, Margaret Jones knew that, too.

That's why he had picked her.

Like their comrade in the SS recruitment poster, she understood the intrinsic value of connecting with the other side.

That's why he knew she would gratefully accept his gift of making her an unofficial spokesperson for their crusade.

That's why he knew she would give him Mark Beckett's home address.

They both knew what needed to be done.

He had recorded their conversation, obviously, and had considered releasing the audio online, but Beckett's public shame had proved much more entertaining.

He played back the discussion one more time, hitting pause just as the Indian copper nudged Beckett aside and took the snowflake's laptop away, like a parent taking away a whiny kid's toy.

He loved that part.

He played the clip a third time and then returned to his map. Beckett really did live in a nice part of London.

CHAPTER 30

Low moved quickly though London's thinning crowds. The tourists and coach parties had long gone, retreating to the warm safety of their hotel rooms, allowing them to preserve their postcard images of England's capital.

Only the night owls remained. Like Low, they basked in the relative anonymity that the gloomy streets granted them. They didn't want to pay an unwanted price for coming out to play. They didn't want to be seen.

Low pulled down his baseball cap and quickened his pace. Eyes down. Mind racing. A plan with too many moving parts, an improvised idea with no clear outcome; Low knew where he was going and why. He just had no clue of what he was going to do once he got there.

A young couple brushed past him, joined together, oblivious to the world around them. Low envied their naivety. He turned right into the street behind the Charles Dickens, which was more of an alley than a street, more in keeping with the cobbled walkways of the pub's namesake. Too far from Leicester Square's clubbers and not close enough to Chinatown's casinos, the alley wouldn't welcome too many stray visitors. The Charles Dickens' circumspect clientele could slip into their home from home with little fuss.

Low appreciated the lack of public interest as he kicked the cellar's trap door on the cobbles. Nothing happened. Low checked his watch and visualised the public castration of an errant pub manager behind Leicester Square.

His heel found the trapdoor again.

There was movement beneath the timber planks. A barrel dragged aside, boots on a staircase, a wriggling padlock, creaking iron hinges. One of the trapdoors flung open.

'Jesus Christ.'

Low edged away from the dingy cellar. Through the hatch, Winston Churchill peered up at him.

'You'd better put this on,' the masked man said.

He threw Low a mask and disappeared down the stairs.

DCI Wickes had almost reached the lift when he spotted the light. Someone was still in the audiovisual room. No one was on the roster to work through the night. Wickes didn't have the staff or the budget for that. He barely had enough to cover the day staff. Even travel and expenses were assessed on a case-by-case basis. Austerity measures had reduced numbers and Charing Cross Police Station was hardly a priority. The area didn't have a murder rate to rival east or north London. And even then, dead teenagers on council estates didn't necessarily lead to a spike in funding. Dead teenagers didn't register with voters – not teenagers with darker faces, anyway.

Wickes peered through a crack in the door and found PC Bishop asleep. The walls were filled with photocopied images of a blurred Winston Churchill riding a stolen moped.

'Time to go home, Danny,' Wickes said. 'Oi, wake up and piss off.'

Wickes gave his constable a gentle dig in the shoulder. Bishop jerked forward and wiped the dribble from his chin.

'Sorry, sir.'

'Why are you still here?'

Bishop started moving papers around, in search of something.

'I'm trying to get a clear shot of the bastard. I'm getting closer. Can't get him in Margaret Jones's street, no CCTV there, but we pick him up later here, three streets away, but he's still got the mask on, head down. But I'll get a positive ID.'

Wickes remembered when he was around Bishop's age, early twenties, idealistic, a clear sense of right and wrong and who the heroes and villains were. Bishop still believed in the simplistic notion of crime and punishment. Track them. Catch them. Convict them.

Wickes was too tired to shatter a young man's illusions. Besides, the job would eventually do that anyway.

'That's good work, Danny, but knock it on the head now, eh?'

'Just five more minutes?'

'Five minutes. And that's your lot. You need to get some rest so you can come back and do all this shit again tomorrow.'

'Yes sir.'

Neither man bothered to say goodbye. They were too exhausted.

In the congested cellar of the Charles Dickens pub, Low squeezed between the barrels. Paul Harvey was just ahead of him, walking towards a velvet curtain. Low held the mask in his hand and decided against putting the bloody thing on. Instead, he grabbed the wispy hair on Harvey's mask and pulled hard.

Harvey spun around.

'What are you doing?'

'What's this shit for?'

'You can't get in without it. No one can. And anyway, it's better for you. You can have a nose without getting spotted and then leave before we both get killed.'

Low considered his other options. He didn't have any.

'For God's sake,' the Singaporean said, pulling the mask over

217

his face. 'Do you have any idea what this man did to my country in World War Two?'

'I don't know. Saved it?'

'No, he fucked it.'

Low put on the mask and the two men edged towards the velvet curtain.

'The place is rammed and I've got staff everywhere, so just collect the glasses and stick them in the sink behind the bar. Don't look at anyone. Don't talk to anyone. And no matter what you do, even if you go for a piss, don't take your mask off.'

Harvey pulled back the curtain. The bar heaved with the same faces. A hundred Winston Churchills. Pinstriped suits. Polished shoes. Matching ties. All drinking. They refilled pint glasses at the bar and paid homage to the Winston Churchill bust on the counter, kissing his forehead.

Bar staff rushed from table to table, collecting empties. Their rolled-up sleeves revealed darker skin tones. The masks betrayed their heritage, ordered to wear the face of white imperialism for minimum wage.

Half a dozen Churchills stood on a long sofa against the far wall. The St George's flag provided a backdrop. They were singing. 'Rule Britannia'. Arms raised, pints in hand, ordering others to join in, the ironic message spreading. These children of white privilege would never be slaves.

Behind the bar, Low shoved his hands in his pockets. He was protecting himself. He couldn't make fists with his hands in his pockets.

Harvey threw a tea towel over Low's shoulder and fixed his mask. The neck had to be fully concealed. The skin was too dark. Too incriminating.

'My staff have to be cleared for these events,' Harvey said. 'If they find out, we're both fucked. Keep that mask on.'

Low was already in the crowd, carrying a tray and moving

his wiry frame between retired villagers and retired hooligans, all living in fear of the foreign invader.

'Get us the same again mate.'

A broad-shouldered Churchill with a tattooed hand shoved a couple of empty bottles into Low's chest. Low nodded and then forgot about the order. He was on his way to the far side of the pub, where the Churchills weren't singing, saluting or dreaming of a white Christmas. They were talking.

Three Churchills were gathered around a small table. Same suits. Same ties. Same shoes. Different demeanour. Calm. Measured. Total control. They huddled, allowing them to communicate in the quietest stage whispers. They whispered because they were used to being listened to, like royalty. They didn't sing bawdy songs on pub tables to attract attention and adulation because their charisma and intellect already commanded both. They exuded authority. Their power came from within, organically, naturally. Some were born. Some were made. But the three Churchills shared an inevitable sense of destiny. They were leaders. Men with St George's flags and yellow vests spoke of standing alone, defiant to the end, ready to defend one's sovereignty, blissfully unaware of the crushing irony. They needed to follow the orders of the small, quiet men around that table.

Low had no reason to bother the three Churchills. None of their glasses needed replacing or refilling. An empty table nearby was messy enough to occupy his time, close enough to listen, but far enough to escape attention. Low pulled the tea towel from his shoulder and began wiping.

'I actually think he makes very entertaining radio.'

The accent was polished and clearly older, but the voice surprised Low.

It was a woman's voice.

'His constant interruptions are grating, alienating. Whenever he talks down to his audience, he does our work for us.'

'Yes, but at what cost?' said an elderly male voice. 'There are too many mutterings, too much interest. Either way, it's a problem. If he goes, he's an overnight martyr and they'll eulogise him for weeks afterwards in the *Guardian*. But if he stays, he'll become truly insufferable, both a crusader and a martyr. This is all getting too polarising and too bloody dangerous, don't you think?'

The two Churchills turned to the other seated at their table. He was reading the news on his phone.

'Ape must never kill ape,' he said, without looking up.

His accent fluctuated between classes. His precise plosives hinted at middle-class affluence, but they couldn't quite cover the wider, working-class vowels of his youth.

His accent was also the only recognisable one at the table. He was at the Altab Ali rally. He was talking to Mistry before she was attacked.

Low resisted the urge to garrotte Billy Evans with a tea towel.

'Not really a time for an anthropology lesson,' the Older Churchill said.

'It's from *Planet of the Apes*, mate. First rule of battle. You don't kill your own. It's too much. Even the hard core like this lot in here will question the whole point of what we're doing if we start turning on our own.'

'I find it amusing that you equate them with us,' the Female Churchill said.

'Yeah, all right, this lot are not like us.'

'No, I wasn't referring to you. I meant us.'

'Absolutely. You know what always fascinates me?' the Older Churchill said. 'It's that this lot actually believe that we are all in this together. We shaped this country over centuries. We financed the ships, the weapons, the opium, trading routes, the East India Company, the takeovers, the occupations, everything. They swabbed the decks of those ships. That's it. We rule. They obey. It's a simple matter of eugenics, evidenced throughout history: the rise and fall of every empire comes down to eugenics. Every empire builds on its elite, ruling class.'

The Female Churchill pointed at his whisky glass. 'Your ice is melting, dear.'

'I'm telling you, every civilised nation depends on its sub-conscious acceptance of eugenics. Once that basic structure is in place, the wealth arrives. And with wealth comes greed and then guilt; guilt that the wealth isn't trickling down beyond the rulers, the true architects of empire. So what happens? There are facile attempts to redistribute, to advocate for that nonsensical drivel about all men being born equal when clearly they are not. They are *not*. Just look around us. One man over there has a pint glass on his head and he's singing a song about England winning two world wars and one World Cup. And there's a chap over there attempting to piss in a plant pot.'

'Oh heaven's above,' said the Female Churchill, clasping a locket on her chest. 'I thought he was watering that weeping fig.'

'Exactly my point – left to their own devices, they're pissing in plant pots. Servants need masters. So we'll allow them to live with us in this glorious country of our creation. But that's it. That's as far as we should be willing to go.'

The Older Churchill downed his whisky. The Female Churchill patted his handed and then squeezed it hard.

'You might want to slow down a little,' she said.

Low arrived at their table and wiped the condensation rings around the glasses.

'Nonsense. Where we failed, where we went catastrophically wrong,' the Older Churchill continued, 'was when we opened up to non-natives.'

He grabbed Low's wrist and pushed up the detective's shirtsleeve.

'Where are you from?'

Low heard Evans giggle behind his mask.

'Leave him alone, Geoffrey,' Evans said, returning to his

phone. 'You can't get the master race to work for ten pounds an hour in central London. They're all students in here. They're not welfare ponces.'

'Well, who are you?'

Low's mask had turned into a sauna. The perspiration stung his eyes.

'You clearly weren't born here, so what are you doing in England?'

Evans looked up from his phone.

'For God's sake, answer him, mate, or we'll be here all night.'

'*Chee bye.*'

Low seemed to hear his utterance after they did, as if caught off guard by his spontaneous speech.

Evans found the hidden barman entertaining.

'What did you say?'

'*Chee bye.*'

'You see what I mean? He's obviously Chinese, from a country that understands the value of preserving both their ruling elite and their racial majority. No one grasps the concept of eugenics better than China, and who's the leading power now? I rest my case. Actually, no, he'd be the dregs of China. They only send away the dregs of a dominant society to other countries. Believe me, if this kid was creating the next Facebook, they wouldn't let him out of their sight.'

'You do have a point,' the Female Churchill muttered. 'I keep telling them this in the chamber.'

Evans was no longer listening. The unidentified barman now had his attention. Something was wrong.

'We don't have any Chinese working tonight,' Evans said.

'What?'

'The staff. They were cleared. None were Chinese.'

Low moved away from the table.

'No, no, you stay there, mate.'

'*Chee bye.*'

222

'Yeah, all right, just stand still.'

Now it was Evans's turn to grab Low's arm.

'Paul, have you got a minute?'

Evans's voice reached the pub manager, who was serving drinks at a nearby table. Harvey turned and heard his own heart smash against his chest. The leader of the Make England Great Again movement had grabbed the arm of a dodgy detective from the Singapore Police Force, who was posing as a barman in a Winston Churchill mask at a private party for far-right fanatics.

Harvey had enjoyed easier nights at the Charles Dickens pub.

'Yeah, hang on, Billy.'

Harvey was on his way. Three tables. Maybe four. But they were too close. He had no time to come up with a plausible explanation. There wasn't one. If Low's mask came off, neither he nor Harvey would leave the pub alive.

Billy Evans wasn't the problem. A big mouth with a chip on his shoulder and a desperate need for fame was a relatively benign threat. He wouldn't be around forever. Such fame was cyclical. But reserved, distinguished figures like those sitting at Evans's table would be around forever. Evans's success depended on his notoriety. They thrived in the shadows.

There was a beer bottle. Half empty. Half full. Harvey focused on it being half full. It was a table away, near the edge, but not close enough to make contact seem unavoidable. Harvey had to shift his body weight to the right, like a balletic boxer, the benefits of being a lifelong pub manager, blessed with the rehearsed ability to duck and dive to avoid beer trays and lunch-time specials in crowded areas. Harvey slowed, just a little, to allow a couple of Winston Churchills to close the gap as they headed his way. The timing had to be perfect to avoid suspicion. And it was.

Their paths crossed at the right table, the one with the beer bottle. Half full. Harvey lurched much further to the right. His thigh jabbed the table. He pushed until the bottle toppled. The beer made enough of a mess to force a dozen people to their feet, hoping that they had been spared damp patches in embarrassing places. Evans stood up to check his suit. Low backed away from the table.

'Oh, shit, sorry about that. I'll get it cleaned up,' Harvey said, turning to Low. 'You. Get a round of drinks for this table.'

Low shrugged his shoulders, miming his confusion to Evans's table.

'*Chee bye,*' he said, one more time, in Evans's face, before slipping into the crowd.

Apart from protecting his identity, Low was grateful that the mask also hid his childish giggling. Being bipolar, his behaviour was often erratic and uncontrollable. He knew that.

Still, he had not expected to use a Chinese dialect to call Billy Evans a cunt.

CHAPTER 31

In the packed Charles Dickens pub, Low ignored their orders. He sidestepped their arm-tugging and shoulder-tapping. He needed to return to his brief sanctuary behind the bar, a chance to examine the crowd, a chance to breathe.

Younger Winston Churchills surrounded him. They only had eyes for their phones. Their Instagram addiction revealed their ages. They were never going to be a problem.

Low was almost at the bar, swivelling his torso, ready to lift the hatch, but he hesitated.

He felt the eyes behind him, over his left shoulder, from a small table; one stool, one Winston Churchill staring at his back.

Low had caught a glimpse on his way through, but it was only when he partially turned, ready to lift the hatch, that he saw Winston Churchill's companion.

He was with a laptop.

In a room filled with like-minded, masked cowards, this Winston Churchill sat alone with a laptop.

Low balled his fists, but couldn't stop the tensing, the shaking. The euphoria consumed him. Low didn't fight the loss of control. He welcomed it, depended upon it. The mania gave him a sense of purpose. When the fireworks exploded, they joined the dots. He saw everything.

In a room with the tightest security, this Winston Churchill had a laptop.

In a room full of noise, this Winston Churchill sat in silence.

In a room filled with rage, this Winston Churchill was calm and measured.

In a room devoted to groupthink, this Winston Churchill was an outsider.

In a warm room, this Winston Churchill wore a long overcoat.

This Winston Churchill had exposed himself.

Low could see right through him.

Low took a step towards the table and Winston Churchill peered up from his laptop. In the eyes of the other man, they recognised themselves. Beneath their masks, they almost smiled at each other.

Low was already calculating his odds. Winston Churchill was tall, but out of shape and seated. He wouldn't stand in time. But a first shot would be Low's only shot. One punch. Pandemonium. They'd pile on and pull him apart, dismembered inside the Charles Dickens pub. No one knew he was here. No one ever would.

But Winston Churchill was making Low's decision for him. His hand was on the move, slipping off the table, towards his coat, right pocket for a right-hander, the right hand that filleted Mohamed Kamal, the right hand that torched Hawker Heaven, the right hand that shattered Low's cheek, the right hand that was reaching for a knife.

Low moved in and pulled the tea towel off his shoulder. He wasn't even sure why. He watched the hand disappear into the coat pocket and realised the wrist was the best option. The hand couldn't be allowed to come out again.

But Low was already too late. His balance had gone. He staggered to the right, away from the table, away from the hand in the pocket. He felt the pressure on his left shoulder again, harder this time, more belligerent.

'Move. Now.'

Harvey's voice pummelled Low's eardrums, overcoming the persistent din of jingoistic World War II songs in the background.

There was another shove in the shoulder, another barked order.

'You've got to get out.'

'No, wait.'

But Low couldn't stop. Harvey's unexpected push had knocked him towards the bar hatch. Low didn't have time to correct his balance. Harvey was already lifting the hatch and shoving the uncoordinated Singaporean through the gap. As the hatch slammed down, Low peered over his shoulder. Winston Churchill's eyes followed him across the bar.

Winston Churchill slowly turned his laptop until the screen faced Low.

The screen was frozen.

Low saw their faces.

They were together, sitting on a sofa, one in the foreground, the other further back and slightly out of focus. The radio host and his protector. Mark Beckett and Detective Inspector Ramila Mistry.

The video zoomed in on Mistry. She was hauntingly beautiful. Beckett was out of the picture. This video was all about Mistry.

And then he dragged his finger across the screen, underlining the slogans as they appeared beneath her delicate face.

SAVE US FROM SHARIA LAW.
SAVE THE NEXT GENERATION.
SAVE OUR COUNTRY.
MAKE ENGLAND GREAT AGAIN.

Winston Churchill was still staring at Low, refusing to look away, giving him a V for victory. Low tried to jump the bar, but Harvey restrained him.

'Look over there.'

227

At the far side of the pub, Evans was holding court with five larger Winston Churchills, pointing towards the bar, pointing at Low.

'They're coming for you.'

'Fuck 'em. He's here.'

The five Winston Churchills clumsily barged their way through the party. Too many identical faces merged and fell away.

'They'll kill you.'

Low figured he had five, maybe ten, seconds before the knuckle-scrapers arrived, which gave him enough time. After that, he didn't care what happened to him.

He ducked beneath the bar, using the counter for both cover and protection. The revolver was taped to the back of his calf, with his sock holding everything in place, safe on the inside, unseen from the outside, an old Tiger trick. Low tore the gun away from his skin, whipping it behind his back, his reflexes taking over.

No more than three seconds had passed and Low was already on his feet, ignoring the five shadows in front of him and turning right, scanning the full house for his joker in the pack.

He picked out the small table and felt his gun grip loosen.

Winston Churchill and his laptop had gone.

'Billy Evans and his guests want to know who you are.'

The gruff interruption of the monkey in the middle had broken Low's concentration, but not his irritation. He examined the five lumps standing before him, wearing Winston Churchill masks and covering most of the bar.

'What?'

'Nah, it's all right,' Harvey said, fidgeting beside Low.

'Was I talking to you?'

'Nah, you were talking to me,' Low said. You wanted to know who I am. But who are you? The Jackson Five?'

The monkey in the middle leaned across the bar, pressing his mask against Low's.

'Do you want a slap?'

'Oh, you won't be able to slap me,' Low said, revealing his gun and aiming the muzzle at just about his aggressor's nose. 'Not after I send your brain through your skull.'

The five masked men backed away.

'Look at that,' Low said. 'Winston Churchill in retreat. A Singaporean hasn't seen that since 1942.'

Low didn't lower his gun until he was through the bar, behind the velvet curtain and deep into the cellar. He threw his mask behind a beer barrel and returned to the street, grateful for the protection of London's nightlife. No one made eye contact after dark in London.

He heard the first bottle smash moments later. The post-mortem had already begun within the bowels of the Charles Dickens. The faint strains of a young man's screaming drifted through the cellar and into the cobbled alleyway behind Leicester Square. Paul Harvey's interrogation had started.

Low retreated to a doorway and swapped the gun for a phone.

'Ramila, call me now,' he said. 'It's not Beckett. It's you. He wants you. He's tired of being humiliated, right? Get away from Beckett now.'

Low hung up and began scrolling for Devonshire's number, when he spotted the only option he had left, leaving the Charles Dickens pub.

CHAPTER 32

Billy Evans tightened his scarf as he watched his driver pull away from the kerb. London in the early hours chilled the bones. But the cloudless sky illuminated the few stars that peeked through. Evans found himself grinning at the stars. They were a status symbol. Kids on east London council estates didn't live beneath starry skies. There were too many homes, too much light pollution. Maybe God knew what he was doing after all.

He didn't want to shine a light on the shitholes below, either.

But Evans had moved on. He lived by Hampstead Heath now. He had doctors, dentists and muntjac deer for neighbours. There were plenty of green spaces for distinguished white faces. He had *Lebensraum*. He had stars.

'Hello, Billy.'

Evans felt the punch before he saw it. He raised his hand to locate the pain: on the side of his neck, beneath the ear, a strange place to be hit.

He was punched again in the same spot, smashing his fingers against his own neck, perhaps breaking them.

Childhood instincts kicked in before common sense.

Muggers.

He was being mugged. But then he remembered his postcode. Residents didn't get mugged on the Heath. And the gangs on his old council estate used knives, not fists. Knives were cleaner and quieter.

'What do you—'

The punch in the ribs ended his opening line. The knuckles poked into the intercostal muscles, temporarily robbing Evans of his only gift. His voice.

Doubled over, Evans raised an arm in surrender, but a succession of swift kicks behind his knees flipped him backwards. He slid to the pavement and offered no resistance as he was dragged behind a parked car.

'Who's the one with the laptop?'

Evans rolled onto his back. A mad Chinaman blocked out the starry night. Evans laughed in exasperation.

'I knew it was you at the pub. You're persistent. I'll give you that.'

'Who's the one with the laptop?'

Evans sat up, resting his back against the parked car. He clutched his ribs, wincing with every shallow breath. He eyed the manic detective.

'Do you have any idea how much CCTV there is in this street?'

Low took note of the cameras. He counted half a dozen on both sides of the road, all within walking distance.

'Wah, you're right. I'd better come down here.'

Low crouched in front of Evans. They eyeballed each other.

'That's better.'

'Yeah, let's be sensible about this. What was your name again?'

'Low.'

'Is that your real name?'

'No, it's my fucking IQ. Do I need to ask again?'

Evans tried to take a deep breath, but the discomfort stopped him halfway.

'I think my ribs are broken.'

'Hopefully.'

'Do you seriously think you're going to get away with this? A foreign Old Bill? Against me?'

Low pondered Evans's question.

'You're probably right.'

Low rested the end of his revolver beneath Evans's right eyeball.

'No, please,' Evans whispered.

'From this distance, you will hear the bullet shatter in that car door before you die.'

'I don't know. I really don't know.'

The muzzle pressed against Evans's eyeball. His blood vessels snaked across his sclera, as if trying to escape.

'You're lying. This one wants you to know. He wants to prove to you that he's a real man, a proper Aryan in your master race.'

Evans screamed as his eyeball bulged. The muzzle scratched his cornea.

'I can't remember his name. Geoff or something, I don't know. I'm not even sure if it's the one I'm thinking of.'

'Address?'

'Ah fuck, how am I supposed to know that?'

Low pushed again, watching as the eyeball filled with blood. 'You're about to suffer a globe rupture. That's what will happen when I push through the membrane. Your eyeball will explode like a soft-boiled egg.'

In a final, pitiful gesture, Evans reached for Low's right arm. A vicious kick in the stomach stopped him.

'North London,' he whimpered. 'Somewhere around Islington, I heard him complain about the traffic once.'

'And you don't know him?'

'We've got three million followers. Thousands of volunteers and he's one of them, one of our volunteers, Geoff something, quiet, weird, most of them are, otherwise why the fuck would they join up?'

Low pulled the gun away.

'But you would have to approve every video, every video editor; everything goes though you. It's your video. Your image. Harvey hired him, but you lot have to approve him, right?'

'Sort of. Look, Paul Harvey helps me out with that. There's too many of them now.'

'Yeah, 'cos you inspired them. You create Geoff and he kills Mohamed Kamal, right?'

'I'm not responsible for that.'

'Yes you fucking are,' Low said, grabbing Evans by the throat. 'You create this shit. You need the tension. The hate. Otherwise, what are you?'

Evans clawed at Low's fingers, but his strength was vanishing. 'I can't breathe.'

'Geoff idolises you. Made videos for you. Killed for you.'

'Please.'

Low tightened his grip. 'You made them all feel special, made them feel like they belonged, made them not feel like the fucking cockroaches they really are, made them feel like they were the superior race again, like the good old days, when people like me and her served you in our little shops. But it's not like that any more, is it? So he's gonna kill her. Do you understand? He's gonna kill the only woman I've ever loved because she's not what he wants her to be. She's not a Paki. She's not a Muslim bitch. She's . . .She's . . .'

Low realised he was crying.

He slammed Evans's head against the car door. Evans slumped over, gasping for air.

Low couldn't see straight. He could only see her, sitting on a sofa, on a laptop screen. Frozen.

He had to reach her first. He had to believe that there was still enough time.

He stood up and left Evans in the gutter.

'You know I'll have you arrested in the morning.'

Low stopped.

233

'What?'

'You'll be arrested in the morning.'

'How's that?'

'You snowflakes are all the same,' Evans said, spitting blood onto the pavement. 'You only see me. You don't see the silent majority behind me. I own Middle England. I am the small businessman. I am the doctors, the teachers, the coppers, the politicians, the people who agree with me but can't say it. I am the voice they cannot have.'

'You're a parasite.'

Evans laughed, revealing his bloodstained teeth.

'I know. And so do they. But they need me. And you'll be amazed what they'll do for me, as long as they see progress being made.'

Low turned around.

'Is that right?'

'You know it is.'

Low crouched down.

'And what is the cause? To make England great again?'

'To make England like us again.'

Evans's bloody phlegm found Low's shoe. Low took out his revolver for a second time and wiped it against his soiled shoe.

'That means no beastly people like me, right? That's what he called us colonials, you know, your great leader. Is that why you all wear his mask?'

'Winston Churchill made our country great before we opened the floodgates.'

'Yeah, he made your country great,' Low said, his finger over the trigger guard. 'Do you know what he did to my country? He left us to the Japanese. We were shot. Raped. Enslaved. You know, all the usual shit that comes with occupation. In other words, he fucked us. And now it's my turn.'

Low whipped his gun across the top of Evans's head, putting the patriot to sleep.

CHAPTER 33

He parked the stolen moped and waited for the song to finish. As the music swelled, he felt his heart soar.

He was so happy. He was almost finished.

He tapped the handlebars, not realising he was singing aloud to Coldplay's Fix You.

He wasn't aware he was crying either.

But then, he wasn't like the others. They didn't know what real devotion was. They didn't understand the sacrifice required. They were caricatures. They were yesterday's football hooligans looking for tomorrow's cause. Cardboard villains. Tattooed knuckles. Shaved scalps. Empty heads. They demanded power, sovereignty and independence, but followed Billy Evans around like puppies.

He had watched them all at the Charles Dickens farce, living in the past, singing World War II chants and playing Wagner as if they understood it, as if the music meant something to them.

He had watched them fawn over Billy Evans, hanging on his every word, unable to take a shit without his permission, unable to see the irony.

He soon tired of their tedious antics. So he focused on his next video, the one of her, the Muslim bitch, the one who had everything, the one who had taken what could've belonged to him.

The dramatic appearance of the undercover Chinese copper had actually entertained him, intrigued him, even. He recognised the devotion, the conviction. They had a lot in common. He was even glad that the copper had presumably spotted the Muslim bitch on screen.

Every little helps.

If the Chinaman knew what was coming next, so much the better. The copper might bear witness to the big event, but couldn't stop it. He liked the potential serendipity. It would be Hawker Heaven all over again.

His voice weakened as he sang the final line. He sounded like a child.

He smiled through his tears. He knew the song was soppy, but it spoke to him.

He switched off the music on his phone and wiped his cheeks.

Sunrise was only a few minutes away and he had to be in the right frame of mind to kill someone.

DC Devonshire saw the shadow first. He happened to be standing near the kitchen window of Beckett's home when he thought he caught an outline, running through the back garden. He stepped away and pulled his gun. The constable that was supposed to be in the garden, standing guard at the back door, was upstairs in the toilet, his bladder finally rebelling against the night air. Whoever was outside had been casing the property for a while, waiting patiently, perhaps for hours. It didn't matter now.

He was on his way.

Devonshire was appalled by his indecision. He didn't know what to do. Every scenario had an obvious flaw. The living room contained a uniformed officer, Devonshire's sleeping wife and Mark Beckett. The back garden contained the man who presumably intended to kill Mark Beckett.

Devonshire was literally caught in the middle. He didn't

want to move. He couldn't move. He couldn't shout a warning, either. He figured that the guy was waiting beside the kitchen window on the other side. Only a brick wall and a few feet separated them.

Devonshire ducked behind the kitchen table and took out his phone.

'He's here,' he whispered.

Within seconds, the uniformed officer and a sleepy DI Mistry were beside him, on their knees. Their elbows rested on the kitchen table, their guns pointed at the back door.

For a few seconds, nothing happened. Mistry rubbed her left eye.

'Are you sure you saw something? It might have been a tree.'

Devonshire adored his wife, but his expression then might have suggested otherwise.

'He's on the other side of that bloody door,' Devonshire said.

'OK.'

'No, wait.'

But Mistry had gone. She moved gracefully across the tiled kitchen floor and pressed herself against the cupboard beneath the sink, taking advantage of its cover. She couldn't be seen from the window above. She was protected. She edged along the cupboard door, her gun cocked, her finger on the trigger, her training taking over.

'Yeah, that's a great combat stance, Ramila, but it's cold out here.'

Mistry's shoulders slumped. The voice belonged to Low. Of course it did.

Mistry peered over the sink and saw a haggard, weary Chinese face staring at her through the kitchen window. His appearance alarmed her for two reasons. First, he seemed scared. And second, he had somehow acquired a gun.

She unlocked the door and Low hurried into the kitchen.

'What the fuck are you doing here?'

Low concentrated on relocking the back door, monitoring the garden through the window. 'He's on his way, I know he is.'

Low was talking quickly, not pausing to think.

'Yes, it's a possibility.'

'No, no, he's on his way. He has to now. I saw the video. He's sick of being put down by people like *you*.'

Low was rambling, hurrying around the kitchen, checking windows and hallways. 'He knows he's got to do it now. He's seen me. He knows I've seen him.'

'Wait? What? Where have you seen him?'

Low paced up and down the kitchen, constantly ducking to peer through the window.

'Charles Dickens. I've seen him. I've seen the next video. There's no time left. He knows we'll catch him now, through Evans, through Harvey; too many loose ends, too many ways of being caught; he's got to finish it now.'

'Low, can you put down the gun?'

Mistry was calm but firm. It was not a request.

'He's on his way, Ramila. Right now. I know he is.'

'Yeah, well, Beckett's in the living room. We're all here. Now put the gun down.'

'Beckett? Please, lah. He's not coming for Beckett. He's coming for you.'

In the living room, Low ordered Beckett to wait in the kitchen. Beckett waited for an explanation from Devonshire or Mistry, but clearly none was coming. Mostly, Beckett wanted to know more about the scruffy Chinese bloke with the strange accent and a small, scratched gun and why he was giving orders.

'Who is this guy?'

'I'm Detective Inspector Stanley Low of the Singapore Police Force, OK? Now go in the kitchen and make me a cup of tea.'

'The Singapore Police Force? What's it got to do with . . .I mean, do you have any jurisdiction here?'

'I don't know. Let me shoot you and then we can find out.'

Beckett looked to DI Mistry for guidance, the officer assigned to protect him in his own living room inside his own house. She nodded.

'I don't believe this.'

Devonshire closed the door behind Beckett. He took a deep breath and then charged at Low, pinning him to the exposed brick wall, a central feature of Beckett's post-industrial décor.

'You've got us fucking fired. You know that, right? Me, Ramila, fired. You're in here with a fucking loaded gun, an illegal gun, interfering with an investigation you've been told to stay away from. Why?'

Beckett slammed Low's spine into the brickwork.

'Fucking why?'

Low didn't resist. It was a calculated risk strategy. He was exhausted. Paul Harvey and Billy Evans had almost wiped him out. His bipolar took care of the rest. He was running on empty. He felt the energy dissipate as the mania drifted away. He hoped to avoid violence with Devonshire.

He wasn't worried about fighting back.

He was worried he'd have nothing left for what was to come.

'You need to calm down, Tom.'

'Bollocks. You need to stop obsessing over my wife.'

'That was over twenty years ago.'

'Yeah, and you're still sniffing around her like a stray dog.'

Mistry tried to step between them.

'Can we not do this again?'

'No, we are doing it. I'm sick of being the spare wheel in this fucked-up whatever it is that's going on between you and her.'

'You need to let go of me now.'

'No, I need to arrest you now.'

Low sighed. 'Please. Don't make me do this.'

'Do what?'

Low's headbutt sent Devonshire tumbling over the coffee table.

'For fuck's sake, Stanley,' Mistry said.

'He wouldn't listen and you both need to listen now.'

Mistry comforted her husband on the Persian rug that complimented Beckett's coffee table. Devonshire pushed her away and pulled his gun on Low. The Singaporean shook his head, almost in sympathy.

'No, no, no, you're smarter than this, Tom. I know why you're doing it, though. You love her. You love a beautiful, intelligent woman and you feel slightly threatened by all that. Even I did, and I'm much smarter than you.'

'Fuck you.'

'But he feels the same. He watched her at the rally. He filmed her, standing up to a dozen bigger white men – racists, fascists, his bloody heroes. She stood her ground against all of them. She's just like the rest of them, just like Jun Li, mocking white men and their traditional values, hating them for taking away the good old days.'

Low pointed at Mistry.

'Women like her ruined that life. Women like Jun Li made fun of that life. These bastards don't want to make England great again. They want to make *men* great again. Working-class white men like him. Forgotten men. Neglected men. And women like Ramila are stopping him. That's why she's a bitch to him. The Muslim bit is for the masses. He only sees a woman standing up to him, standing up to all of them, and she's a brown woman some more, married to a white man, ticking all the wrong boxes. That's why he's made a video all about you.'

Devonshire dabbed his swelling nose. 'What video?'

Low slumped onto Beckett's faded sofa.

'The video he'll put out after he's killed you. I saw it at the Charles Dickens.'

Devonshire lowered his gun. His head hurt, but the anger was subsiding.

'Why did you go there?' He said, finding his holster.

'Harvey. I knew he could lead me to Evans. And I thought Evans might lead me to his fanboy, the one making the videos, but he didn't have to. I saw him, sitting alone at a table in his Churchill mask, editing a video about Ramila.'

'He was in his mask in the pub?'

'They all were. It was a private party for the movement. Your friend Billy Evans was there, and some of his backers, all in Churchill masks.'

'Jesus.'

'Yeah. And then I saw our guy with his laptop and I knew. He knew, too.'

'Knew what?'

'We saw through each other. He knew he didn't have much time.'

Devonshire wasn't convinced.

'Doesn't mean he's coming now. That's ridiculous. Everyone in London knows where we are now. Ramila was on that bloody radio show.'

'It's worth the risk for him,' Low said. 'He's running out of time. If we don't get him, Evans's monkeys will. He can't keep killing Asians in their name. Bad for the image, hits their funding. Now it's just a matter of who catches him first.'

'Does Evans know who he is?'

Low rubbed his face. His body craved sleep.

'He said he didn't. He might be lying, but it wasn't really in his interest to lie to me.'

Mistry found it hard to swallow. Her throat was dry.

'You've seen him?'

'Yeah. Just now.'

'And where is he now?'

'Where I found him. In the gutter.'

Mistry coughed, but failed to clear the tightening sensation at the back of her mouth.

'Did you?'

Low felt like he'd been stabbed.

'You really think that of me?'

'You said you wanted justice for Jun Li.'

'I do. Evans didn't kill her.'

The awkward silence was interrupted when Beckett tapped on the door and politely asked if he might be allowed back into his own living room.

'I just wanted to get my phone,' he said, hurrying over to a side table.

Beckett avoided eye contact with the Chinese stranger sitting on his sofa. The stranger unnerved him. Beckett picked up his phone, keeping his head down.

'Wait,' Mistry said. 'What's the phone for?'

Beckett stopped at the door. 'Just wanted to make a quick call.'

'It's a bit early. It's not even seven o'clock. You're not calling the radio station are you? No more interviews.'

Beckett stared at the Persian rug that he'd bought in Portobello Road, a treat for himself after being voted the most popular radio host in a *Guardian* poll.

'Fair enough.'

The radio host turned away from the detectives. Mistry noticed his apprehension.

'So who are you calling?'

'Just a friend.'

'Who?'

'Do I have to tell you every person I call?'

'If you're not making the call in our presence, yes, especially after the stunt you pulled with Margaret Jones.'

'It's just family.'

'You just said a friend.'

'It can't be both?'

242

Mistry confronted her perspiring host.

'No. Who are you calling, Mr Beckett?'

'I'm sure there's a privacy law or ruling on this something.'

'Who are you calling?'

Beckett looked away.

'My son,' he mumbled.

'You have a son?'

'Yes.'

'You never told us you had a son.'

'You never asked.'

'Don't be a smartarse. There's no public record of you having children.'

'Because it's not something I want recorded in the public record, for personal reasons, and for protective reasons, once the show took off.'

'How old is he?'

'Eight.'

Mistry felt a pang of sympathy.

'Same as my son. I take it you and your partner are still not together.'

'No, we never were. It was a drunken thing, bit of a mistake, really. You know.'

'Didn't quite fit the social crusader image?'

'I just want to protect my son. You're a mother. You should get that.'

'I do.'

Mistry regretted her sarcasm.

'Go and call your son. In fact, we should probably call ours, too.'

Devonshire checked his watch.

'Yeah.'

Low was no longer listening. He was no longer watching Devonshire and Mistry chat on speakerphone, but he could see their son.

'Protect your son,' he said. 'You gotta protect your son.'

His rambling caught Mistry's attention.

'That's your first instinct. Yours, Devonshire's, even Beckett's. Protect the next generation. That's what he said. Save the next generation. He underlined it.'

Mistry broke off from the three-way phone conversation with her son and husband.

'Who?'

'Save the next generation. That's what he wants to do. That's what needs to be done, now more than ever; foreigners coming over here, swamping us, stealing our jobs, stealing our people.'

Low snarled at Devonshire.

'Fucking our people, diluting the stock, turning us into a country of coffee creams, can't have that; once that happens there's no way; his people are literally wiped out, they no longer exist, the race is literally over. And you two, sitting there with your perfect mixed-race marriage, your perfect postmodern family and your perfect-picture postcard life for the bearded hipsters, you're the ones he hates most, 'cos you don't even pick a side; at least the Muslims and the Chinks and the Pakis who stay with the right colour, at least they're consistent, but you fuck things up for both sides. You ruin the next generation on every side.'

Devonshire whispered to his son that he'd call him back shortly.

He didn't want his beloved boy to overhear the ranting of a madman.

'He could've killed you at any time,' Low said, speaking faster. 'You're the public face of the case, a brown face with a white partner, but that's not enough. He's done that already. Kill another opinionated brown woman for what? No, this way is better, this way he gets two birds with one stone. Destroy the emasculating Muslim bitch and save the next generation. Killing you is easy. Not enough. Not enough pain. He wants you to feel pain like he fills pain. You can't do that if you're dead. You need to be alive to see him kill your son.'

CHAPTER 34

He stroked the little boy's head. The half-caste was beautiful, just beautiful, having everything that he'd never had. Black hair. Brown eyes. Olive skin. Mixed race. Loving parents. Liberal parents. The kid belonged everywhere.

He belonged nowhere.

But that would change soon. He just had to be patient. They would be here soon.

'What's your name?' he asked.

'Benjamin,' the boy replied.

Even the half-caste's small, delicate voice was angelic. He ran his finger along the boy's flawless cheek.

'What's your full name?'

'Benjamin Devonshire-Mistry.'

'Benjamin Devonshire-Mistry,' he repeated softly. 'They even gave you both names. That's the real proof, isn't it? Accepted by both parents, both cultures. So lucky.'

He was grateful for the mask. His tears couldn't be seen behind the mask. He was furious with himself. He was wavering.

'Where's Granddad?'

He heard the fear in the half-caste's voice. Smart kid. Sharp senses. Kids always have the best radar. They pick up every vibe, every feeling, every emotion, every rejection. He remembered that. Nothing gets past a kid.

'Your Granddad's resting in the kitchen, having a nap. He asked me to look after you and the shop until your mother gets here.'

'Are you my Granddad's friend?'

'I'm your mother's friend.'

'What about my daddy?'

'No, just your mummy. Shall we see if she's coming? Come on.'

He took the half-caste's hand. They left the two plastic stools behind the shop counter. The half-caste seemed reluctant to leave them behind. His grandparents had always sat on those stools, reading the newspapers between customers, trying to improve their English, always trying to fit in.

He led the half-caste to the shop's front door. The glass was full of faded special offers and leaflets for local services and takeaways. He turned the 'open' sign to 'closed' and peered through the glass.

'It's too early to close,' Benjamin said.

'What?'

'We only close when it's dark, except in summer. And it's not summer.'

'Wow, you really are a clever boy. They must be so proud of you.'

'I don't like your mask.'

He felt the half-caste's hand tugging against him. They had really produced an intelligent, intuitive child.

'It's OK. I told you we were going to do fancy dress and make your mummy jump when she comes in. Do you have a mask?'

'Yeah, Iron Man. I'll get it.'

The half-caste tried to run away, but he pulled him back. Now they both had tears in their eyes. He wasn't prepared for this bit. She was taking too long. Why the fuck was she taking too long?

247

'No, no. It's OK. We can get the mask in a minute. Let your Granddad sleep. Let's pick some sweets now, talk about our favourite superheroes and then you can put your mask on, OK?'

'OK.'

He tried to blink away the sweat stinging his eyes and grabbed a handful of chocolate bars from the counter.

'I don't like those ones,' the half-caste whimpered.

'They'll do for now.'

As they returned to the stools, a knuckle tapped on the glass door. A figure peered into the shop. He clamped his hand across the top of the boy's head and pushed him beneath the counter.

'Shh, let's play hide and seek.'

He didn't notice the tears streaming down the boy's reddening face. He was peering through the doughnuts in the display case at the end of the counter, focusing on the silhouette outside the shop.

'You open, Dave? It's me, Gary.'

He thought about responding, but decided that any voice that didn't belong to Dhaval Mistry might arouse suspicion.

He raised a finger to his lips, demanding silence. As an added precaution, he placed his other hand over the half-caste's mouth. He enjoyed the warm tears trickling down his skin. That was the added bonus of not wearing gloves. For the first time, he could feel everything.

Behind the counter they huddled together, not moving. There was another tap on the door, but less forceful, more out of hope than expectation. He heard shoe soles swivelling on tarmac, scraping away, and then nothing.

He returned to the weeping half-caste. Too many tears, not enough options left; he needed to improvise, to stall just a little longer.

'Who's Iron Man?'

He removed his hand from the half-caste's mouth. The half-caste didn't answer, but his confusion had stopped the crying.

'Who's Iron Man?'

'He's a superhero.'

'Ah, like this guy,' he said, tapping his mask. 'Do you know who my superhero is?'

The half-caste shook his head.

'No, of course, you don't. OK, let's sit on the stools again. I'll tell you all about my superhero and then you can tell me about yours, OK?'

The half-caste nodded. They crawled back to their stools.

'My superhero is called Winston Churchill. He was a real-life iron man. He saved my country. Do you know what his superpower was?'

'No.'

'Belief. He believed that he could never be defeated. He would do anything to preserve his way of life. But that's still not enough. Do you know what else a good superhero needs?'

'No'

'A villain. And Winston Churchill's villain was a man called Adolf Hitler. They were the perfect hero and villain because they were almost the same. They believed in the superiority of their own people. They went to war for the same thing. The same thing. But when you lose the war, you are a monster. When you win the war, you are a patriot.'

He took out his beloved twelve-inch German dagger.

'I am a patriot.'

He waved the blade in front of the half-caste's face. The half-caste's eyes widened as he followed the dagger through the air.

'All superheroes have weapons. This is mine. Touch it.'

The half-caste poked his finger against the silver eagle above the handle.

'No, no, you have to touch it like this.'

He ran his finger along the edge until his flesh opened. His blood trickled along the polished steel. He watched the half-caste pull away in terror.

'It's OK. Even superheroes get hurt sometimes. Like Iron Man. The best superheroes are never perfect. One half might be perfect, but the other half isn't. That's why they wear uniforms and disguises.'

He stared at his dagger.

'I am not perfect. Not like Churchill. But I am a patriot.'

He nodded to himself.

'I am a patriot.'

He caressed the half-caste's porcelain skin one more time.

'I'm sorry. I thought it'd be over by now.'

He pointed his eagle towards the ceiling. In the corner, a scrap of a paper chain clung to the plaster, a long-forgotten, pathetic attempt by the Mistry family to celebrate a foreign country's cultural festival, to be accepted.

'Look at that old Christmas decoration,' he said. 'Can you see it?'

The half-caste nodded.

'OK, let's play a game. Let's see how long we can look up at the Christmas decoration.'

He stood up and made his way around the dead grandmother's stool.

'Now close your eyes and think of your favourite Christmas present.'

The half-caste hesitated.

'Close your eyes. I'll close mine.'

The half-caste closed his eyes, only to hide the crying. He held the dagger at the half-caste's throat, ready to do the unspeakable, ready to do as instructed by the blue eyes in the framed poster.

'Can you see the present?'

The half-caste couldn't speak through the sobbing.

'Can you see it? Can you see your Christmas present?'

The half-caste started shaking.

'Can you see your fucking present?'

The front door exploded. Shards of glass skidded across the shop floor. The open and closed sign flew through the air. A figure ducked and ran through the doorframe.

He saw the gun before he saw the face behind it.

'Put the knife down now,' DC Devonshire said.

Devonshire's training suddenly meant nothing. All those courses at Hendon Police College, weapons-handling, firing ranges, they vanished.

The targets never included a little boy's face.

His boy.

His son.

Crying.

Crying because he was scared. Crying because he was smart. Crying because he knew he was dying.

Devonshire stepped towards the counter. The glass crunched beneath his shoes. On the other side of the counter, Winston Churchill pressed the blade against Benjamin's throat. Devonshire was close, but not close enough. He wasn't a marksman. He was a rookie detective who had never pulled a weapon on a suspect before. He was a father in fear. He was the cornered one.

With his left arm, Winston Churchill grabbed the boy by the throat and dragged him backwards, edging away from Devonshire.

'Please. Don't.'

Devonshire's sobbing betrayed his impotence. He was never going to pull the trigger. The margin for error was too much, the possible consequences unbearable. Both men knew it.

Winston Churchill kept moving, dragging the half-caste until they were out in front of the counter, standing on broken glass and facing a broken copper.

He had won this battle. He was ready to win the war.

'Where is she?'

'Who?'

'Your wife.'

Devonshire aimed his semiautomatic pistol at Winston Churchill's sweet spot, middle of the forehead, right above the eyes. His target had actually done the detective a favour. In moving around the counter, Winston Churchill was no longer at an angle, diagonally across from Devonshire with an obstacle between them. Only inches separated them now.

This was the simplest of standoffs, the easiest, cleanest shot. But it might not be an instant shot. Devonshire had no way of knowing. He wasn't a gun nut or a pathologist. He had no idea of reaction times after the bullet entered the brain.

Maybe there wasn't enough time to slice his son's throat.

Maybe there was.

Devonshire was almost sure. But he wasn't certain.

'She's not here.'

'Of course she's here. She's his mother.'

Devonshire couldn't settle his internal argument.

Distract him. Shoot him. Contain him. Shoot him. Engage him. Shoot him. Shoot him. Shoot him. Shoot him.

Be a fucking man and shoot him.

But Devonshire was more than a man. He was a father.

'All right, all right, I'll get her if you put the knife down.'

Winston Churchill tilted his head to the side, emphasising the futility of Devonshire's request.

Devonshire took one hand off his gun and raised it towards Churchill, palm up, a conciliatory gesture. 'OK, OK, I'll call her, all right? I'll take out my phone and call her. To do that, I've gotta lower my gun.'

'Daddy?'

It was the first time Benjamin had spoken since his father had smashed through the door, his real superhero.

It was the first time Devonshire had heard his son's voice.

It was the first time Devonshire had heard his own heart breaking.

'It's OK, Ben, I promise. We have to do this. We have to get your mother, OK? We all need to stay calm.'

Devonshire brought down his left hand and pointed towards the inside pocket of his jacket. Winston Churchill nodded. Devonshire pulled out his phone and held it up for approval. His right hand continued to hold the gun, but both men knew that his aim was no longer steady.

'Now, you know that I have to look down when I dial. And we both know that in that moment, you could stab my son and perhaps me, before I get a chance to aim and hit you with a fatal shot.'

Devonshire's voice was flat. His calmness surprised him.

'But we also know that you'll never kill me before I've had a chance to empty this gun. I promise you. I will live long enough to kill you. Do you understand?'

Winston Churchill didn't move.

'Do you understand?'

Winston Churchill nodded.

Devonshire smiled at his son and then peered down at his phone. They all watched his fingers as he tapped the screen.

'Don't worry, Ben,' Devonshire whispered. 'It's over now.'

Winston Churchill felt the pain before he heard the bang. The bullet passed between his right clavicle and humerus, shattering both bones instantly and tearing open his brachial artery. His arm flung outwards, against his will, as if controlled by an external source. The dagger fell to the floor. Everything was moving. The half-caste running one way, the detective running the other, meeting in the middle, hugging, embracing in a way that he didn't understand.

If he reached for the dagger, he could still fix this. There was still time. But his right arm was moving away from him again. He was sure he heard cracking. He was aware of his own screaming. He was turning, spinning, against his will; everything was against his will now.

And then he saw her face and understood everything.

She had taken the shot that her cowardly husband had refused. She had weighed up the risks and taken the decision to blow his shoulder in half.

She was a mother.

And mothers always know best.

In the kitchen, behind the shop floor, Low was tending to Dhaval Mistry's head wound when he heard the shot. He dropped the tea towel, the chair falling away behind him. Dhaval's unfinished tea and the boy's soggy cornflakes spilled across the kitchen table.

Low remembered her words.

Stay with Dad. We have to finish this.

For once, Low had listened. He hadn't learned, but he had listened, to the angry daughter, the terrified mother and the anxious wife.

Winston Churchill never stood a chance. But Low had to be sure.

He ran through the doorway streamers that separated the public shopkeepers from the private family. No one else hung streamers from shop doorframes any more. But the Mistrys still did. The streamers reminded them of a simpler time, when streamers were the only protection needed from the other side.

Low cocked his stolen revolver, recognising Billy Evans's blood on the barrel. He kept low, his hamstrings aching in protest, his adrenaline rising to the challenge. The crying worried him, but the screaming shocked him. He ran through the aisle, passing the shop's shelves, aiming at the two moving images spread out across the broken glass. One cried. The other screamed. Both were male.

Behind the counter, a mother shielded her son from the violence. Her work was done. For now. The broken boy would need years to be put back together again.

On the shop floor, the wounded animal yelped in pain as he was kicked.

'You held a knife to my son's throat, my fucking son's throat.'

DC Devonshire kicked the masked man again and Low shoved his gun into the waistband of his jeans. Devonshire was doing the job for him. Low thought about Zhang Jun Li punching a bedroom door filled with the melting photos of her dead boyfriend. A traumatised father was about to get his revenge, thanks to the sterling efforts of another.

Winston Churchill was going to die.

But he couldn't.

Not like this.

Ramila Mistry's heart couldn't be broken a second time, not by another copper thinking with his balls.

Low grabbed the collar of Devonshire's suit jacket, the surprise attack catching the avenging father off balance. Devonshire clattered into a stand filled with birthday cards, landing hard on his back, stealing the oxygen from his lungs. Pride tried to drag him to his feet. Low reached for the gun.

'Stop,' he said.

'No, don't give up. Never surrender.'

Winston Churchill's goading caught everyone off guard. Low spun around, his gun in the wrinkled face of a World War II hero.

'I'm not shooting you through a fucking mask.'

Low yanked off Churchill's head and confronted a smirking face.

Younger face.

Familiar face.

'It's my favourite Chinese detective.'

Low saw him in the Charles Dickens, another masked man in the corner, the neglected one, and then he saw him again in the Charles Dickens, unmasked, still in the corner, still the neglected one.

'The barman.'

'My name's George.'

'Yeah, not Geoff. George. The one who takes orders all day long. So predictable.'

Low left the barman from the Charles Dickens to nurse his wounds, preferring to focus on a mother and son behind the counter, still hugging, a reassuring image in a room filled with blood, hate and violence.

'You know what isn't predictable? The sound a Chinese girl makes when she's on fire. It's not really a scream. It's more of a whimper, like the sound a baby bird makes when you squash it in your hand.'

George made a fist, slowly, miming the action in the air.

'Stabbing is different, though. When you stab a Paki through the heart, you see the terror in his eyes. He knows he's dying. He's like a little boy, a little blubbing boy – well, a bit like him just now. Little blubbing Ben. I should've cut your throat shouldn't I, Ben?'

Devonshire was already on his feet, but he still wasn't quick enough. Low's raised left hand held him back. Low's right hand was steady, the blood-stained gun poised, his finger on the trigger, ready to do what was needed, what Zhang Wei demanded, what George wanted, what they all really wanted but could never say in this politically correct swamp of their own creation.

But Low lived in the darkest place with no fixed rules: no limits, only justice. He took a step closer.

'You see, they won't do it,' George said. 'But I think you will. Even though they are the boy's parents, they won't do it. But you and me are different. We know what we are capable of.'

'You have no idea what I'm capable of.'

'I know what I saw in Chinatown. I saw you. Impotent. Knowing that you could do nothing was the greatest night of my life.'

The fireworks burned so brightly. Low gave chase, but they

were too fast, too luminous, too many. He couldn't keep up. The images besieged him. Stabbed boy. Burning girl. Pregnant girlfriend. Goading killer. Laughing killer. Mocking killer.

'I killed her because of you, Skull Face. I know who you really are. "Fuck you, *ang moh*." That's what you said. On my video. *Ang moh* means white man, right? I looked it up. Only you would know that. You saved her at the rally, didn't you? *Skull Face*. You gave me the video. You made them angry. So I killed a mouthy Chinese bitch, just to balance things up,' George said, grinning.

'I set her on fire because of you.'

Low was no longer listening. He was on his knees, jabbing the muzzle against the roof of George's mouth, listening to George choking. Retching. Instructing.

'Do it.'

Low's finger brushed the trigger, ready to squeeze, hoping for a silence that he knew would never come.

'Do it,' George shouted. 'Fucking do it.'

'Stanley.'

Her measured voice was enough. It always was.

The next sound was metallic and grating as Low withdrew the gun, dragging the barrel across George's teeth on its way out. Low blocked out his whining to watch a reunited family embrace.

He no longer envied Mistry or her husband and son. He knew that he couldn't miss what he didn't deserve.

CHAPTER 35

DCI Wickes's office was filled with unfamiliar faces. Every Charing Cross employee had been invited to the impromptu party, but every off-duty copper in London seemed to be drinking Wickes's beer and stealing his pizza. In a quiet corner, Low sat alone, content to be overlooked. It was almost reassuring to know that he polarised police stations in two different countries. In Singapore, he was one of their own. They had to put up with him. In London, he was either the enigmatic Chinaman with a gift for criminal mind games or a bipolar sociopath with a flair for violence. Low wouldn't disagree with either description. Nor did he particularly care. The enigmatic Chinaman and the bipolar sociopath were left alone. He was too aloof to be considered good company at a piss-up.

Low recognised the uniforms toasting each other beside the drinks table. PC Bishop and PC Cook were like loan sharks, back in Singapore. They always came as a pair. Cook, the more junior officer, tried to balance three beer bottles. Bishop wasn't interested in playing the fool. He preferred to stand back, the only quiet face in a rowdy crowd. Low noticed their beer was non-alcoholic. He admired their restraint.

By the whiteboard, plain-clothes detectives took group photos beside the CCTV photocopies, clippings and maps;

the evidence of London's latest monstrosity. None of the photos would ever be fit for publication. Too sensitive. Too honest.

Across the room, DI Mistry and DC Devonshire sat in silence, their beers untouched. Low caught Devonshire's eye and nodded. Devonshire raised his bottle in gratitude. Mistry did nothing. She didn't have to.

A door opened and DCI Wickes marched in, clutching two bottles of champagne. His office erupted.

'Ladies and gentlemen, if you'll give me a moment,' he said, plonking the champagne on the table. 'Cook, stop juggling those bloody beer bottles.'

Cook did as he was told.

'OK, I'll keep this short,' Wickes continued. 'We've got him.'

He waited for the cheering and fist-pumping to fizzle out.

'George Davis, a full-time barman at the Charles Dickens pub and a long-time volunteer at the Make England Great Again Movement. He obviously matches the physical description in all the CCTV footage that Bishop pulled together, even if Bishop never got us a clear image of the bloke. God knows how he managed that.'

Bishop responded to the inevitable jeering with a two-fingered salute.

'But we've taken samples. We're testing his coat, gloves and mask. Forensics are confident of getting a match from either Hawker Heaven, the Charles Dickens or from the clothes of Margaret Jones and Detective Inspector Stanley Low.'

The sudden mood change was as obvious as it was awkward. Low didn't actually mind the tension in the room. He felt right at home.

Wickes took note of the underlying resentment.

'Now, look, whatever else has happened, I have to accept – and you have to accept – that Inspector Low's work has helped to save a little boy's life, the son of two officers in this room.

So wherever this party ends up later, I expect you to treat him like one of the team.'

Cook piped up.

'You mean get him pissed and leave him in a ditch?'

'Exactly. Now, I've spent fifty quid on this champagne and if it's not gone by the time I get back, I'm taking it home to Mrs Wickes.'

Wickes accepted the backslapping as he made his way through sweaty, red-faced officers, stopping at Low's table.

'You didn't have to say that,' Low said.

'I know. I didn't want to say that.'

Low respected Wickes's decency and integrity, but his sudden abruptness was out of character. Wickes sat across from Low.

'What happened to the gun?'

'Dumped it.'

'What happens if he mentions the gun at trial?'

'Charge me with possessing an illegal firearm.'

'Why are you so antagonistic?'

Low shrugged. 'I'm a product of my environment.'

'You come from one of the safest countries on the planet.'

'Only on the surface.'

'Yeah? What's underneath?'

'Men like me.'

Wickes appreciated the inspector's honesty. Low came from an archaic, simplistic world of right and wrong. No nuance. No subtlety. No crime. It worked. Wickes's liberal bosses despised countries like Singapore not because they were illiberal, but because they worked.

'So who's gonna bring him up first?'

Wickes seemed surprised at the question.

'He's the only reason you're talking to me. You're not here to wish me a pleasant flight.'

If nothing else, Wickes admired Low's intellect. There really was nothing else to admire.

'We haven't got him. Not quite. He won't talk.'

'Wait for forensics. And then he won't have to.'

The station's celebrations continued around both men. Wickes watched Cook fail another bottle-juggling attempt. The chief inspector envied his team's euphoria.

'He says he's not done yet.'

Low rubbed his forehead repeatedly, but it made no difference. His mind was already alive to the possibilities.

'Yeah, too easy,' he mumbled. 'Too bloody easy.'

'What?'

'All that scheming, all those videos, just to lead me straight to her son, straight to him, for us to kill him in a murder-suicide. Too easy, too stupid.'

'We've already charged him with the kidnapping and attempted murder of little Benjamin,' Wickes said, glancing across at little Benjamin's parents. 'So he's not going anywhere.'

'But he won't talk about the murders?'

'Not a word. Nothing. He ignores me. He ignores his solicitor. Whenever I mention the murders, he keeps saying the same thing.'

'What?'

'I'm not talking to anyone except the Chink.'

CHAPTER 36

George Davis didn't like his naked body rubbing against the surgical gown. As he was so tall, the gown didn't quite reach his wrists or ankles. He was uncomfortable at the prospect of exposing his flesh to strangers.

He liked the interrogation room, though. It was small, grey and boxy, with barely enough room for a table and four chairs. He was squeezed in beside a slight, ferrety solicitor and there was little distance between them and the uniformed officer standing guard at the door.

The cramped conditions made him look even taller. He was more imposing, a giant among lesser men. He didn't need to stoop. He could straighten his back and appear less socially awkward.

He smiled as DCI Wickes kept his promise. The chief inspector returned to the claustrophobic sweatbox with that Chinese curiosity.

Davis peered up at the clock above the door. He was ready.

But Low kept him waiting, refusing to sit. He read aloud the highlights from Davis's file.

'George Davis, born in Walthamstow, east London, forty years old, left school at sixteen, went to work with father Harry Davis at Spitalfields fruit and veg market, left after two years, odd jobs, bar work, more bar work, then saw Billy Evans give a speech at Victoria Park, which made you cum in your pants, join Make England Great Again and get yourself your first steady full-time job at the Charles Dickens pub. Now you've got a nice one-bedroom flat in west London.'

Low looked at Wickes for confirmation.

'It's being searched now,' Wickes said.

Low dropped the file on the table and took his seat.

'Well, that's all clichéd enough. Why didn't you kill the old man?'

Davis's solicitor scribbled on a notepad and slid the paper across the table. Davis pushed it back.

'What old man?'

'Dhaval Mistry, the boy's granddad. He's not white. He's not native.'

'He's British.'

'Not British-born though. You've could've offered another sacrifice for Aryan supremacy, but you left him alive.'

'He's as British as me.'

'But he isn't, is he? He came here in the 1970s, one of the original Indian immigrants. He turned your nation of shopkeepers from white to brown. He should've been top of your list.'

'Why? He's no different to me or him,' Davis said, pointing at DCI Wickes. 'We know what role we have in British society. Our place. Maybe their caste system helps. They believe that some are just born better, which is true. It's not politically correct, just genetic reality. History shows that we are the high caste.'

'British people?'

'White people.'

'You don't seriously believe that.'

'Don't need to believe it. History proves it. Look at our former colonies. Look what they were before we arrived. Look what they were after we left. Have you seen India or Pakistan lately?'

'Have you seen Singapore lately?'

'You kept our laws, our language and our civilised culture.'

Low grinned at the lanky man in a surgical gown.

'So you've read a few history books.'

'Only the right ones.'

'I get it. You're a smart racist.'

'No, I'm a smart patriot. That's why we're universally despised, inspector. We have to be. We remind the Left of what people can never be and we remind the Right of what people really are. And neither side wants to look in the mirror.'

'So your profound conclusion is what? Make England white again?'

'No, make England great again. I think the slogan is sincere. I really do. You look at the earliest days of mass migration, when it was only the select few, when air travel was reserved for the rich, transport was easier to monitor and borders were easier to control, that was the best. The early migrants were grateful just to be here. There was racial tolerance, but never acceptance. Didn't need to be. Everyone knew their place in society.'

'Like a caste system?'

'Yeah. And it worked.'

'Yeah, it worked. My people were racially abused in Chinese takeaways. And anyone brown or black was beaten up on the way to school. Other than that, we were invisible. We didn't exist.'

Davis shrugged.

'You can't make an omelette.'

'Without breaking a few immigrants?'

'I like that.'

Wickes crossed his arms.

'Let's get back to the murders of Mohamed Kamal and Zhang Jun Li, shall we?'

'In a minute,' Low said, focusing on Davis. 'I read your file on the way in. Your mother died eleven years ago, not long before you joined Evans's mob.'

Davis grinned.

'Yeah, one led to the other. If she were alive today, I'd probably have my own fruit and veg stall now in Spitalfields market. Is that the best you can do?'

'No, I'm more interested in your father. Harry Davis. He was a local villain last time.'

'Yeah.'

'Got three years for grievous bodily harm, another eighteen months for demanding money with menaces; he was a well-known gangster around London.'

'Yeah.'

'But he's not a gangster now?'

'He's an old man now.'

'Must have been tough growing up?'

'Not really.'

'Was he violent?'

'He gave me and Mum the odd slap if he thought we'd been out of order.'

'So it was a dysfunctional family?'

Davis laughed loudly.

'No, it was a working-class family in the eighties. Is that really all you've got? I expected better than this.'

Low felt the eyes of all the men in the room. Even the uniformed copper at the door seemed fidgety. Low was trying to connect dots that he couldn't see. He tapped his finger on the table, refusing to break eye contact.

'It's not just race, is it?'

'No.'

'Yeah, too simple. That's for the others, in their Winston Churchill masks at the pub, that's not you. It's not only race, otherwise you'd have killed the granddad. You'd have killed me outside Hawker Heaven and the girl's dad. No, you killed the girl because she humiliated you on social media. You. Charlemagne. And why are you Charlemagne, by the way? I get the Leonard one, the name you used on radio – Churchill's middle name; that was you just messing with us in your red phone box opposite Parliament, but Charlemagne is bigger. Charlemagne is a king.'

Davis giggled.

'Yeah, I'm not sure about that either. A French king, a leader of European people seems off for you.'

Low turned to Wickes.

'Search for a different Charlemagne on your phone. See what comes up.'

Wickes passed his phone to Low. The Singaporean nodded his approval.

'Ah, the Charlemagne Regiment, the French volunteers who signed up for the SS to fight against their own people,' Low said, reading from the screen.

'Very good,' Davis said.

'Yeah, that's the ultimate, right? To bring local and foreign together, friends and enemies, left and right, different languages, different countries, they are polar opposites except for one thing. Race. They are the same race. Or they have the same beliefs about race and culture.'

Low's eyes widened.

'They don't mix. They don't interbreed. They don't dilute the races. The older immigrants didn't do that, did they? People like Dhaval Mistry; these people were just as prejudiced as you. They stuck with their own kind. They all did back then. Same in Singapore. Same everywhere. Your parents. My parents. Ramila Mistry's parents. But not Ramila. She comes along with her liberal university education and her tolerant views and she shags a nice, middle-class white boy. That bastard kid of theirs is neither cream nor coffee. Can't have that. And the other one, the pretty Chinese girl, not only was she shagging a Muslim boy, she was mocking you for it on social media, rubbing your nose in it, the bitch. There's you, home alone, wanking over

266

Mein Kampf, and they're all out there, shagging between the races, making half-blood babies, in your country.'

'No one knows their place any more.'

'Exactly. But your dad did, didn't he? He was one of the pioneers. Harry Davis. He wasn't just a local villain. He was one of the first National Front boys, an original fascist, long before it became fashionable. There wasn't a minority group in London he wasn't prepared to kick the shit out of, right or not? It's all on file. He must be so proud of you now.'

'I don't know.'

'No, but you knew back then, eh? Detained with him at thirteen when your lot had a riot with the anti-Nazi League. At fourteen you were putting bricks through Asian shop windows. Then you and your mates started beating up homosexuals at Gay Pride rallies in London, all textbook stuff, trying to impress your father, your absent father, always on the run, in prison, whatever. But you couldn't be Harry Davis, not really. You're tall like him, but you haven't got his bulk. His aura. He walks into a pub and he's Harry Davis. You walk in and you're nothing. A barman. No one notices. So you must go further, become a lackey for Billy Evans. But it's still not enough. No validation from Gangster Daddy. Still looking for acceptance when he's sitting there in his own piss, the old Gangster Widower, reminiscing about the good old days, dreaming of a white England. But you're not a man like him. You clean pubs. He owned pubs. Controlled them. Like Billy Evans. They both had what you never had. Power. Respect. Acceptance.'

Low noticed the slight change in Davis's demeanour. It was small: a shift in body weight, a head tilt, a widening of the pupils, but it was enough.

Wickes made the mistake of interrupting the Singaporean.

'Shall we take a break?'

Low waved the chief inspector away, forgetting where he was, forgetting the power structure in the room, forgetting everything except the man in a white gown, absorbing the internal explosions, channelling the mania.

'No, it's about *acceptance*. It always is with these racist fuck-wits. It's not about other colours being accepted, it's about the primary colour no longer being accepted. You're ignored, sidelined, right? For smart, confident people, this isn't a problem. They don't feel threatened. But for the rest of you, racial dominance is all you've got. Being born into a world where most of the people look the same as you is the best you could ever hope for. It's the only advantage you've got. But you don't even have that any more, do you? No one's willing to stay in their boxes any more, are they? Everyone's fighting back now. Everyone has rights now. The women. The blacks. The Pakis. The Chinks. The gays.'

Low spotted fear for the first time, behind the eyes.

'Yeah, they can all come out now, stand up for themselves, speak for themselves, but you can't, can you?'

As Low raised his voice, Davis sipped water from a plastic cup on the table.

'Not in your world, you can't. They all can and you hate them for it. Women. Muslims. Pakis. Gays. They have rights and protections. They have acceptance. All of them. Women. Muslims. Pakis. Gays.'

'That's enough now,' said Wickes.

'No, it's more than enough, it's too much, right, George? How can women, Muslims, Pakis and gays have a better life than you, in your own country? But it's not about your country, is it? It's about your world. It's tough to be those things in your world, right? You don't hate them for what they are. You hate them for what you are. What you can't be. Not in Harry Davis's world. He wouldn't accept that shit, would he? He went to war against it, just like you. Luckily, you're not a woman, or a Muslim, or a Paki, are you? So it's just a process of elimination.'

'Fuck you.'

Low leered at the naked man in the white gown.

'Yeah, you would, right? Enjoy it, too. Nice Chinese arse like mine, something forbidden and exotic, not quite a Nazi stormtrooper but good enough, right? But you can't. Your dad would kill you. So you made your little videos in protest against those who have the basic freedoms you don't, in protest against the sin within. You joined the very fuckwits who were making your life a misery, hiding in plain sight, a closet gay hanging out with homophobes. Was it a good cover for your dad? Did you think you could pray the gay away? Or did you just dream of fucking a guy in a Winston Churchill mask?'

The roar was primeval, catching everyone in the interrogation room by surprise. Davis was on his feet, flipping the table towards the two detectives. As the plastic cups of tea and water toppled, Wickes grabbed the file off the table. At the door, the young, startled officer drew his weapon for the first time in his career. His shaking hands betrayed his inexperience.

Low stood between the gun and Davis.

'No. That's what he wants.'

Their heavy breathing echoed around their confined, shared space. Davis's shoulders slumped, as if defeated. He wiped his eyes.

'I can see you're very emotional, Mr Davis,' Wickes said. 'But please sit down.'

Wickes instructed the officer to holster his gun. The other men returned to their seats. The terrified solicitor was the last to do so.

'May I suggest—' he began.

'No you may not,' Low interrupted, returning to Davis. 'You know one of the biggest stains on my society?'

Davis took a deep breath before speaking.

'You?'

'Homosexuality. It's still illegal – well, the act of male sex is, anyway – in this day and age. Illegal. Can you believe that?'

Davis looked down at the table. 'Section 377A of the Penal Code.'

'Yeah, it is. I thought you might know. And it's death by stoning in Brunei now. I mean, that's real oppression, proper denial.'

'My dad said it's the only thing religion ever got right.'

'So you never told him?'

Davis lifted his head and gazed at the clock above the door.

'When I was thirteen, maybe fourteen, we were in the pub together. He was pissed, so he wouldn't remember. But he said to me, if I ever killed anyone, he'd visit me in prison until his last breath. But if I turned out to be queer, he'd break every bone in my body. Those were his exact words.'

'So you took out your anger against your father on—'

'Anger?' Davis interrupted.

He appeared genuinely shocked.

'There's no anger. I love my father. He just wanted what was best for me. And he was right. You can't be gay in my world. He knew that. He wasn't being homophobic. He was being protective.'

'That's got to be the most fucked-up example of filial piety I've ever heard,' Low muttered.

'What?'

'It doesn't matter. You killed two people, young people, because you couldn't get Daddy's love?'

'No, because he was right. And our movement is right. If we don't stay in our boxes, we pollute each other. We contaminate society. I've stayed in my box my whole fucking life, for my father, for my country – why couldn't they do the same?'

'So you went after the Mistry family because they had a mixed-race son.'

'Half-caste son. Diluted two races.'

'How did you find him?'

'Followed her home from Mark Beckett's place.'

'So you were never actually gonna kill Beckett then. He was just bait.'

'I thought about it. To win this war, I know how far we've got to go. We've got to be truly reprehensible.'

'Ah, like your heroes in the Charlemagne Regiment. You seriously expected Mark Beckett to join Make England Great Again?'

'No. I seriously expected to kill him. It needs a heinous crime, something truly unspeakable, to force people to pick a side. You know that.'

'So why didn't you kill him?'

'It's still white on white. It's too much.'

'The French did it. They turned on their own and joined the Nazis, in your beloved Charlemagne Regiment.'

'Well, that's the French for you. We're not ready for that. Not yet.'

'And Neo-Nazi Daddy wouldn't have approved, right? Much easier to set a young Chinese woman on fire, right?'

'Yeah, it was actually.'

'Yeah, Zhang Jun Li, much easier, especially being an outspoken, educated Chinese woman who was sleeping with a Muslim Indian.'

'Yeah. Though I'm glad you saved her father. He hadn't done anything wrong.'

'And the boy?'

'What boy?'

Low clenched his fists.

'Mohamed Kamal. Twenty-two years old. A Singaporean scholar, whole life ahead of him. That. Fucking. Boy.'

Davis fidgeted in his seat.

'Oh him, yeah. Seems so long ago now. He worked at the pub with me.'

'We know that.'

'Yeah, well, what happened was, I caught him one day

271

praying to Allah on our pub property. He knew he wasn't supposed to do that, not with our clientele. Same story again. Wouldn't stay in his box. So I followed him home and it just sort of happened. We had a row, a bit of a fight and that was it, more of an accident, really.'

'The knife?'

'Took it from the pub.'

'And now?'

'Long gone. In a drain somewhere.'

'If it was an accident, why didn't you panic? Why did you hang around to write "MEGA" on the wall in the kid's blood.'

'I didn't panic. In fact, that's the one thing I learned from killing people.'

'What?'

'I really liked it.'

CHAPTER 37

A small crowd had gathered in a darkened room, craning their heads to catch a glimpse of George Davis signing his confession. He paused to take in his reflection. He grinned. He couldn't see them on the other side of the one-way mirror, but he knew they were there, celebrating, patting each other on the back, toasting the Chinaman.

At the back of the room, DI Mistry and DC Devonshire had joined Low and DCI Wickes. They didn't speak. Exhaustion had overtaken elation. Mistry had wasted enough time with Davis. She wanted to get home to her son.

Her traumatised, wounded son.

Her stomach tightened as the man who'd held a knife to her little boy's throat scribbled away at his statement. Had someone handed her a petition to bring back the death penalty, in that room, at that moment, she might have signed it.

She decided to call her son, to remind her of life rather than death, but her phone was already ringing.

'DI Mistry. Oh, hello. What did you find? Really? What else is there? Where was that? On the wall? And nothing else?'

Low observed Mistry's change in tone, from assured to confused.

'OK, well, hang about, speak to the neighbours and I'll call back in a bit.'

Mistry peered through the glass, looking Davis up and down. 'Strange,' she whispered.

'What?'

Low was already at her side, reading the bad news.

'The team at his flat. They said it was spotless, almost like a show flat. No mess anywhere, barely any food, even the bed didn't look slept in. There was a desk, a laptop, a router and some cables, a TV, but that's about it.'

'He was meticulous,' Devonshire said. 'He's cleaned up. He knew we'd get there at some point.'

Low wasn't convinced. 'Not enough time from going to the pub, seeing me, going to your house. It's too ad hoc, too much rushing. What was on the wall?'

'A framed Nazi propaganda poster. World War Two. Usual shit.'

'Who owns the flat?'

'Still checking,' Wickes said. 'But Paul Harvey's name is on the lease. It's got be owned by their backers. Pubs don't give their barmen flats in the West End. Would cost a fortune.'

'He's keeping up appearances,' Low said. 'Anything personal in the flat?'

'Only one thing, really. There was a photo of him and his dad on the desk.'

'Of course there was.'

Low pushed his way through the star-struck onlookers.

The door to the interrogation room slammed hard. Even the officer on guard winced. Low picked up his chair from before, the one that faced Davis, and flung it against the wall. The horrified solicitor tried to disappear, tortoise-like, into his own cheap suit. Davis placed his pen on the table and sat back, enjoying the unexpected entertainment.

'Two lives, two flats,' Low shouted.

'What?'

Low was around the table and in Davis's face, peering into the eyes of a dead soul. 'Two lives, two fucking flats.'

'What are you going on about?'

But Davis failed to convince. He acknowledged his solicitor's presence for the first time. His eyes drifted across the room, following the nervous black copper at the door, the inept solicitor, the chief inspector barging in and reaching for the screaming Chinaman.

'Two flats, two fucking flats, one for work and one for show, one for killing and one for Daddy.'

'Inspector Low, back away.'

DCI Wickes's orders were ignored. Low didn't see Wickes's hand on his shoulder, or the solicitor's hand scribbling accusations of assault in his notepad or the copper's hand grabbing his gun, hoping not to draw it on anyone, unsure of the target.

'Two lives, two flats; one for straight, one for gay.'

'You're mental.'

'And you're coming out of the closet – tonight, right now, to him, just him.'

'What?'

'To Daddy, tonight. I'm gonna drag you out of the fucking closet.'

'No you won't,' Davis said, but the fight was deserting him. He saw his father over and over and over again. The football. The pub. The rallies. The fights. The violence. The hate. Endless, limitless hate. His father's intolerance was inexhaustible. The hate never went away.

Davis accepted the violence. They always did. Mother and son. That was their life. That was all their lives. But he couldn't take the hate, not after his mother died. She wouldn't have minded. She would've still loved him, probably, maybe, but she certainly wouldn't have hated him, not her own son. But he would. He told him as much, reminded him, every time he got drunk in dying pubs, archaic working men's clubs, on the settee, after hours, that same vile, drunken, purple face, the same threat of violence.

I'll break every bone in your body.

You hear me, boy?

I'll break every fucking bone in your body.

Perhaps Harry Davis knew. Perhaps he saw something. Perhaps that's why he kept reinforcing the message, over and over and over again: intolerance will be met with intolerance. It always returned to hate.

A father's hate.

Davis couldn't see straight. Tears blurred his vision. The Chinese monster was still in his face, raging, unrelenting.

'I fucking will. I'm calling him now,' Low said, pointing at the dumbstruck copper at the door. 'Call Harry Davis.'

'No,' Davis said. He was crying now.

'You can't do this, Low,' Wickes said. 'Nothing's being recorded. It's inadmissible.'

But Low had blocked out everything expect Davis, probing his pain.

'Don't care. Get Harry Davis. Bring him in. I'm gonna tell him myself, in this room, that his golden Nazi boy is gay.'

'Fuck you – no.'

'Then tell me where you really live.'

'It'll be over.'

'It's already over,' Low said, towering over the cowering Davis, their noses almost touching.

'I can't.'

'Queer, poof, homo, faggot, that's what he'll call you, and then he'll beat the shit out of you and then he'll kill you.'

'No.'

'He will. You know he will. He'll kill you, right here in this room, I will leave him alone with you in this room tonight, I swear, if you don't tell me.'

'Please.'

'Call his fucking father. Now.'

'Hornsey House, eleventh floor, number sixty-one, Field Street,' Davis said, whimpering like a cornered puppy. 'Please don't tell him.'

No one else spoke.

Davis's pitiful weeping was the only sound in the room.

'OK, OK,' Wickes said, trying to compose his thoughts. 'OK, we'll need to continue the interview, once we've sorted warrants and searched the flat, so you're not going anywhere.'

Wickes pointed at the solicitor.

'And I'll, er, send Cook and Bishop over to Hornsey House. Yeah, let's do that. Bishop knows the route inside out, from central London to north London. He's done the CCTV mapping. '

'Makes sense.'

'Yeah it does,' Wickes said, tapping Low on the shoulder. 'Yeah. Well done, inspector.'

'Thank you, sir.'

'You coming?'

'Yeah, right behind you.'

Low waited for the chief inspector to leave the interrogation room before picking up the chair he had earlier thrown against the wall. He pushed it under the table, until the seat brushed against Davis' legs.

He was still crying. With his head tucked into his chest, his gown soaked around the neck.

Low pulled a ball of used tissues from his pocket and handed it to Davis. He watched Davis clean himself.

Pathetic.

They always were.

'You have no idea how many people I've met like you in Singapore. That's how I knew. Two lives. One straight. One gay. Some even keep two flats. One for themselves, one for the homophobic family. Just like you. But they're ashamed of their society, not each other. That's the difference.'

'Yeah, that is the difference. My father can still be proud of me.'

Low took a last look at Davis, weeping into his tear-soaked gown.

'He should be. No son ever did more to please his dad.'

Low headed for the door, stopping to speak to the police constable.

'Filial piety, eh, officer?'

'What?'

'Filial piety. It means – oh, forget it.'

The police constable whispered into Low's ear.

'I don't want to be out of line, but how did you do that?'

Low stopped in the hallway. His sigh echoed along the narrow corridor.

'My psychiatrist said it best. You know how a lab rat ingests poison until his antibodies produce an antidote?'

'Sort of.'

'Well, I'm the lab rat. Goodnight.'

'Goodnight, sir. Do you know I grew up near Hornsey House?'

'Really,' said Low, barely listening, trying to leave.

'Yeah. Strange place for him to have a flat.'

'Why?'

'No white people.'

Low turned back. 'What are you talking about?'

'Well, I can say it because I used to live on a council estate nearby. It's a shithole. Even we moved out.'

'Who's "we"? Policemen?'

The officer looked away. 'No, black people. There might be a few Africans, I suppose, but they'd mostly be illegals – a few refugees, Syria, Iraq and all that. He'd stick out like a white ball on a snooker table.'

Low was already running, back past the police constable, through the door into the interrogation room, hands on the table, confronting the man with two faces. Same man.

Different face.

George Davis was a man with two faces.

He was no longer crying.

He was laughing.

Low clenched his fists, but directed his fury elsewhere, pounding against the one-way mirror.

'Evacuate Hornsey House. Now.'

CHAPTER 38

By the time they arrived, the small field in front of Hornsey House was full of dazed residents wrapped in blankets. Low was out of the car first, not waiting for DC Devonshire to park. Devonshire quickly gave up trying in a narrow street filled with too many emergency vehicles flashing too many lights. He mounted the pavement and clipped the tiny fence that protected the feeble shrubbery of a fading housing estate. DI Mistry thought about following Low, but there really was no point.

Hornsey House wasn't letting anyone into its tall, grey, imperious block.

Hornsey House was still on fire.

Eleventh floor.

His floor.

One flat was gutted.

His flat.

Fire crews had worked quickly and methodically, containing the blaze. Judging by the soot-stained walls, the flames had licked four, maybe five, floors either side of the eleventh floor, shattering windows and stealing lifelong memories, but there was no chance of the drenched building being engulfed.

The fire crews had done their job. So had Low.

Mistry and Devonshire busied themselves with the evacuated

residents, offering empty platitudes and hollow small talk. Some cried. Most didn't. They were immigrants. They weren't blessed with the privilege of innocence. Families sat beneath trees with bare branches, as if seeking shelter that wasn't there. In the shadow of a brutalist tower block, everything was stripped back to black.

Mistry watched the mothers comforting babies and toddlers, sitting on a frozen mud patch, reassuring them that they had found a better life here in north London as fire crews hosed down whatever was left of their homes.

Mistry thought of her late mother. She thought of her own response when George Davis held a knife to her son's throat. She thought of the similarities between the two women. They were prepared to sacrifice the same thing for their children. Everything.

She knew that these kids would be fine. Eventually. They still had their mothers.

At the ground-floor entrance, Low tried to force his way through the police cordon.

'No chance, mate,' said a uniformed officer, raising an arm to block Low's path.

'I'm with Charing Cross Station,' said Low.

'I don't care if you're with Arsenal Football Club. No one is going in.'

'Did you get everybody out?'

'Yeah. We were here for at least ten or fifteen minutes evacuating every floor – eleventh floor first, obviously. We were all out on the grass when it went off. Every resident seems to be accounted for. They haven't reported anyone missing. You really from Charing Cross?'

'Yeah,' Low whispered, peering up at the smouldering tower block.

The young constable offered his hand.

'That was a good shout from you lot.'

'Yeah.'

Low wasn't really listening. He stepped back to take in the devastation. The scorched right side of Hornsey House gave the impression of a giant black eye. She was wounded, unsteady on her feet, but she'd survive. Her walls would stand firm.

George Davis had failed.

'Excuse me, step aside, please.'

'Get out of the way.'

Low heard them before he saw them. Two firemen. They pushed open the doors at the main entrance of Hornsey House, wheeling out a trolley, checking the white sheet for any gaps. They were thinking of both the children outside and the dignity of the blackened corpse.

'Come on, move.'

The fireman's tone was abrupt, irritable. He had lost one on his watch, a blot in the copybook, a stain on his conscience. Forever. The police constable lifted the cordon. Low stepped aside as the stretcher passed. He could live with death, but not defeat.

The body had beaten him.

George Davis had succeeded.

An ambulance reversed into the narrow path, flinging its back doors open. Two paramedics took over, lifting the stretcher away from prying eyes and possible viral video clips in the morning. The ambulance meandered its way through Citizen Road, the siren wailing, accelerating towards Holloway Road, where they'd be less traffic and more space at such an ungodly hour. Then the ambulance would cut the siren and grant the dead a little peace.

'You told me everyone got out?'

'I thought they did,' the police constable said. 'They told me they counted every resident out here.'

'Well, they obviously didn't.'

In the far corner of the grass field, beside the road, a

uniformed officer crouched beside a tree, his back against its trunk. His blackened hands and face made him hard to make out in the darkness. As he lowered his head, his helmet fell to the floor. His shoulders started shaking.

PC Bishop had never cried on duty before.

CHAPTER 39

'You lost your fucking war. It's over,' Low said, pushing past the others.

DCI Wickes considered stopping the Singaporean, but no one inside the interrogation room was thinking straight any more.

Besides, Davis *had* to know. He *needed* to know.

It was all they had left at Charing Cross Police Station, the only crumb of comfort before they made preparations to bury one of their own.

PC Cook would not die in vain.

The dopey, harmless kid would not be remembered as a pawn in Davis's psychotic game. Wickes was desperate to communicate that message to Davis on behalf of his team, all watching on the other side of the partitioned wall, mourning their colleague. Craving justice.

But Wickes was a law-and-order man, a proud advocate for tolerance and fairness. He wasn't the man for a monster right now. There was only one psychopath in the room, but Low ran Davis a close second.

Wickes knew he was a good copper, but he'd never have Low's way with words.

'You didn't get a Muslim, a Paki or a refugee. You didn't even get a dark face,' Low said, leering at Davis across the table.

'What?'

'Yeah, your homemade device went off.'

Davis grinned at the revelation.

'But it was like you, fucking amateurish. Blew out your flat, but that's about it. You didn't get your nine-eleven moment. You barely got a moment. You killed one man. That's it. Just one man.'

Low raised a finger, stopping himself from making a fist, directing his anger. Davis shrugged.

'Oh, well, better than nothing. That's two, at least. Or three, I suppose.'

Low shook his head.

'Nah, he was white. You killed a white man, you flaccid little fucker. You killed a white policeman; young, handsome, beautiful girlfriend, loved by his parents, everything that you're not. Everything that you'll never be.'

'No.'

'Fucking yes. And he'll be everywhere now, because he was white, because he was good-looking and because he was a policeman. You know how that shit works. He'll be a darling of the right-wing media for weeks – your media – he'll be a national hero. He'll get plaques and foundations and park benches in his name. He'll get a hero's funeral. His death will achieve more than any living copper, any living politician. He'll unite left and right, the neo-Nazis and the latte lovers, in their revulsion. And he'll bring together the people he died for. Muslims. Immigrants. Refugees. They'll light candles for him. Pray for him at mosques. They'll remember him and hate you. All the hate, on every side, every fucking colour, will be directed to one cause. You.'

'What colour was his girlfriend?'

'White. You haven't even got that straw to clutch. You didn't get white killing brown. You didn't get your race war. You got nothing. Except life in prison, where they'll all be waiting for you. And for what? The love of Homophobic Daddy?'

'He will be proud of me.'

'Will he?'

'I supported his beliefs, like a proper son.'

'Did you?'

'Yeah, I did.'

Wickes handed Low a mobile phone.

'Let's see,' Low said, turning to Wickes. 'Is this the number?'

Wickes nodded. Davis stared at the phone.

'What are you doing?'

Low raised a finger to his lips.

'Be quiet. I'm trying to make a call.'

'Who's he calling? Wickes, who's he calling?'

'Oh, hello, is Harry Davis there? Can I speak to him please?'

'No, no, no, no, no, no, no.'

George Davis was on his feet, reaching out for the phone, grasping at thin air. Wickes moved quickly, grabbing Davis's arms at the elbows, pinning them to his back. The officer standing guard at the door joined Wickes, but Davis was freakishly strong like his father, a chip off the old block, refusing to succumb, fighting to the very end to preserve Harry Davis's bigoted values.

'Must be a girlfriend,' Low said, baiting his trapped prey.

'Put the phone down,' Davis shouted, struggling to free himself. 'Put the phone down. Put the phone down.'

'George, please, it's really hard to ...Oh, hello, is that Harry Davis? It's an honour, sir,' Low said, walking towards the door. 'I'm Detective Inspector Stanley Low and I wanted to talk to you about your son's sexuality.'

'Fuck you,' Davis screamed, spitting across the table. 'I'll fucking kill you. I'll fucking kill all of you.'

As Davis fought to escape, Wickes jabbed him in the ribs, a sly rabbit punch, and pinned him against the table. Face down. Hard.

Low waited at the door.

'Sorry about the language, Mr Davis. I don't know where he gets it from.'

Under the weight of Wickes's hand, Davis managed to turn his head to watch the odious Chinaman ruin his lifelong dream. He had never been naïve. He had never expected love from a father devoted to the suffering of others.

Just recognition.

Perhaps even acceptance.

But that was gone now. Only hate remained.

And no one did hate better than Harry Davis.

'Anyway, as I was saying, let me tell you about your son,' Low said, glaring at his broken murderer.

At that moment, grieving officers on every floor of Charing Cross Police Station took solace in the reassuring sound of George Davis's screaming.

CHAPTER 40

DCI Wickes found PC Bishop in the audiovisual room, still wearing the uniform covered in the blood of his dead partner. The flickering images on a dozen computer screens glowed against the side of his blackened face, revealing the night's horrors.

Wickes took the chair next to his traumatised officer. The wall behind the computers was still covered with hundreds of photocopied images, a masked killer frozen in time.

Winston Churchill at a traffic light, head down, Winston Churchill on the road, hiding behind a crash helmet, Winston Churchill riding into shot, out of shot, always too blurry, always too far, always Winston Churchill, always the mask, never the man.

Wickes patted Bishop's knee.

'I read your statement. You did everything you could.'

Bishop didn't look at up.

'No I didn't. He's dead.'

'You got everybody else out.'

'Except him. I told him not to go back in. But he said he heard something.'

'He did.'

Bishop looked up at the chief inspector for the first time.

'He heard the sound of a baby crying,' Wickes continued. 'It looks like Davis had a smart speaker in the room. He'd programmed it to play a crying baby. Or somebody did, anyway. Who knows? Probably hoping to take out the neighbours. They were all Asian on that floor. But it ended up being PC Cook.'

'John.'

'Yeah, John,' Wickes agreed.

John was their friend and colleague. PC Cook was a crime statistic.

'Anyway, he tried to force the door. There was a trip wire. Cheap homemade device, but Davis had doused the room in petrol, like Hawker Heaven. Amateurish.'

'Amateurish? He's dead. Didn't look amateurish to me.'

Bishop dragged a sleeve across his face. The chief inspector took another look at the images.

Winston Churchill was everywhere, all over north and central London. Similar mopeds. Same clothes. Long overcoat. Black gloves. Crash helmet. Riding goggles. He was mapped from one crime scene to another.

So many images, so many cameras, so many opportunities to rely on the technology that was supposed to make up for the extra men that Charing Cross Police Station would no longer get. Austerity had decimated Wickes's resources. He didn't get the men he wanted.

He got machines instead and they had failed him.

He didn't get the men he wanted.

He got men like PC Bishop.

There were so many cameras, sightings and images. They were all the same. Winston Churchill. Long overcoat. Black gloves. Crash helmet. Riding goggles.

That mask.

Every image came with that mask.

'Why did you delete the other images?'

Both men appeared surprised by Wickes's question.

'What?'

'Why did you delete the other images?'

Wickes pointed at the photocopies, dragging his finger from left to right to underline the quantity.

'You gathered hundreds. Maybe thousands. I had my suspicions before, but I ignored them. That was my mistake. Your mistake was being too thorough.'

'I don't understand.'

'Yes, you do. No copper can be that unlucky. No copper can be that incompetent. And you're neither. You've always been good for me. Reliable. Thorough. Got the job done, never a problem. And then suddenly, you can't pull a single image of him, anywhere in London, either with him putting the mask on or taking it off. You always lose him just before he dumps the moped, or just before he arrives at wherever he was going.'

'He knew where the cameras were.'

'George Davis was a functioning nutcase. I'll give you that. But there are half a million CCTV cameras in London. He doesn't know the location of all of them.'

PC Bishop picked out the anger in his boss's voice. Wickes rolled his chair closer.

'Then Mistry and Devonshire told me you broke down outside Hornsey House. All coppers react to a tragedy, but you had a public breakdown. It was deeper, almost visceral. And then as soon as you're done with your statement, you're straight in here. Maybe checking the images one more time, just to be sure, or maybe genuine grief and guilt, for what you did in this room. But that's when I knew.'

'Knew what?

'Are you a member?'

'Of what?'

'Make England Great Again.'

Bishop seemed disgusted at the suggestion.

'No.'

'You wouldn't be the first racist copper from your background.'

'Oh, right, because I'm white, working class and grew up on a council estate, I've gotta be a Nazi, right?'

'No. I'm white, working class and grew up on a council estate. But the job can do it. I've seen it before, more than once. All the things we see and can't comment upon. Racial tension. Vietnamese people smugglers. Muslim gangs. Black gangs. We know the knife-crime stats. We know how one-sided they really are. They don't know what we see every day, what we put up with. You wouldn't be the first.'

'With all due respect, sir, please don't patronise me. I've worked in the community with every race for almost ten years, me and John.'

'You did. And you also deleted images of George Davis without a mask. We can't scratch our arses in London without a camera catching us. I can – and I will – have the footage checked again.'

Wickes took in the hundreds of photocopies of blurred CCTV images pinned to the wall and shook his head.

'So why did you do it?'

Bishop refused to answer.

'Why did you do it, Danny? I will have the footage checked again. All of it.'

Bishop suddenly sat up straight in the chair.

'Do you remember Gary Nelson?'

Wickes was caught off guard by the sudden belligerent tone.

'Who?'

'Gary Nelson.'

'No, I don't.'

'Nah, you wouldn't, because he was a knife victim who didn't die. I mean, there are so many of them now, every day, that even the media can't keep up, unless the victim is white, then there's a bit of attention for a week. Gary Nelson was white. But he didn't die, so he didn't count. Got stabbed in the back while he was sitting in a park with his mate, smoking a bit of puff. The knife tore through his spine, his spleen and his bladder. He's in a wheelchair now, pisses in a bag every day, his whole life fucked,' Bishop said.

'And he's my cousin. We practically grew up together, went to Tottenham games together, got pissed together. The only difference was he was the smart one in the family. He'd just finished university – biochemistry, ended up getting a first-class degree, a white kid from a Tottenham council estate and he gets a first-class degree. Unheard of. So he meets up with his old mates one last time before he goes back to uni to do his doctorate or whatever it was, and he gets stabbed in the back for no reason at all. None. It happened so fast they couldn't even see the fuckers in the hoodies – three of them. They were off through the park while he's almost bleeding to death on the kiddies' slide.

'But that's not the end of it. It gets even worse. He's written off in the local papers, on social media. Everywhere. White council-estate blokes smoking puff in a park, one gets stabbed, so he's a chav. White trash. Gotta be, right? He's not a science genius, not a university scholar, not the pride of his whole family. He's a piece of shit. He's a council-estate gang member, a druggie who got what he deserved. But I knew what it really was, because I deal with this shit every day. It was a gang initiation. Stab a random geezer in the back and get accepted into the gang. So they pick my little cousin. Could've been anyone, but they pick my little cousin. Three blokes. Hoodies. No description, but we don't need one, do we?'

'What do you mean?'

'You know what I mean. I've given you a basic description

and a motive. So when you see their faces, what colour do you see?'

'I'm guessing you want me to say black.'

'You don't have to say it. Black. Brown. The crime stats say it for you. I can't even say it to my own aunt when she asks for my help in catching the bastards. I have to tell her the truth. He didn't die, her boy. He didn't die. Sorry about that, but he didn't die, which is a problem because he won't be prioritised. No resources, not enough coppers, and he didn't die. We've got too many dead kids to worry about. And the only description they gave was dark, either brown or black, which makes it even harder, because they are nearly always brown and black, aren't they? But we can't say that either. The stats can say it. But we can't say it, can we? Political correctness doesn't allow it. We have to spend our days making sure we call black, Asian, gay and transgender people by their right names to keep the leftie media happy, so we haven't got any time left to actually fucking catch anyone. So I have to lie. I have to lie to my own aunt. And tell her that we'll catch the bastards who left her son in a wheelchair when I know that I'm talking complete bollocks. These fuckers rule London and they know it.'

'So what? You thought George Davis would reduce their numbers a bit?'

'No, I thought he would – you know.'

'No, I don't know.'

'Say what we can't say any more. Why is it so wrong to want it like it was before, before they were stabbing each other all over London, before they were running through Borough Market shouting "*Allahu Akbar*", how is that wrong? How is wanting to feel safe, like we used to, wrong? I kiss my wife goodbye every morning and wonder, "Is it today'? Is today my turn? Am I gonna get in the way of someone else's religion? Am I gonna be on the wrong end of a blade because of some poxy gang ritual?" Why is it so wrong to not want to live in this shit? Because it's pretty fucking clear to me that we just can't live together.'

'So you deleted his images?'

'Yes, I deleted his images.'

Bishop was shouting. Wickes allowed his officer's words to settle in the tiny room before responding.

'Were there many?'

Bishop sighed.

'No, there weren't many. Maybe two or three, only one could've made a positive ID, perhaps, and there was a grainy one of him without a mask in the street. Couldn't see his face clearly, but it was him coming out of a building.'

'Where?'

Bishop stared at the images on the wall.

'Where?'

'Walking down a path outside Hornsey House,' Bishop mumbled.

'You could've given us his home address?'

'Yeah.'

'Where he planned everything, where he planted a device that killed John Cook.'

'Sir, I can—'

'No, I'm not interested,' Wickes interrupted. 'Save it for your new statement.'

Wickes watched Bishop bury his face in a crumpled, blood-soaked uniform.

'You know, a psychiatrist will say that you've probably suf-fered enough. But you haven't. Not for me. And not for the usual reasons you might think, either. It's not the destroying of evidence or even the betrayal. It's the choice you made. When you sat in that chair, you were given a chance to make a real difference. But you chose a monster instead of your own police force.'

'You don't have a cousin in a wheelchair thanks to them,' Bishop said, his voice cracking.

'No, I don't,' the chief inspector said, pushing his chair under the desk. 'But I have a dead policeman, thanks to you.'

CHAPTER 41

Within days, Mark Beckett was back on the London Call-In breakfast show, sharing a studio with the woman who'd given his name to a psychopath. He hadn't wanted to return. He had even offered to resign. But he had a contract.

Now he had an improved contract and a book deal, his side of the *MEGA Murderer* story, as George Davis was now being called.

On the other side of the studio, Margaret Jones pushed her microphone aside to check her complexion in a compact mirror. She dabbed a little powder on her cheeks. Since her harrowing ordeal, the viewing figures for their in-studio live-cam had doubled. She, too, had a book deal, but she was under pressure to release her title ahead of Beckett. She had polarised her audience even further. She still had her loyalists, but a few on the fringes had drifted away, unable to reconcile her betrayal. Even with a knife at her throat, Jones had given up a white man, a leftie snowflake of a white man, but a white man nonetheless.

She needed an issue to get them back on side.

Fortunately there was always an issue on talk radio, always a button to push.

The light on her microphone blazed. She leaned forward, looking straight at Beckett across the desk.

'Thank you for staying with us here on London Call-In, with the most popular breakfast show in Britain,' she said. 'This morning, we're discussing a sensitive issue, one that has obviously had a direct impact on my life. Knife crime.'

Jones paused, making sure the microphone picked up her dramatic sigh.

'What are we going to do about knife crime? When are we going to speak the truth about the stats? This morning another fatal stabbing in north London; that's five in a fortnight. The victim? Black. The suspect? Black. The response? Vanilla. Why can't we call it how it is when it's clearly a black-and-white issue. Well, it's not, is it? It's a black issue.'

Beckett peered up at the middle-class faces on the other side of the glass, holding their cameras, all benefiting from their white privilege, every one of them profiting from the racial divide, all blissfully unaware of the irony.

'Margaret, you know exactly what you are doing and that depresses me more than the startling crime stats,' Beckett said. 'We both do. That's why we were targeted for clear, but very different reasons. That man, and I refuse to utter his name on air, saw me as opponent, hated my views on tolerance, equality and social fairness. He saw you as an equal, a comrade, someone who will speak on his cause's behalf on national radio. Does that not bother you, Margaret? After all that has happened, do you not have a conscience? Every time you stoke the racial fires, you incite them. The plankton. You give them a voice. I've said this time and time again. And it sickens me that I'm still saying it now, after everything that has happened, to both of us.'

Jones was pleasantly surprised that her co-host had taken the bait so quickly. She now had an easy chance to shore up her fan base before the commercial break.

'Safety sickens you? Law and order sickens you? Free speech sickens you? The right to be protected – they all sicken you? Which one of our inalienable rights sickens you this morning?

I resent the accusation that I am inciting anyone by calling for tougher sentencing against those stabbing our young people in this country, whatever bloody colour they are. If I'm guilty of anything, it's encouraging the hardworking men and women of this country to throw away their paper shields of political correctness and speak the bloody truth. That's not a crime.'

'No, but there are consequences.'

'Good. There should be. We should shame them, out them, catch them and string them up from the nearest lamppost for all I care. What do you think, listeners? We're taking your calls after the break.'

The microphone lights went off. Jones pulled off her headphones and grinned at her flustered colleague.

'That went rather well don't you think?'

They gathered outside the Charles Dickens pub. Their numbers had dwindled since George Davis's arrest, but the imagery retained its potency. They didn't need the numbers. They had the masks.

Winston Churchill was back.

He was everywhere, standing in the doorway, in front of the stained-glass windows, on the pavement, raising a pint in one hand and making his characteristic sign with the other.

They all stood together, making a 'V' for victory.

Winston Churchill's symbol had become George Davis's symbol. Two misunderstood men were united by a grand gesture, a willingness to visit the darkest corners of humanity to bring back the nation's natural state of being.

They had made England great again.

The MEGA website's new videographer asked the Winston Churchills to stand closer together, side by side, to give the illusion of greater numbers. He needed to make dozens look like hundreds once the clip was judiciously edited. He had a lot to live up to.

His predecessor had been a natural with digital editing tools.

As they gathered for the recording, they started singing, spontaneously.

'One Georgie Davis,

There's only one Georgie Davis,

One Georgie Davis,

There's only one Georgie Davis.'

Inside the Charles Dickens pub, Billy Evans drummed his fingers along to the tuneless chant. He enjoyed the irony. There wasn't one George Davis. There were hundreds of them, thousands perhaps, disillusioned, middle-aged nativists, ready to fight for a cause that they still naively believed was about them.

Their leader knew the cause wasn't about him either. But Evans wasn't naïve. He accepted his place in his beloved country. England was about tradition, structure, loyalty and an underlying acceptance of one's place in society. Structure was the key. Without that class structure, England lost the very essence of what made it special, what made it different from those feral cesspools elsewhere, the ones that refugees would always seek to flee. In some ways, Evans admired the refugees, the immigrants and even the illegals.

They knew what England really was, too. It's only when they got ideas above their station that they started fucking things up for everyone. But Evans was different. He was smart. He knew his place.

His phone rang. He sipped his beer before answering.

'Hello, I hope it's not an inconvenience,' he said.

'It's always an inconvenience.'

The irritable voice was educated, refined and female.

'It's about funding,' Evans said.

'It usually is.'

'This Davis thing has been a bit of a setback.'

'On the contrary, I suspect he might just prove to be the panacea for our current social ills, in the long term,' she said.

'So what should I do now?'

'Step back. Let them do the work for us. They'll continue to stab each other. It's in their nature. They just need to get a few of us along the way. Then we'll get that critical mass, that nationwide revulsion. The tide will turn and we'll finally get shot of these savages.'

'Hopefully.'

'It'll happen. And you will get your funding. Anything else?'

Her clipped tone underlined her impatience.

'No, that's it,' Evans said.

'Good. I've got to prepare for a select committee.'

She never bothered to say goodbye.

Evans sat back and took another sip of his beer. They were still singing outside the Charles Dickens pub. He closed his eyes and listened to his members chant the name of a racist killer.

Evans felt a lump in his throat.

He bloody loved his country.

DCI Charlie Wickes fussed over the daffodil bulbs in his back garden. He knew the spring flower was a bit of a cliché in an English country garden, but he planted the bulbs every year none-theless. Daffodils reminded him of his first date with his wife, Janet. They were the only flowers a police cadet could afford.

Wickes leaned back on his heels and wiped a muddy arm across his forehead. His knees were buried in the flowerbed and covered in soil. He didn't mind. He loved his garden. At the end of every major case, he planted seeds and bulbs, whatever the season. He always found something for the right time of year. He wasn't spiritual or religious, but he liked to start afresh, to clean his hands in the soil and begin again.

He intended to spend as much time as possible in the garden in the coming weeks. It wasn't the crimes that bothered him, but the coppers involved. He had dealt with the deranged for most of his career. George Davis was unusual, but hardly unique.

Only PC Cook visited his dreams.

Inspector Low just disturbed him when he was awake.

'I don't how you expect me to get the mud out of the knees of those trousers,' Janet shouted from their outdoor wicker furniture.

She was reading a travel brochure.

'I'll throw them away,' Wickes replied.

'No, you won't. We're not made of money. We'll be skint when you retire.'

Wickes considered his wife's playful digs. She had wanted him to retire for years, but he had always resisted. Now he wasn't sure. His resolve was weakening.

'Seen anything you like?' he said, changing the subject.

'Yeah, an Asian cruise.'

'Sounds lovely,' Wickes said, getting up slowly. His back ached.

'Yeah, stops at Thailand, Malaysia and Singapore.'

'Singapore?'

Wickes's voice rose sharply, surprising them both.

'Yeah. What about it? It's in China, right?'

Wickes smiled.

'I've just been working with a bloke from Singapore.'

'What? A copper?'

'Yeah. Sort of.'

'We could visit him in Singapore then. What's he like?'

Wickes brushed the mud off his trousers. He had no idea how to answer.

Low held the shop door open as an elderly West Indian woman waddled through with two bags of shopping. Low smiled at the name slapped across the plastic bags.

Mistry Mini-Mart.

It was old-fashioned marketing for an old-fashioned man.

Dhaval Mistry waved at the woman through the window,

insisting again that the bandage on his head was really not as bad as it looked.

'I'm fine, Mrs Griffiths, really,' he mouthed, tapping the bandage.

'She's not,' Low said, peering at the woman through a gap in the homemade leaflets on the door. 'She can buy that lot for half the price in Tesco.'

'But she won't get my special service.'

Both men laughed at the unfunny joke, eager to delay the awkward silence that had to follow. Mistry straightened his newspapers, making sure the corners of every one aligned. Gujarati shopkeepers didn't cut corners.

'Look, Stanley.'

'It's OK, Dagenham Dave,' Low said, continuing to follow the old lady's progress as she passed the terraced houses, all painted and paved to hide their council-estate origins. 'It's fine.'

'No, what you did, for Ramila, for little Ben.'

'It's my job, Dave.'

Mistry pretended to tidy some Mars Bars.

'How did you know he'd come here?'

'Same reason why your daughter left me in Singapore,' Low said, tapping his forehead. 'Up here. Good for some stuff, but not the stuff that really matters.'

'Yeah, you always were a mad bastard.'

Mistry offered a hand, but hugged Low instead.

'Thank you, Stanley. Thank you. I couldn't have lost them as well.'

When they separated, Low noticed a tear in Mistry's eye. He also saw something else, but couldn't place it.

Benjamin Mistry-Devonshire ran through the kitchen streamers, brandishing a blue lightsaber.

'Use the Force, Luke.'

The boy whacked Low in the kneecap.

'Ow, shit,' Low said, rubbing his leg.

'Mind your language,' Ramila Mistry said, following her son onto the shop floor.

'I used to love that programme,' Dhaval Mistry said.

'They still show it in Singapore.'

'It always was a backward country,' Ramila said.

'They must be if they're taking me back. Where's Tom?'

'Too much paperwork at the station. He wished you a safe flight.'

Low chose not to pursue the obvious lie.

'Yeah, he's not bad actually,' he said. 'I quite like him.'

'No you don't.'

'Yeah, all right, I don't. But that says more about me than him, right? He's a good man. You did good, Ramila. Really. I'm happy for you.'

'Take care, Stanley. Get the help you need.'

'Never,' Low said, embracing the woman he would try to stop loving.

Dhaval Mistry needed to cut the tension.

'Do you want a bag of crisps?'

'Not from you, too bloody expensive,' Low said, pulling away from Ramila.

'Bloody Chinese, all the same.'

'Hey, I could've been your son-in-law.'

'No chance. I would've killed you first,' Dhaval Mistry said, laughing as he threw a bag of salt-and-vinegar crisps across the counter.

Low caught them, but could no longer see them. He was edging away, drifting, following the fireworks, chasing them across the darkness.

'Filial piety, eh?' he said. 'Asian fathers and their daughters.'

'That's right, only the best for my little girl. You think I'd let her marry a Chinaman?'

'Stop it, Dad.'

'Nah, he's right.'

'Of course I'm right,' Dhaval Mistry said, chuckling politely.

'There's a racial hierarchy. There's always been a racial hierarchy with us: whites on top, and then everyone else,' Low said.

He was mumbling to himself, running after his thoughts.

'Chinese would never come before *ang mohs*, not with Indians – never. Most Indians wanna be *ang mohs*. They would always pick *ang mohs* over Chinese. There's a hierarchy, a racial hierarchy, always has been. You can move up, not down, Indian to *ang moh* is a step up, Indian to Chinese is a step sideways.'

'I was only joking,' Dhaval Mistry said, alarmed by Low's abrupt mood swing.

'No, you're right. You step up, not down. Have to. No choice.'

'Stanley, wait.'

The buzzer above the shop door was still ringing as Low ran past the terraced houses and disappeared from view.

CHAPTER 42

In the chilly morning air, Zhang Wei sat on a bench and pulled a handful of bread scraps from a plastic bag. He enjoyed feeding the birds. They brought life to a place for the dead.

He was pleased with his daughter's headstone, a near-identical match to her mother's.

They had always shared clothes, swapping tops and trousers. They were a similar size. Now they had similar headstones.

The City of London Cemetery had been his wife's one and only choice. They had visited potential plots together, before she was even sick. They weren't morbid. They were Chinese, always practical, in life and death. They were *kiasu*: scared to fail, in life and death.

And Zhang had really tried his best with her instructions.

Green. Quiet. Wet.

She wanted water nearby, just like Penang Island. Just like the *kampong* of her childhood, growing up with the tree ferns beside a stream. She went to her grave loving her adopted country, a loyal, grateful immigrant to the end, but she wanted to return to her Malaysian roots. Even if the return was symbolic.

Zhang had bought plots for the whole family at the back of the cemetery, away from the grand, arched entrance and the crawling east London traffic. The walk was further, but worth it. His girls had the River Roding on one side and a riding school on the other. Life surrounded them. The walk left Zhang exhausted, but he didn't mind. He had nowhere else to go.

He spent every morning on the same bench, beneath a magnificent English oak tree.

'It's a good spot.'

The footsteps, crunching through the leaves, made Zhang jump, but the voice bothered him more.

'Inspector Low?'

The Singaporean stood over Zhang, blocking his view of the headstones. Low's appearance surprised Zhang. Same clothes. Same hoodie. But he had shaved, brushed his hair. He had almost made an effort. Almost.

'Yeah. Can I sit down?'

Low didn't wait for the answer, joining Zhang on the bench. The sparrows and pigeons pecked away at their stale breakfast on the immaculate lawn. Zhang was careful not to throw any bread near his family.

'Yeah, it's a really good spot. Peaceful. You have found a corner that is forever England.'

'I didn't pick it. My wife did.'

'I can see why.'

Zhang threw a handful of crumbs, enjoying the birds' company.

'Why are you here?'

'Pay my respects before I go back to Singapore.'

'Thank you.'

'Do you think you'll go back to Malaysia?'

'Go back to what? Everything I have is here,' Zhang said.

'Yeah.'

Low checked the zip on his hoodie. He always struggled with the English weather first thing in the morning.

'It's cold.'

'You get used to it.'

'I never did.'

Zhang rolled a lump of bread around in his hand.

'I saw the news. You caught him.'

'Yeah, that must have been tough, having to read all the details.'

'Not really. I can't be hurt any more,' Zhang said, nodding towards the graves. 'They're already dead. My whole life was for nothing.'

'Yeah. That's the one thing they'll never understand, right? The *ang mohs*,' Low said, glancing over his shoulder at the serene woodland. 'Filial piety. The Chinese way. We look after our children when they're young and then they look after us when we're old. That's the deal.'

'Not for me.'

'No. That's why you killed him.'

Zhang struggled to breathe. He squeezed the bread in the palm of his hand as the birds gathered around his feet, waiting for crumbs that didn't arrive.

'What?'

'Mohamed Kamal. You killed him,' Low said.

His tone was almost flippant.

'That's ridiculous. Why would I?'

'You would've never let your precious girl marry Mohamed Kamal.'

'He confessed to the murders. That animal, he confessed to it. I saw it on the news.'

'He confessed to stabbing Mohamed Kamal through the heart, looking him in the eye as he stuck the knife in his chest, following some mad obsession with impressing his father, but he didn't. Kamal was stabbed twice in the back. By a coward, or by accident, or by both, I don't know, but he wasn't stabbed by George Davis. He was stabbed by you.'

Zhang couldn't speak. He didn't have to. He was already crying.

'Filial piety eh? Filial bloody piety,' Low said, shaking his head. 'Parents and their children, wanting different things for themselves, for each other, seeing the world in a different way. You didn't want what she wanted. Couldn't accept it.'

Zhang wiped his nose on a handkerchief.

'Did you always know?'

'I knew you were lying at Hawker Heaven about something, but I put that down to the eternally terrified immigrant, doesn't want to rock the boat, doesn't trust the police and the authorities and everything. Plus, when it comes to money and business, us Chinese are secretive bastards, right? That's why there's no CCTV in Dansey Place. We don't want cameras in the back streets of Chinatown. But even then, I couldn't understand why there wasn't a single sighting of Davis around the area and why he'd be there anyway, at that time, just to kill a kid he worked with in a pub. It wasn't a grand statement. It was too random. Everything he did was calculated. But then, Hawker Heaven happened and the radio thing and we all got distracted.'

'No, Hawker Heaven did not *happen*,' Zhang said, squeezing the stale bread between his fingers. 'My daughter was burned alive.'

'Yeah, but why was that?' Low said, turning to face Zhang on the bench. 'What caused her death, really? She had lost the love of her life. Have you any idea what that feels like? No of course not, you had the love of your life. You even got to bury her in a beautiful corner of Epping Forest. But your daughter didn't. She had her love stolen, so she vented on social media and brought out the trolls, the monsters, and one of them came for her, because of you. You killed her boyfriend, because she saw her life with a Muslim and you didn't.'

'I'm a traditional Chinese,' Zhang whimpered.

'No, you're a traditional fucking bigot. You're no different to George Davis. At least he's honest. We're not. We're full of shit. We hide our racism, right? We protect our monoculture so much we even get praised for it, for saving our heritage. *Ang mohs* go to Europe and set up British bars and it's cultural imperialism. But we set up Chinatowns all over the place and we're preserving our culture. No one will criticise people of colour, not in the current climate, so we manipulate it. And we profit from it. And that's fine. Everyone knows their place. And then your daughter comes along and she doesn't know her place. She's the next generation, with her liberal views on diversity. And she wants to marry a Muslim and you cannot take it.'

'I was thinking of her. You know we cannot mix. Just look at Chinese and Muslims, Singapore and Malaysia, hundreds of years of fighting over race, religion, whatever – you think we can bring that into our house and everything will be fine? Cannot.'

'So what does that mean? Only Chinese is good enough? I'm Chinese. Would you let her marry a man like me? I'm a mess. He was a top student.'

'He was going to drop out,' Zhang said, his voice rising. 'He was going to quit his degree to be a DJ, a bloody nightclub DJ. And she was going to follow him. She was training to be a doctor, a degree that we had saved for, me and my wife, our whole lives, so she can be a doctor, and she tells me she's going to quit, to follow her boyfriend around shitty nightclubs.'

'He was a scholar. He could've done anything.'

'In Singapore? Please. He wasn't Chinese. No chance.'

'So it's race, again,' Low said. 'Strip away all the politics, all the psychological bullshit, it all comes back to fucking race. Again.'

Low pulled out the revolver from his right pocket and rested the weapon on his lap. Chen's gun.

Low hadn't thrown it away. Of course he hadn't.

He released the cylinder. Five bullets. Fully loaded.

Zhang was suddenly aware of the early morning breeze. He was cold now, shivering. His body stiffened. He reached out for the armrest at the end of the bench and clamped his fingers around the splintered timber, his knuckles turning white. He edged away from Low, instinctively mindful of the gap, as if a few extra centimetres might improve his chances.

'So what happened?'

Low's voice was eerily calm.

'What?'

Low checked the bullets a second time and flicked the Taurus 905, locking the cylinder into place. He kept the weapon at waist height, beneath the sight of any weeping mourners behind them. They were at the quietest corner of the cemetery, off Nursery Road. Only the dead could see the revolver.

'How did you kill him?'

Zhang took a final look at the headstones and then turned away. He didn't want his girls to hear.

'It was an accident.'

'Yeah, I thought so.'

'She came to me, told me their plans and I lost my temper. I said she was wasting her life and our lives, too, her mother's life. I shouldn't have said that. She swore at me. She'd never done that before. She said she was disgusted with me, using her dead mother to make her feel guilty. She said her mother had fallen in love with a hawker and that was OK, but she couldn't make her own choice. So I spoke to him instead, a few days later. We were unpacking the vegetables in Dansey Place. I told him to leave my daughter. He said no. I offered him money, a thousand pounds. He told me to go fuck myself.'

Zhang smiled at the memory.

'He was tough, like I was, back in Penang last time,' Zhang said, rubbing the back of his calf, finding the scar, the teeth marks of a dead man. 'He really was tough. If my wife's father had tried to bribe me, I would've said exactly the same. So he got angry, pushed me out of the way. I had a knife that I used to cut open the vegetable boxes. And that was it. I lost control.'

'No, you didn't. You were in complete control. You had the sense to write "MEGA" on the wall, to throw everyone off.'

'That wasn't for me. That was for her. I didn't want Jun Li to know what really happened. I was protecting her.'

'Filial piety, right?'

'Always, until the end.'

Zhang sat up straight and rubbed the back of his calf again, feeling for the scar, tracing the outline of his pain one last time.

'So what happens now?'

'Yeah, what does happen now?' Low said, almost to himself. 'Well, I go back to Singapore and George Davis goes away for killing three people. That's about it. Or he gets life for killing two people and the police get accused of covering up a killing between minority races. And that'll lead to Billy Evans's boys rioting in the streets. Mosques will be torched. Angry young Muslims will retaliate. And George Davis might get his race war after all.'

Zhang threw the last of his bread to the birds. Low pushed the crumbs away from his feet.

'They really love that bread,' he said, before returning to Zhang. 'And we'll lose face. Me and you.'

'Yeah.'

'We're Chinese. We can't lose face.'

'No.'

Low opened the revolver a second time and removed four bullets, leaving one in its chamber. He flicked the cylinder shut and shoved the four bullets into his hoodie pocket.

He held out the gun.

'This belongs to the guys you know. From Chinatown. I don't need it any more.'

Zhang hesitated.

'Take it,' Low insisted. 'I'd never get it through customs anyway. You know they always stop the Chinese because of the weird shit we bring back.'

311

Zhang smiled.

And then the old man took the gun.

Low stood up and buried his hands in his hoodie pockets. Dark clouds had gathered over the cemetery. Rain was on its way. As he stomped his feet in a pitiful attempt to keep warm, Low peered across at the final resting place of Zhang Jun Li and her mother. They really were beautiful headstones.

'Yeah. I can definitely see why you chose this spot,' he said. 'It's perfect.'

Low pulled his hoodie down until it covered most of his face and headed down the gravel path. The sparrows and pigeons continued to feast on the bread scraps until a gunshot sent the birds scattering to the English oak tree towering over the cemetery bench.

Glossary of popular Singapore terms and Singlish phrases

ah beng:	Young, unsophisticated Chinese man.
ah lian:	The female equivalent of an ah beng.
ah long:	Loan shark (in Hokkien).
ah pek:	Uncle (in Hokkien), usually a man over 60.
ah pu neh neh:	Crude Hokkien term to describe Indians.
aiyoh:	To express frustration, impatience or disgust.
ang moh:	A Caucasian (literal Chinese translation is 'red hair').
bak kut teh:	Pork rib soup (literal Chinese translation 'meat bone tea').
buay tahan:	Buay (Hokkien) for "cannot" and tahan (Malay) for 'tolerate'– means cannot stand something any more.
guai lan:	Difficult person (literally 'strange dick' in Hokkien).

chee bye:	In Hokkien, the rudest term for vagina.
chio bu:	A rude term for an attractive girl.
dosai:	A pancake made from rice flour, often served with a spiced vegetable filling.
Filial piety:	In Confucian, Chinese Buddhist and Taoist ethics, filial piety is a virtue of respect for one's parents or elders.
Half past six:	Something or someone a bit daft, term is a sexual reference to the position of a 'weak' male organ.
hong bao:	Red packet, usually filled with money.
kakis:	Friends.
kampong:	Village.
ka ni na:	Crude Hokkien term, literally 'fuck your mother'.
kelong:	A colloquialism for cheating, corruption or fixed, often used in a sporting context. (In Malay, kelong is a wooden structure above the sea).
kiasi:	In Hokkien, kiasi means 'scared of death', a criticism directed towards someone for being cowardly.
kiasu:	Kiasu: Singaporean adjective that means 'scared to fail' in Hokkien.
lah:	Common Singlish expression. Often used for emphasis at the end of words and sentences.

laksa:	A South-East Asian dish, consisting of rice noodles served in a curry or soup.
lum pah pah lan:	When a plan goes wrong. In Hokkien, literally means 'the testicles hitting the penis'.
Majulah Singapura:	In Malay, Onward Singapore. Majulah Singapura is Singapore's National Anthem.
makan:	Malay word for 'meal' or 'to eat'.
mat salleh:	In Malay, a colloquial term for a Caucasian.
nasi padang:	Padang steamed rice served with various choices of pre-cooked dishes, originally from Indonesia.
parang:	A large, heavy knife – or a small sword – used as a tool or a weapon in Malaysia and Indonesia.
roti prata:	A fried pancake usually served with a fish or meat-based curry.
shiok:	A fantastic, wonderfully pleasurable feeling.
siao:	Crazy in Hokkien.
siew mais:	Cantonese dumplings.
tahan:	In Malay, to endure (something).
talk cock, sing song:	To speak rubbish or banter, chat with someone.
tekan:	A Malay term to hit or whack someone, but not always in the literal sense. Tekan means to abuse or bully.
wah lau:	A mostly benign expression that can mean 'damn' or 'dear me' in Hokkien.